The Contessa's Brooch

P. J. MacLayne

The Contessa's Brooch
Copyright © 2019
by P.J. MacLayne

The Contessa's Brooch is a work of fiction. All names, characters, events and places found in this book are either from the author's imagination or used fictitiously. Any similarity to persons live or dead, actual events, locations, or organizations is entirely coincidental and not intended by the author.

ISBN-13: 978-0-9985014-9-9

Published in the United States of America.

Acknowledgments

To all the usual suspects—thanks for your help in getting this story out of my head and into the hands of readers. To Cornelia Amari, for her support, encouragement, and editing assistance. To K.M. Guth for her wonderful covers. To Amy at Author E.M.S. for her help in getting my books into the hands of the readers. And finally, to all those wonderful people out there who enjoy the stories and tell me so.

Chapter 1

The tires of the Charger bucked as they dug into the winter-dead grass in front of the Aldridge—now Eli's—house. I clutched the steering wheel and Jake cursed as he grabbed the dashboard. The books in the trunk banged against the walls of the compartment and I imagined their neat stacks disintegrating. We'd taken his car instead of mine because his trunk had more room for my purchases. But I had more important things to worry about.

"When I let you drive, I didn't mean you could abuse my car," Jake complained. He let go of the dash and ran his hand across his short brown hair.

The Charger was built to take worse punishment than that, so I ignored him as I flung the door open and climbed out. A police car blocked the driveway, dominated by two fire trucks, as gray smoke rose from behind the grand old Victorian house—giving me more than enough reason to pay no attention to him. I did notice he reached over and turned on the emergency flashers. Which was good, because the driver's side of the car infringed on the traffic lane.

I didn't recognize the young officer approaching me, and that meant it was the new guy. Great. Why did it have to be the rookie? All the other cops knew me for one reason or another and might give me some leeway. The rookie was an unpredictable factor. Of course, tough-guy Jake stayed firmly planted in the passenger's seat. He didn't get along with law enforcement. For good reason. He'd done time for assaulting an officer of the law. Several of them. Still, he'd back me up if things got out of hand.

The rookie stopped a few feet away from me, his right hand resting just above his gun belt and his feet planted in the proper position. Not straight ahead, but pointed out. Alright, he got an A-plus for form but if he thought he could intimidate me, he was wrong, even if he was bigger than me. Hell, I'd gone toe-to-toe with certain members of the FBI.

"You'll have to move the car, Ma'am," he said. "You're impeding traffic."

Two cars sailed by on the road, the drivers slowing to gawk. I understood the rookie's agenda, but I had one of my own. "I'm Harmony Duprie. I represent the out-of-state owner," I said, waving one hand towards the house. "I need to make sure the property is undamaged."

If he followed procedure, he wouldn't tell me anything. But I had my suspicions. There had been a string of grass fires throughout the city. It looked as if this was another one and the house itself was fine. Anything more and every fire truck in the city would be scattered around the property. I'd been working with Police Chief Sorenson to find a pattern, but we were striking out. In my head, I mapped this fire with the rest, but it didn't help.

"I'm sorry, but I'm not at liberty to tell you anything. You'll have to wait for an official news release like everyone else."

Did he think I was a reporter? Hadn't he been to the library yet? The points I gave him for correct posture vanished.

"Can you at least tell me if the house is involved?"

That was Chief Sorenson's fear. That whoever was setting the fires would move to bigger targets and bigger thrills.

A slight breeze wafted a hint of pungent smoke our direction and I covered my nose and mouth with my arm. I glanced toward the house to make sure the flames hadn't crept any closer and noticed the curtains moving on the third-floor window. I thought we'd sealed the frame well enough to stop the wind from seeping in, but I'd have to double-check. Either that or the resident ghost was checking out the action, too.

The rookie hesitated, and I leaned forward to read his name badge. I couldn't keep calling him rookie. If I slipped and unintentionally used that in our conversation, I'd lose any chance of getting on his good side. But with the long shadows being cast by the late afternoon sun, I couldn't see it clearly.

He blinked, and his eyes wandered over my shoulder. I swiveled to follow his gaze as three firemen, covered in soot and dragging assorted equipment, strolled around the side of the house, headed towards the fire trucks. One pointed our direction and waved. Despite the dirt and grime covering his face and clothes, he looked familiar. When he removed his helmet, I was sure.

"Hey, Pete," I called and waved back. A few years back, Pete Zamora had been one of the rare male high school volunteers at the library. When I first started working at there, I'd been closest in age to the high-schoolers and became their unofficial liaison. Sure, he signed up because he had a crush on a girl who volunteered, but that didn't stop him from pitching in with the best of them. I hadn't seen him around lately, but the rumor mill reported his hiring by the fire department.

"Stay right there," he yelled, then turned and had a private conversation with the other two men. He handed one his shovel, the other his helmet, and headed my direction, taking off his heavy coat on the way. His biceps bulged under his tight t-shirt. Behind me, the rookie cop sighed.

"You're the last person I expected to see here, Miss Duprie," he said with a grin when he was a few feet away. "I hear you finally made boss at the library. Figured you'd never leave the place."

I'm not short, but I had to crane my neck to look him in the eye. "The job is temporary," I explained. "and I was running an errand when I spotted the emergency vehicles here. The house is owned by a friend."

"Oh, it's the one you restored? Nice job. We got here in plenty of time. There's no damage, although you might want to clean the windows on the back side."

I didn't even ask how he knew I'd been the one responsible for fixing up the house. The Oak Grove rumor mill never sleeps.

"But wait until tomorrow at least," he suggested. "Let things cool down. We need to make sure the fire doesn't flare up again."

"I can do that." With the way my schedule looked, it might be a few days before I came back. And I'd be doing more than washing windows, depending on how much smoke seeped into the house. Eli deserved to find his house in the same shape it was before he signed the purchasing agreement.

Pete dug into his pocket. "Hey, is this yours?" He held a small oval object in his hand.

I didn't recognize the item but took it to examine, scraping dirt off the front. It looked like an old-fashioned brooch with a Celtic knot design. I turned it over to check the back and saw the pin used to fasten it to clothing was missing. "Not mine, but this looks old. Mind if I show this to a friend who has an interest in jewelry?"

"No problem. One of the guys spotted it in the back yard. I thought I'd see if I could reunite it with its owner."

Did the wife of the original owner drop it way back in the 1920s? Or was it even older than that? I flipped the brooch back over and wondered if there was a hidden meaning in the design.

"Well, I gotta get back to work. Nice to see you again, Miss Duprie."

"You too, Pete. Drop by the library sometime. We've got a new book by that author you like, James Caboodle."

He grinned. "I'm halfway through it already. Now I really have to go. Later!"

He turned on one heel and headed towards the fire truck. The rookie cop behind me sighed again.

"Now will you please move your car?" he asked.

He didn't seem impressed at all by my connections. If he knew of my relationship with Police Chief Sorenson he might be, but I didn't like to be pushy. Besides, there wasn't a reason for me to stick around.

I fluttered my eyelashes. "But of course! Have a good rest of the day." I stuck the brooch in my coat pocket and returned to the car.

"Change of plans," I said as I dropped into the driver's seat. I fastened my seatbelt and adjusted my glasses. "You get to help me carry the books to my place. I'll bring them back later." They were housewarming gifts for Eli, along with the bookshelf Luke and Joe were refinishing.

Jake arched an eyebrow. "You're awfully calm, Angel."

No matter how many times I asked him, I couldn't get Jake to call me by my name, Harmony, instead of the sweet nickname he used back when we were more than friends. But now was not the time to argue about it again.

I started the engine and pulled into the street after waiting for a few cars to go by. I recognized Rena Oleksandra's car, one of the library volunteers, and wondered what she was doing out this way.

"The house is fine." I dug into my pocket and pulled out the brooch and handed it to him. "But look what a fireman found."

He took it and held it in his open palm, bouncing it into the air a couple of times. "Junk," he pronounced. "Good junk, but the weight is wrong. It's plastic, maybe from the sixties or seventies."

"You think it's been laying in the yard all that time?"

"Not likely. If I had to guess, someone cleaned out their mother's house, gave the brooch to a kid to play with, and they lost it."

It made sense. I'd seen plenty of neighborhood kids wander through the yard while we were fixing up the house. Crestfallen, I took the brooch back and tossed it into the center console along with a few scraps of paper I needed to throw in the garbage.

❀ ❀ ❀

Like a wayward teenager, my anxiety levels rose every time Chief Sorenson showed up, even if I hadn't done anything wrong. It was no different when he strode into the library Monday morning even though he was on my turf. Since I was busy helping Mrs. McCartney track down information on problem pregnancies in goats, I nodded his direction and inclined my head towards the office. I didn't want to make him hang around the front desk while he waited.

Besides, a few of the patrons would be unhappy if he spotted them. I saw Harry, one of Oak Grove's small homeless population, duck behind the magazine racks in the reading room.

Once Mrs. McCartney was all set up with a search page, I returned to my office. The Chief had helped himself to a cup of coffee from the pot I kept on my credenza and was staring out the window that overlooked the alley. Not much happened out there most days except for a stray cat or two nosing around the dumpsters.

"I understand you got to witness our latest incident first hand," he said without turning.

I added coffee to my own cup to warm it up. "Not really. The fire department had it out before I arrived. I've already added it to my spreadsheet, but there's still no discernible pattern."

When he turned, his lips formed a tight line. "Hinds is talking to a state fire investigator."

Claire Hinds was the fire chief. Oak Grove's first female fire chief, and as smart as they come.

"That sounds like a good idea. We can use a fresh perspective." I sat at my desk and logged back into my computer. "My research indicates our offender is either a member of the department or one of the volunteers. I hate to think it's true."

"I'm aware of the current theories. That's what worries me. If this outsider comes in with that idea in mind, he or she will ignore potential evidence trying to prove the preconception."

For a researcher that was a cardinal sin. "What are you going to do about it?"

He took a deep gulp from his cup. "If you weren't so busy, I'd ask you to be our representative to assist in making local connections. Make sure they get the whole story."

Chief Sorenson wasn't a man who handed out compliments, and I felt as if I'd won the grand prize. I pondered the suggestion. He was right, I'd be the perfect person for the job, but didn't have the time. But who else could? I frowned. "Freddie would be the obvious choice."

He raised an eyebrow.

I sighed. "But he could easily be dismissed as being prejudiced in favor of our guys."

"I came to that same conclusion."

"I can't think of anyone else right now. Let me sleep on it and get back to you."

He finished off his coffee and stood. "I appreciate your time, as always. I'll be in touch."

Chapter 2

"Spill it," I demanded after the waitress refilled our drinks. Water for me, coffee for Jake. She hovered too close as she filled his cup. Typical. "How did the job interview go?"

That's why I'd invited him out for a late supper, to grill him for details. He knew it and avoided the topic for the entire meal because he could.

His boss had set him up with a connection in Cleveland. Not to force him to leave, but there wasn't enough work available to keep Jake busy. The bars in town had fewer fights in the winter than in the summer, and bouncers only worked on the weekends. Even picking up the occasional shift as a bartender didn't satisfy Jake. Or support him. I suspected Eli slipped him cash on the sly. At least, that's where I hoped he was getting money. I didn't want to hear any alternatives.

"Don't know." Jake shrugged. "The guy had a great poker face. He said he'd be in touch, but I'm not holding my breath."

Coming from Jake, a self-taught expert at reading faces and body language, that was one heck of a compliment.

"I think I'd like working for him," Jake continued. "He doesn't let customers abuse his staff. Doesn't matter how much money they spend."

"He told you that?" I asked.

"No, one of the waitresses. I got there early enough to have an ice tea before the interview."

And scope out the joint ahead of time, no doubt. As well as the other employees. "Did she meet your standards?"

His brown eyes twinkled, and he winked. "No one can match you, Angel."

I snorted. "Whatever."

"I felt old, compared to most of the employees. The waitresses looked barely out of high school. If that's what the manager is shooting for, I don't have a chance. Unless he's looking for a father figure. I'm not old enough to be a father figure, am I?"

Was he serious? I decided to run with the joke angle. I leaned forward, examining his full head of light brown hair in the dim light. "I have noticed some gray hairs," I said, working to keep a straight face.

There was something about 'hair dye' in his muttered response.

I didn't let him off easy. "And are those wrinkles around your eyes?"

Jake frowned. He did have a few wrinkles, but he'd earned them the hard way, in prison. "Rub it in, why don't you? You still look as good as you did when we met."

I'd gained a few wrinkles myself, but it was sweet of him to say that. "You're going to have every woman in the place wrapped around your little finger in no time flat, Jake. Maybe one or two of the men as well. Like always. If you get the job, I mean."

The waitress, a brunette about my age, chose that moment to come over and refill his barely touched cup of coffee. Her arm grazed his as she reached for the cup. I was willing to bet she winked at him as she set the overfull cup back on the table. He maintained a straight face until she wandered back to the kitchen. Then his characteristic killer smile took over.

"Any bets on her number being on the back of the bill when she brings it?" he asked.

I should hope not, since I planned to cover the meal, and wasn't sure if I'd pass it along. The phone number, that was. It would only inflate his already swollen ego.

"Nope. I never bet against you." I considered reaching out and patting the back of his hand, but I didn't want to give him the wrong impression.

Without losing his smile, he shook his head. "Not that it matters. She's not my type."

He lied. His type was any female between the ages of eighteen and sixty, and both of us knew it.

A fire truck zipped down the street with no sirens on. I checked the time. Seven-thirty. The volunteers were right on schedule for their practice run. It was good some things remained normal.

A large family came in and took seats at the table behind us. I love kids, but these were out too late, over-tired and over-stimulated. They kept switching seats and running around their table, bumping into ours several times.

Jake leaned forward. "Ready to get out of here?"

Boy, was I ready. At least our waitress had good timing because she dropped the bill on our table as she hurried past to refill drinks for another couple. Without even checking the back for a phone number, I dropped enough cash on the table to cover the bill along with a generous tip. It was a sign of the times that Jake didn't even try to grab the bill from me. We stood simultaneously and hurried out of the restaurant.

"So, how was your day?" he asked as we strolled to the parking lot.

It would have been nice to have someone to share my concerns about the fires with, but my arrangement with Chief Sorenson demanded absolute secrecy. Still, Jake was a friend, so I picked another topic. "I'm worried about Janine and her mother. I haven't heard from her for over a week."

"And?" he prompted.

"The last time I talked to her she mentioned the doctors changing her mother's medications because they weren't working." Janine's mother was fighting stage four breast cancer.

"And?"

I sighed. "And I'm worried that her mother is dying. I mean, she is dying, but that her condition has worsened. That's the only reason that I can come up with to explain why Janine hasn't been in touch."

Jake stayed silent as he opened the passenger door of the Charger and held it for me. He didn't say anything until he crawled into the driver's seat, fastened his seatbelt and turned on the engine. "And?"

"It's time for me to start job hunting again. When Janine returns after her mother passes, she'll want her position as chief librarian back."

"You don't have to work." He feathered the gas pedal as he waited to pull onto the street. The volunteers were returning from their practice run and the stream of traffic behind them meant we had to wait longer than normal. "And if Janine is as smart as I think she is, she'll make a permanent position for you," he added.

"I'll drop a hint or three." I knew the library's budget intimately. Unless someone left, it held no wiggle room to create a spot for me. But Jake was trying to comfort me and I didn't want to discourage him.

Lost in my worries, I didn't see it happen but heard the honking of horns and the scream of metal against metal.

"Shit!" Jake shifted into park and killed the engine. Before I figured out what occurred, he opened his door and jumped out of the car.

It was a slow-motion disaster, like watching an old film played at the wrong speed. Brakes squealed as three cars piled together. Headlights and taillights shattered, and broken shards gleamed in the streetlights when a fourth car joined the chain of destruction. A pickup stopped just short of the bumper of the fourth one.

Jake rushed to the middle of the street, waving his arms over his head and yelling. Traffic came to a complete stop in both directions. I considered joining him, but he didn't look as if he needed help. Instead, I dug into my purse for my cell phone, dialed 911, and wondered how jammed the switchboard was.

"Where is your emergency?" a familiar voice said in my ear. Thank heavens Allison, our most experienced emergency operator, answered.

I explained the situation in as few words as possible.

"We've got the cavalry on the way," she said. "If it's safe, stay in your car and wait for them."

"I wasn't involved. Is there anything I can do to help in the meantime?"

"Keep clear of the scene," she answered. "We don't want civilians getting hurt."

Even if it made sense, it hurt my feelings. There had to be a way for me to help. But Jake had the traffic situation handled and all I remembered about first aid was limited to scratches and bruises.

The least I could do was move the car, so it wouldn't be in the way when the emergency vehicles arrived. If the cops wanted our witness reports, we'd be tied up for several hours. Thankfully, Jake left the key in the ignition and no one blocked the parking lot behind me.

With the Charger parked, I joined the small group of onlookers gathered on the sidewalk. Some were busy taking photos and videos, no doubt to post on social media. I kept my eye on Jake in case he needed help. But he'd been joined by an off-duty cop and the sirens screaming a few blocks away announced the imminent arrival of the professionals.

The volunteer firemen were the first to arrive, then the police, and finally the paramedics. They swarmed the street, triaging the folks needing medical attention. One officer relieved Jake of traffic duty while another put out cones to block the street. It was all so well-organized it seemed anti-climactic.

A burst of wind heralded the arrival of the predicted snow and I shivered as I zipped my jacket. The crowd began to wander off, driven away by the cold. A few of the hardier ones, mostly female, stuck around to watch the proceedings. I knew the type. Freddie had told me the ones who chased after cops were called badge bunnies. I wondered if the term applied to women who chased after fireman, too.

Not my worry. It looked as if a few of the guys enjoyed the attention, making a show of helping folks from their cars or directing traffic. Unimpressed, I considered heading back into the restaurant to warm up and escape from the diesel fumes. Maybe get a cup of cocoa or something. One for Jake too. The windbreaker he wore surely wasn't keeping him warm.

He finished his conversation with a policemen and headed my direction. "We're clear to leave," he said. He jerked his chin toward the officer in charge. "He knows where to find us if we're needed."

"Not that I'll be much help. I didn't see the first cars hit." I handed him the key to the Charger. "I was thinking about something else."

"How well do you know the library volunteers?"

"Why do you ask?"

"I thought the lady in the first car looked familiar, so I asked the cop her name. It was Rena Oleksandra. She's one of the volunteers, right?"

Oak Grove is a small town, but it was a strange coincidence, seeing her outside of the library twice in such a short span of time. I couldn't remember the last time I'd run into her in the grocery store or anywhere else. "Occasionally. She doesn't come in as much since she got a job. Why?"

"Huh. Funny thing. It was almost as if she braked deliberately when she didn't need to." Jake shrugged. "Or she spotted something in the street I didn't."

Chapter 3

"Interesting observation."

For a big man, Chief Sorenson moved quietly. I hadn't heard him walk up behind us. In unison, Jake and I turned to face him.

"What are you doing here?" I asked. Surely a fender bender—or a series of fender benders—didn't require his presence.

He arched an eyebrow, but a small smile touched his lips. "Is there a reason I shouldn't be?"

I realized he wore civilian clothes, not his uniform, so he was off-duty. Had he been in the neighborhood or at home relaxing and monitoring his scanner or did someone call him? "Of course not," I sputtered.

"Now that we have that cleared up," he said, then turned to Jake, "Tell me about the initial collision."

The snow started falling in earnest, so we moved the conversation to my apartment. Chief Sorenson had suggested his office, but Jake would be uncomfortable there. Besides, my coffee tasted better than the sludge the pot in his office made. I hoped the coziness of my place would allow the chief to relax. I gave him the recliner while Jake and I made do with the loveseat—after I'd moved my newest stack of books to the bookshelf. As soon as the first cup of coffee hit the chief's hands, he started the interrogation-I mean, the conversation.

"What makes you think the collision was deliberate?" The chief put his cup on a coaster and pulled out a small notebook and pen. Even in the informal atmosphere, his commanding presence made me sit straighter.

Jake leaned against the back of the loveseat and casually draped one arm across the top, but I sensed the tension in his muscles. There was no friendship between the two men. "I didn't say the crash was deliberate. I said it appeared the brakes in the first vehicle were applied for no reason."

"Care to elaborate?"

"I was keeping a close eye on the traffic, flowing slowly but smoothly. The light down the street was green and there was plenty of space between Ms. Oleksandra's car and the one in front of her. No one jaywalked and I didn't see a dog or anything run across the street. The car didn't just slow down, it came to a full stop."

"Sounds deliberate." Chief Sorenson flipped the page in his notebook.

"I can't say. Did she step on the brake instead of the gas? Did she sneeze? Was she aware of the car behind her?" Jake cocked his head. "I can't answer those questions, although I'm sure your officers will ask them if they haven't already."

"She claims the car in front of her braked sharply and she barely missed hitting it."

Jake shook his head. "Not that I saw."

"And the other cars?"

"Slow reaction speed? On the phone? Not paying attention? Take your pick."

"What's your take on this, Miss Duprie?" Chief Sorenson asked.

I shrugged. "I didn't catch the initial crash. The last two cars tried to avoid the collision, so they barely touched bumpers."

"From the reports my officers gave me, that's fairly accurate."

Was he complimenting me again? It made me uneasy, wondering what favor he wanted. "Your officers could have handled these questions, Chief. Which tells me there's more to this than it looks like. What's up?"

He picked up his cup and drained it before setting it back on its coaster. "Will both of you promise not to share this with anyone else?"

He trusted me, so it was Jake's presence that bothered him. I could practically hear the adrenalin flowing faster in Jake's veins as he dropped his pretense of being relaxed and leaned forward. "I promise."

Chief Sorenson's eyes met mine and I nodded. Jake's word was good. This time.

"It's not surprising," he said, "when major events end up on social media. But we don't have any of those around here." He glanced my way. "Not often, anyway."

I stared at an interesting spot on the wall behind him. I had an unfortunate history of being involved in recent major events.

He continued. "It's not even unexpected when things like our recent grass fires make the news."

Jake leaned forward a bit more.

"But an entire internet channel dedicated to these events bothers me. And the fact the channel has a large following makes things worse."

My laptop sat on the coffee table, charging. I reached for it as I asked, "What's the site?"

Jake jumped in. "And I'm guessing some of the videos show the fires being set."

Chief Sorenson grimaced. "You nailed it." He scribbled something in his notebook, tore the page out, and handed it to me. "That's the web link."

My fingers flew over the keyboard as I logged in and linked to the proxy site I used to hide my tracks. I didn't want my activity to be logged anywhere. "Who's posting the videos?"

"The information on the site says they're in Alaska."

"Fake." I shook my head. "I'm not good enough to track the source. But I know who is."

"Eli," Jake said.

"And Lando and Scotty. Two of Eli's employees,"

21

I explained to the chief. "They're the reason the program you bought from Eli is so secure. Not only do they write software, they can hack it."

The connection to the site was slow and took forever to load. "How did you hear about the channel?" I asked.

"Officer Atwood's son found out about it at school. He was watching it the other night when his father caught a glimpse and questioned him."

Of course, teenagers knew about the channel. But what did the fires have to do with tonight's accident?

The first video finally popped up. It was grainy and shot through smoke, so there wasn't much to see. There were a few clear pictures of the firemen at work, but the video kept going back to focus on the insignificant flames.

"No narration," I said.

"None. So, no voice to identify."

"How many are there?" Jake asked, leaning against my shoulder.

"I've found twenty."

I counted in my head. Too many. We hadn't had that many fires reported. "They aren't all local."

Chief Sorenson frowned. "I didn't recognize the location in a few. They might be from out-of-town incidents."

"Have you talked to Chief Hinds about this?"

"Not yet. I wanted to have something solid to present, not rumors and unsubstantiated theories."

That was reasonable. I browsed to the second video, and it was much the same as the first. Blurred focus, out-of-center shots, sickening-fast zooms as if someone just learned to use the camera on their phone.

But the big question still hadn't been asked or answered. "What's this have to do with the accident?"

His lips formed an impossibly tight line. "There's already a video of it online. I created a fake email account to follow the channel and be notified of new postings."

He was more tech savvy than I'd given him credit for. "Which came first? The call from dispatch or the email?"

"Dispatch. Thankfully."

While we talked, Jake took over my laptop. "Now there are two videos from tonight."

The chief grunted. "I thought I heard the notification bing."

It only made sense to watch both of them. One at a time, of course. The first one was a slow scan of each car in line, focused on the damage. It looked like something an insurance agent would use to help determine a payout and only lasted a minute or so. When it finished, Jake hit the replay button and swiveled the laptop so Chief Sorenson could see.

"Did you spot anything interesting?" he asked when the video finished playing.

"It was taken on the opposite side of the street from where Harmony and I were," Jake pointed out, "But there's nothing illegal about taking a video in public, right?"

"For the most part, correct. I'll spare you the details. How about you, Miss Duprie?"

"It was weird that all they showed were the cars. Oh, and the legs of people. It was like they wanted to avoid people's faces. Or they didn't want people to know they were recording."

Chief Sorenson nodded. "Let's see what the second one shows."

Jake and I got up to stand behind the recliner, so we could all watch at the same time. I expected more of the same, out-of-focus, grainy and jumping from one spot to another. As we waited for the video to load, I checked the clock. If Jake and the chief didn't leave soon, I'd be running short on sleep in the morning.

It started playing and the picture was as clear as a commercial production. It began seconds after the initial collision and panned to show the subsequent bumps. But it didn't cut off after the last car. The view switched to the gathering onlookers, zooming in on their faces.

"Shit!" Jake snarled as the focus changed once again and settled on him as he directed traffic.

"You're doing a good job for an untrained civilian," Chief Sorenson commented. "You'll be an internet sensation if this goes viral."

Jake paled. "Can Eli get the video taken down?"

There were any number of reasons that Jake might not want his face to become a nationwide phenomenon, but with Chief Sorenson in the same room, I couldn't ask about any of them. "I'll mention it. But that won't get rid of the original."

He muttered a few choice swear words. I didn't blame him. I kept an eye out for a picture of myself, but so far, I hadn't appeared on screen. It was illogical that I felt disappointed by my absence.

Chief Sorenson didn't say anything, but he'd listened in on our conversation while he kept his eyes on the screen. The action had switched to following the paramedics and firemen, especially the younger guys. It made me wonder out loud if a woman did the filming.

"That's a possibility. Notice how the recording skips right past the two female paramedics and concentrates on the men? But it isn't enough to eliminate a male."

In my head, I tried to count how many times the camera switched to each man. I'd met many of them, and the few I didn't recognize I assigned a number to. But I soon lost track and made a mental note to review the video a second time when I could take notes. There were two of the guys that seemed to get more attention than the others, Pete being one of them. I didn't recognize the other man, a paramedic.

"What does this accident have to do with the fires?" Jake asked when the video finished.

I had a theory but wanted to hear the chief's first, so I kept my mouth shut.

Chief Sorenson hit replay and Jake cringed when his image showed up.

"Perhaps nothing and it was no more than a coincidence. Good footage, keep the interest in the channel going." The chief blew out a deep breath. "If Ms. Oleksandra doesn't admit to causing the accident and why, we're at a dead end unless

Hennessey and his staff can get us information on who is posting the videos."

He meant Eli, of course, not Jake. Since he rarely used anyone's first name, it kept things interesting when several people shared the same last name.

"It's more than one person," I pointed out. "The first recording was filmed at the same time as the beginning of the second. Either two people posted to the site or one person knows who's posting and gave his video to them."

"Agreed." Chief Sorenson nodded. "And it's possible more will show up. I requested the officers at the scene to ask bystanders to share their photos. But will that make it easier or harder to find out who is responsible for the fires?"

A tiny ding had all three of us reaching for our phones. Chief Sorenson was the winner, or loser, depending upon your point of view. Jake and I returned to the loveseat to give him his privacy. After typing a return message, he stood. I wondered if he would update us on new developments.

"Please let me know if Hennessey gets that information," he said. "In the meantime, try to avoid trouble."

'Try' being the operative word. I didn't go looking for trouble—well, not often—but it had a way of finding me.

"Of course." I grinned. "Don't I always?"

Jake coughed, and I was tempted to punch his arm. Chief Sorenson almost smiled as he left. He was gone before I remembered to ask him the rookie's name.

Chapter 4

I scooped up the empty coffee cups and piled them in the sink, hoping Jake would get the hint it was time for him to leave. Instead, he pushed back in the loveseat and crossed his legs, like he was settling in for a long conversation. His fingers tapped on the seat cushion, revealing his nervousness. "Do you think you can reach Eli first thing in the morning?"

"Who are you afraid of, Jake?"

He grimaced. "Afraid isn't the proper word. Let's say I try to be suitably cautious. Remember, I shared a cell with some not-so-nice people."

True, but they weren't the people I had in mind. "Oak Grove isn't much of a hiding spot and you've been here how long? And no one has bothered you yet."

He lifted an eyebrow. "Are you sure?"

Guilt flooded over me. What kind of friend was I, not to consider that real criminals might want to seek revenge for something that happened while

Jake was incarcerated? But logic took over. Those people could find out where he was by searching his name on one of those shady internet sites. A random video shouldn't provide them with extra information. Besides, wouldn't I have heard something through the rumor mill?

I crossed my arms and glared. "Are you trying to play me, Jake?"

"You've always been able to see right through me," he said, avoiding my eyes. "No, no one from my prison days has come looking for me, but the longer I stay, the more likely it is they will. I can handle them, but…"

"Say it, Jake."

"You. I'm worried about you."

I'd never thought about it, but it made sense. If someone was looking for a way to get to Jake, I'd be an easy target. Well, I'd look like one, anyway. Unless someone did their research, they'd never know about my meager self-defense skills or Betsy, the Beretta that traveled everywhere with me.

Sleep didn't come easily once I'd convinced Jake to leave and I went to bed. I lay in the dark, reviewing my limited security. Being on the third floor helped, as did the better-than-average lock on the door. The number of times law enforcement types dropped by would be a deterrent to any bad actors keeping an eye on me.

None of that ensured my safety. I'd been

abducted before and had no desire to repeat the experience. So, I tossed and turned and finally fell asleep long after midnight.

❋ ❋ ❋

If Eli followed his normal routine, he'd be at work before anyone else got to the office. We often used the time to talk as I glanced through the morning paper and drank my first cup of coffee. Still, I worried I might wake him as I listened to his phone ring too many times.

"Good morning, beautiful," he answered at the last moment before I hung up.

A rush of warmth ran through me like it always did whenever I talked to him. "Good morning to you too, handsome. How did the meeting with the potential client go?"

"I don't know yet. They seemed impressed by the software but wanted to review their budget before committing. Standard business."

He seemed comfortable with it, so I didn't push the subject. "I need a favor that requires your special skills," I said without pussy-footing around. "But tell me if you don't have the time to do it."

"Just a minute." The distinctive squeak of his office door told me he'd closed it. "This sounds interesting."

"How would you feel about Lando and Scotty coming here and doing some side work for me? And you, of course," I added hastily. Although it would be weird paying him. "If you can afford to take a break."

"They'll be insulted if you offer to pay them. Especially Lando. I'm convinced he has a crush on you. What's the job?"

"I need a website hacked."

"Okay."

His bland one-word response wasn't the reaction I expected. I wished we were video chatting, so his face would reveal what he was thinking. I bit my bottom lip and waited for him to say more.

"We can do that from here," he said. 'Here' being far away in Florida.

"True, but it would kill two birds with one stone if you came to Oak Grove. I miss you." And it was true even though he'd visited at Christmas.

He chuckled. "I can't imagine you killing one bird, let alone two. And I miss you too. You don't have to invent an excuse if you want me to come."

"I want you to and it's not an excuse. The request came from Chief Sorenson. He wants to know who's posting the videos. They show the grass fires that have been plaguing the fire department."

That got his attention. "Holy shit."

"Yeah. And Jake wants the newest one taken down."

There was a long pause. "Why?"

"He's featured in it."

"What's the link?" Eli's voice was tight.

I gave him the web address, and listened to his keyboard clicking, followed by silence, and then a low whistle. "It has a lot of views," he said.

"That's what he's afraid of."

I heard his fingers tapping on the computer keys again. "This will take more than a couple of minutes. Let me check on what the guys are up to today. I'll get back to you soon."

I wanted to continue chatting, but once he'd gotten involved in a project, he had no desire to talk to anyone. "Love you, Eli."

"Love you too, Buttercup," he said but he sounded distant. Lost in whatever he saw on his computer screen was my guess. I smacked my lips loudly in the approximation of a kiss and ended the call without waiting for a response.

Talking to Eli, even for a few minutes, always made my day brighter. I even tried to whistle as I drove to work but ended up humming instead. Dolores, my salsa-red Jaguar, hummed with me. Well, her engine purred along, as usual.

Even though Eli hadn't committed to coming to Oak Grove, I started making plans for his trip. He'd stay with me, of course, because the house wasn't furnished yet. Lando and Scotty could either camp out at the house—all the utilities were on—or stay at The Towers, Oak Grove's best hotel. Paid for by me, naturally.

I couldn't figure out how to get time off to spend with them. I'd be a terrible hostess if I worked every day they were here. Or maybe they'd be so involved in their work they wouldn't notice my absence.

The library was only a block away when sirens screamed nearby. My heart raced as I glanced in my rearview mirror to make sure I wasn't being pulled over by a cop. But the only vehicle behind me was a beat-up pickup truck. Mr. Harnish was on his way to the nursing home to have breakfast with his wife.

I tapped my brakes in warning as we approached the intersection. His hearing was bad, and I didn't want to be part of an accident if a fire truck hurtled around the corner. Which is exactly what happened. We both came to a safe stop and waited for the traffic to clear before proceeding.

Curiosity got the better of me. We'd gotten enough snow, so I couldn't imagine the firemen were headed to a grass fire. And it was only one truck, not the vehicle they sent out for medical emergencies, which meant a small fire. I decided to follow them at a safe distance, for research, of course. I just wouldn't get to work as early as normal.

It soon became obvious I wasn't the only one chasing the action. A small procession formed behind me. Was this normal behavior or a new phenomenon connected to the videos?

The fire truck led us toward the edge of town and stopped in front of a ranch-style house. I parked down the street to keep an eye on things and wished I had a police scanner. Three firemen hopped out of the truck carrying extinguishers and headed toward the back of the house. The house next door and a wooden fence blocked my view.

But that didn't stop other onlookers, cell phones held in front of them like the Holy Grail. They scurried as close to the scene as possible and clustered on the sidewalk near the back of the fire truck. One guy, bolder than the others, edged through the yard toward the back. I grimaced. Just what the firemen needed, a civilian getting in their way. At least the unofficial contingent of volunteers who showed up to fires with bottles of water for the firefighters weren't there. They were a problem at times, and a blessing at others.

More sirens splitting the air promised help. I craned my head to determine what kind. The two police cars speeding down the street seemed like overkill.

The vehicles screeched to a halt alongside the fire truck. With the sun in my eyes, I needed to squint to identify the officers who hopped out. Officer Smith I recognized right away, but the other officer required a second look. The rookie. And I still didn't know his name.

They pushed the onlookers back a safe distance from the fire truck. Just in time, because two of the firemen returned to grab axes and other equipment. The sweet smell of burning wood mixed with a chemical stench drifted through my open window. I still couldn't imagine what was burning, but it had to be a small fire because the hose remained coiled on its rack.

I assumed none of the late-arriving looky-loos set the fire. And the way they clustered together, comparing notes, eliminated the potential for a unique video. They'd all look the same. I was wasting time when I needed to get to work. I coughed to clear my lungs of a particularly acrid puff of smoke and pulled back into the street at the first opening in traffic.

Refreshing the web page for the tenth time didn't help. No new video appeared on the list. So much for my theory the fire had been set deliberately for publicity. Why else would someone start one in a small pile of brush? With the snow covering the top of the stack, the blaze was almost out before the firemen got there.

That was the story from the gossip mill, anyway. I'd heard it from three library patrons so far. Slow news day. No one had died, gotten divorced, or had a baby, so the fire was the only thing to gossip about. Old Mrs. Edwina even mentioned how many fires there had been recently, and in all the years I'd known her, she'd never come up with an original thought, bless her heart. Someone out there was putting the pieces together and spreading the word. Or were they creating the pieces?

In the privacy of my office, I reloaded the web page one more time. Still nothing. I snuck a peek at my cell phone. No missed calls, not even the ones I anticipated from Chief Sorenson and Eli. I was tempted to break my own rule and turn the ringer on so I wouldn't have to trust I'd feel the vibration. But that would set a bad example, and I had an image to uphold. If not for me, for Janine when she returned.

What I really wanted to do was hop into Dolores and head over to the cop shop to chat with Chief Sorenson. Or go home and clean in case Eli showed up. Or take a trip to the fire station to introduce myself to Chief Hinds and swap information. Instead, I attacked the stack of mail I'd been avoiding all morning. Mostly junk, but I needed to open every envelope to make sure I didn't miss anything important. Part of the job I refused to foist off on anyone else. Besides, shredding junk mail was cathartic.

My moment of Zen was disturbed by loud but happy voices outside my office. I rolled my eyes and put the rest of the mail in a neat stack before pushing my chair away from my desk. I'm okay with a low rumble of conversation in the library, but some older patrons got antsy at the merest drop of a pen. The noise level had risen well above that, and the front desk staff didn't appear to be trying to stop it. That left it up to me.

I opened my office door and saw my staff clustered around a lone man. I smiled despite the noise. Pete's unexpected appearance came as a welcome surprise. But when he looked up, caught my eye, and frowned, I realized there was more to the story.

It took Pete fifteen minutes to extract himself from the group and make his way to my office. A line creased his forehead as he perched himself on the edge of the chair on the other side of the desk.

He reached into his pocket and tossed a small, roundish object on top of the stack of paperwork. "Did you lose this, Miss Duprie?"

It was a reflex action to lean over and pick it up. One I regretted right away, because instinct told me this was evidence, now contaminated with my fingerprints.

"It's not the one you gave me the other day, if that's what you're thinking." It was a copy of the brooch he'd given me the day of the fire at Eli's house. "The clasp on that one is broken." I tried to remember if it was still in Dolores' center console or if I'd tossed it in the garbage. "This one isn't. Where did you get this?"

He sighed. "That's a relief. One of the guys found it at the scene of the fire this morning. They mentioned seeing your car there, too. It bothered me."

"I'm not your firebug." Although the idea would have crossed my mind if we traded places.

Red rose in his cheeks. "I didn't want to believe it, so that's why I came to you first."

"You haven't mentioned it to anyone?"

"No. I came up with a story about checking out the pin online."

I didn't know who I needed to talk to first, Chief Sorenson or Chief Hinds.

Chapter 5

Chief Sorenson adjusted his desk lamp to direct the light at the two plastic sandwich bags. I'd used a marker to label them as one and two and slipped a brooch in each. Freddie leaned over his shoulder and peered at the evidence.

My short lunch break evaporated while I waited for the chief to finish meeting with members of the city council. The vending machines at the station offered nothing in the way of nutrition, so the chief's secretary snagged me a piece of pizza from someone's desk. Still, my stomach was dangerously close to growling as I waited for the two men to reach a conclusion.

"Who else has seen these?" Chief Sorenson asked without lifting his head.

"Besides Pete and the other firemen? I showed the first one to Jake but not number two."

Freddie grimaced. Neither man liked Jake. "And what did he think?"

"That it's costume jewelry. Older, but not valuable. But what are the chances of finding two copies of the same piece from the 1970s?"

"What does the internet tell you about it?" the chief asked.

I'd gotten busy at work and hadn't even looked yet. "It's on my to-do list," I admitted, studying a speck of dirt on the floor.

That earned a stare from Chief Sorenson. "The library keeps you that busy?"

"Most days, yes. I don't want anything to slip through the cracks in Janine's absence."

"You should have mentioned it. I'll find someone else to pull the monthly reports together."

Not a chance I'd give up that duty. It was too fascinating, reading the data and manipulating it into a form that non-experts could understand. Besides, I needed the income once Janine returned. "You don't have to. I know what you need and it only takes me a few hours. It would take you forever to train someone else."

He shrugged and didn't argue. I appreciated that.

"Let me know if you change your mind. And I'll let you get back to work, unless you have a theory about these I should hear?" He raised an eyebrow.

I shook my head. "No, I hoped the two of you would have an idea."

"I'll assign a team to search the last few scenes to see if there are more of these pins," Freddie said. "Determine if this is a coincidence or a pattern."

Chief Sorenson nodded. "Make it a joint team. One officer, one fireman for each site."

I wished I'd thought of that.

"Let's ask Chief Hinds to have her personnel watch out for more of these at any new fires." Freddie poked at one of the bags. "Or any similar jewelry."

"My liaison with the State Police can check their database for other reports," the chief said.

They had it handled. I stood, a useless third wheel. "I've got to get back to the library. We're expecting a shipment of books." We got a few new books almost every day, but they didn't need to know that.

Without glancing my way, the two men nodded. I scooped up my purse, straightened my spine, and lifted my chin. Not that they noticed. They were too busy comparing the pins section by section. I didn't want to destroy their fun by telling them I'd already done that, and yes, they were a perfect match.

I worked late to make up for my long un-lunch break, not wanting anyone to complain about me not earning my paycheck. Since Eli hadn't gotten back to me, there wasn't any reason for me to rush home. Sometimes things went that way, depending upon how business was going. He didn't talk about it, but he was still concerned someone who worked for him was leaking information to his competitors. I worried too because I couldn't help him figure out who.

Dolores' headlights melted away the darkness on the trip home. I took the long way, reluctant to return to my empty apartment. Being alone didn't have the same appeal it had before I met Eli.

But as I drove down the side street, I spotted light where it didn't belong. I remembered turning off the light in my kitchen when I left that morning.

My options were limited. I imagined myself sneaking up the stairs, Betsy in hand, and throwing open my door to confront the intruder. Or charging up, Freddie by my side, and a dozen of Oak Grove's finest backing us up. But if the trespasser carried his own gun and bullets flew, innocent bystanders might get hurt. And if I'd mistakenly left the light on, I'd embarrass myself and make Freddie look like a fool.

Of course, the visitor might be Jake. He dropped by once in a while when I didn't expect him, and always found a way to let himself in. There was one way to find out. Call him. Not as exciting as the other choices, but more sensible. That's what any self-respecting chief librarian would do.

Instead of parking in the driveway, I pulled in along the curb and turned off the lights, but left the engine running. I checked my mirrors and studied the street in front of me. Empty. I didn't even see Mr. Callahan out walking his dog, his excuse for sneaking a cigarette. The quiet made me twitch. It felt as if the world was waiting for something terrible to happen.

I retrieved Betsy from my purse and laid her in my lap before pulling out my cell phone. In the dim light provided by its display, I scrolled through my contacts to find Jake's listing. Sure, I had his number memorized, but didn't want to misdial.

By the third ring, I switched the phone to my left hand and stroked Betsy's handle with my right. At the fourth ring, I verified the safety was on. At the fifth ring, I plotted how to rescue Jake from whoever held him hostage.

But before the sixth ring, I heard a faint click and the familiar "Hey, Angel."

Just because he answered didn't mean we were in the clear. "Hey," I said, pretending I wasn't about to have a panic attack, "Where are you?"

"Your place. Trying to find a decent show. When are you going to get cable?"

Never. I rarely watch T.V. and Jake knew that. "Why didn't you call me and tell me? You gave me a heart attack when I saw my lights were on."

He had the gall to laugh. "I've got to keep you on your toes. You're getting complacent. Not watching your surroundings, staying with the same schedule, taking the same route to and from work. Have you forgotten everything I taught you?"

Guilty as charged, but it was hard. Besides, the bad guys who might bother me were in jail. I had no reason to worry.

He didn't wait for an answer. "How soon will you be home?"

"I'm just down the street. See you in a few."

"I'll have a glass of ice tea waiting."

Yes, even in the dead of winter I was a sucker for a good glass of ice tea. I couldn't brew it in the sun like I did during the summer, but I'd mastered the trick of getting the perfect strength on my stovetop. A glass before supper sounded perfect.

As I parked Dolores in the garage, I wondered what Jake wanted.

The worry increased when he served me supper—warmed up Mama D's lasagna that tasted like heaven. But where was his car? I hadn't spotted it on the street where he normally parked.

I hid my anxiety through the cheesecake and coffee. As he carried my dishes to the kitchen sink, I broke.

"What's going on, Jake?"

There was no smile on his face when he turned around. "I'm leaving town tomorrow."

If he got the job in Cleveland, that was good news. This didn't feel like good news. "Where are you going?"

"It will be better if I disappear." He reached out and stroked my cheek. "At least until Eli can get that video taken down."

My faith in Eli's hacking superpowers had gradually faded during the day as the clock ticked out the passing time and he hadn't called to announce his success.

"Give him a day or two to work on it," I urged.

"It can't wait that long. I won't put you or anyone else in danger. I'll make a big show of leaving so there's no doubt I'm gone. Get a squad car to follow me to the city line or something."

Torn between believing him and suspecting he was being over-dramatic, I asked, "Is it that bad?"

"Not yet. And maybe never. I'm not willing to take that chance."

I took a deep breath. "Who is after you, Jake?"

He claimed the tale needed to be told with the help of alcohol. Two beers for him and red wine for me. Just a basic Pinot Noir I picked up in a rush a few days earlier. Jane, my favorite cousin and liquor distributor, sighed when she rang it up, suggesting I try something new, but I didn't have the time to rummage through her selections.

With the TV turned to the weather station for background noise, he settled himself on the loveseat, and quickly drained one can of beer. With the second can in hand, he started talking. I expected a tale from ten or fifteen years ago. I was wrong.

"You were there," he said. "You saw the kind of people I associated with in West Virginia."

Yes, I remembered. That was only a few months ago when an FBI agent had blackmailed him into going undercover for them.

"Anyway, to help my cover and fit in, I hung out with a waitress from the bar."

Interesting. He didn't use the word date.

"Don't worry, I made sure she was over eighteen."

Was that his way of telling me they'd had sex? Why should I care? We were only friends, at my insistence. I had Eli. Jake needed someone.

43

"She wasn't local either. She moved to Charleston from someplace in Tennessee. And I told her I came from Atlanta."

I bet she'd been a sucker for his fake southern accent.

It hit me like a sledgehammer. "Shit, Jake, is she pregnant?"

He took a gulp of his beer as I emptied my glass of wine.

"No, nothing like that. I'm careful. But she turned out to be one of those clingy women. The type that as soon as you pay them any attention, suddenly you're their soulmate. She was looking for a ring within a couple of weeks."

I didn't understand the problem. Jake could handle the issue without leaving town. Especially if the girl thought he was in Atlanta. "So you dumped her. She'll get over it."

He grimaced. "That's what I figured. But just before I left town, I heard she went crying to her mommy about it. Turns out she's as crazy as her daughter and threatened to track me down and make me pay for hurting her baby."

I wanted to laugh, but he was serious. I poured another smidgen of wine to cover my smile. "She isn't the first unhappy mother you've dealt with."

"No, but this one is a biker. And she has friends who are bikers. Not the weekend doctor and lawyer casual ones. I mean the hard-core kind of biker. The kind to get revenge and ask questions later."

I wasn't aware we had any hard-core bikers in Oak Grove. At least, I'd never seen any or read anything about them in police reports. "What are the chances this girl will ever see the video? And I can think of another way for you to hide. Change your appearance. Dye your hair, grow a beard. A full one, not the scruff you're so fond of."

"That might work." He rubbed the hair on his chin. "What do you suggest? Black, blond, or red?"

Red would be hard to maintain and blond too close to his normal hair color. Black it was. His beard, once he grew it, would need to be dyed too. Did they make coloring just for beards? "Have another beer. I'll make a run to the drugstore and get what we need."

Chapter 6

I stripped off the flimsy plastic gloves that came with the dye and tossed them in the garbage can. Jake was still Jake, but a new and improved version with black hair. The beard might make a difference but would take a week or two to grow.

Still, I stepped back and walked around him to admire my work.

He studied himself in a hand mirror. "I hate it," he said. "I don't look like me. But I guess that's the point."

"It brings out the color of your eyes." A little flattery might help. But that gave me another idea. Glasses. "Wait here."

Like there was any place for him to go in my small apartment. There were several pairs of my old glasses stuck in a drawer. The prescription would screw with his vision, but if they changed his appearance, we could pick up a pair of low-level cheaters from the drugstore.

The first ones I found sported pink frames,

bought on a whim, worn two or three times. While they would be a fun joke to play on Jake, I didn't think he'd find them amusing. I dug deeper. The perfect pair with heavy black frames was in there somewhere.

When I found them, he was pretending to comb his hair while staring at himself in the mirror. The lines on his forehead made it clear he wasn't happy. I thrust the glasses at him.

He slipped them on and grinned. "I forgot how blind you are, Angel." He squinted in the mirror. "I can't see a darn thing!"

My eyesight wasn't *that* bad.

He slipped them down his nose so he could peer over the top. "Makes me look like a professor."

Not the ones I had in college. He was better looking. But I wasn't about to say that out loud and inflate Jake's ego.

"Hmm. They help. Now if you wear button-up shirts instead of your polos, you can pull this off."

He groaned. "I'll get laughed at if I show up to work in a dress shirt."

"Or maybe the customers will think you're management and pay more attention to you." His work as a bar bouncer and occasional bartender wasn't always easy.

"That's a thought. But I can't wear these." He pulled off the glasses and handed them to me.

"Of course not." I put the glasses on the counter. "You can pick up a pair at the drugstore. Or make a trip to the costume store in Pittsburgh and get some with plain glass for lenses."

He grinned. "You keep surprising me. No wonder I love you."

We'd had this same discussion too many times. And hadn't we just talked about him having sex with another woman? I glared at his reflection in the mirror.

"As a friend. I love you as a friend. Your heart belongs to Eli." He chuckled.

I hoped he meant that.

After Jake left, headed to a late shift, I checked my phone once again. Still no message from Eli. If he'd hopped the first available commercial flight—or pulled the corporate plane out of its hangar—he'd already be here. There wasn't a missed call or message from Lando and Scotty either. I restarted my phone to make sure it wasn't frozen, and as I waited for it to load, I pulled up the fire website one more time.

Nothing had changed. Eli and the boys hadn't pulled off a miracle. And no new videos either, which I didn't understand.

The logical thing was for me to call him. And got his voicemail. Even the sound of his voice in the recorded message made me feel better. The message I left in response had nothing to do with the issue at hand and everything to do with making him miss me.

The morning brought gray skies, heavy snow, and bad news. The Pittsburgh airport closed due to the weather. Eli and the guys wouldn't be coming. And Freddie wouldn't be able to comb the locations of the fires to search for more brooches.

My work schedule didn't include Saturdays, although I often went in to catch up on whatever I'd missed during the week. After sweeping off my steps and helping Joe and Luke shovel the sidewalks, I decided to stay home and clean house. An all-day deep cleaning splurge would distract me from my worries.

I started in the kitchen. The refrigerator, specifically. It didn't smell, and nothing was out of date, but it needed rearranged. I kept my condiments in a specific order, from most used to the ones rarely used. Jake didn't pay any attention to the system and put things away anywhere they fit. While straightening it out, I wiped down every shelf and bin.

As I rinsed out my sponge, it took me a moment to realize that someone was knocking, as the sound mingled with the classic rock on my headphones. I danced my way to the door and remembered to peer through the peephole before opening it. I'd half-hoped for Eli, but it was just Pete.

But how did he know where I lived? I'd never had a fire in my apartment. There didn't seem to be a reason not to open the door, so I did.

"What brings you out in this weather?" I asked, more cheerfully than I felt. I hated being interrupted in the middle of cleaning.

He stomped his feet to shake off the snow that stuck to his boots. "Can I come in?"

I stepped back to make room for him. A blast of winter air accompanied him in the door, making me shiver as I reached to close it. "Coffee?" I needed a cup to get warm.

"Sure." He shrugged off his jacket and I snagged it to hang on the coat rack. I didn't want melted snow all over the floor.

Like most first-time visitors, he glanced around, checking out my apartment. It was never what anyone expected. Small but neat, with packed bookshelves everyplace there was room. Used furniture and only a few knick-knacks. If they only knew me by my car, my apartment came as a shock.

He followed me into the kitchen and I started a new pot. I skipped the expected niceties. "What's going on?"

"I'm looking for advice and you are the best person to ask."

Although I made a habit out of helping the high-school volunteers, he and I had never been close. "Why me?"

He swallowed, hard enough that his Adam's apple bobbed. "Because you hang out with Detective Thomason."

Cleaning could wait. The day had suddenly gotten interesting.

"But not in an official capacity," I reminded him as I watched the coffee trickle into the pot. "And

I'm not a lawyer so I can't give you legal advice."

"That's not what I'm looking for."

Blunt was the best way to go. "What's the problem?"

He waited until I'd handed him a filled mug. "Promise not to tell anyone. It's not just me, and the other guys don't want to be identified, but they agreed to let me talk to you."

"I promise, unless it's something illegal." A tickle of worry asked if he and his friends had set the fires.

He shook his head. "Nothing like that. Just personal. We don't want to waste police time. They're busy enough. Can we sit?"

I was slacking on my duties as a hostess. After we'd settled ourselves—I insisted he take the recliner—he told me the story.

"We're not sure when they started. The crazy emails. I deleted the first few I received, figuring it was spam. They sounded like a pre-teen writing love notes to their first crush. I thought it was weird. Or funny. I couldn't decide."

"You said you talked about it with the other guys."

"Not right away. Not even when they came more frequently. Then one of the other guys joked about getting them. We compared notes and five of us had received them."

"And so, you came to me."

"Nope. Not until whoever sends the emails started attaching photos of us. First, they were pictures of us while we were working, but yesterday I received a photo taken when I was at the grocery store. And Terry got a picture of him at the gym."

"Have you asked your IT department to trace who's sending the emails?"

He snorted. "Department? Neither of the two guys who support our computer stuff work on the weekends. And it's not like this is an emergency."

It might be, but I didn't want to alarm him.

"Is the same person sending all the emails?" I refilled my coffee cup, plotting how to tackle the problem. Lando and Scotty taught me about tracing emails, but only basic stuff. Like how to see the actual address an email came from.

"No. We figure at least three different people sent them."

Or one person using three different emails. "Can I see an example?"

Pete pulled his phone from his pocket. "I saved a couple. Let me log in."

It only took him a moment and he handed me his phone. He was right, the email read like it was written by a twelve-year-old. An immature twelve-year-old. Or English wasn't their first language. I didn't recognize the email company.

"There's no picture with this one." I handed the phone back to him, not wanting to scroll through his emails.

"You know what I look like," he joked.

What I really wanted to see is if a second email came from the same address as the first. And if it sounded like it was written by the same person. He tapped his screen a few times and handed the phone back.

"Here you go."

It was a bad picture, grainy and out of focus. I guessed it had been taken from a long way away. But it was Pete, no doubt about it.

The message, although still filled with bad grammar and emojis, felt different. Darker. Needier. Almost threatening. Not in words, but in context. My previous job with our local authors had taught me a lot about that. No wonder Pete and his co-workers worried.

RU ready 2B my frend? I wait for U avery nite but U neva come. Why dont U rite back? Please talk to me, At least I can see U work (smiley face) I (heart) U. A string of hearts, flowers and smiley faces followed the text.

I didn't forget to check the address it came from. It was different from the first but still a company I didn't recognize. The situation was beyond my limited skills. I needed the experts more than ever. But I still hadn't heard from Eli.

I sent Pete home with a promise to check into the emails and a request for more information. I needed the additional emails to study for clues and to share with Eli and the guys. And I needed to find out if the emails and pictures qualified as stalking or not. My first instinct was to call Freddie, but I'd made that pesky promise. The one not to tell anyone. Eli wasn't law enforcement, so he didn't count.

It took only a few minutes to find the laws on stalking. Deciding whether or not the emails qualified would take several lawyers, a judge and a jury. From the emails I'd seen, it seemed impossible to decide if there was malicious intent. And Pete didn't appear to be worried about bodily harm. After all, he was about six feet tall and built to handle heavy fire hoses, what could a little kid do to hurt him?

But on the internet, there's no way to know if the person at the other end is fourteen or forty-four years old. Pete and his co-workers might not be worried, but I was. I'd made the leap between the emails, the videos, and the fires. Lots of dots but I needed help to draw the connecting lines.

Time to try to reach Eli again. It had been over twelve hours since I called him, so I wouldn't come off as being pushy. I hoped. But the streak continued. His voicemail picked up immediately. I didn't bother leaving a message.

That left me with two choices. Research the emails on my own or pick up cleaning where I left off. I knew my limitations. That meant cleaning.

Chapter 7

By late afternoon, the snow had stopped and my urge to clean had been sated. Although the shelves at the grocery store might be on the barren side this late in the day, I only needed a few things. Enough to get me through two or three days if Eli showed up.

My frustration grew as I fought to get by inconsiderate shoppers who left their carts parked in the middle of the aisle as they browsed as if in search for treasure. The new cereal they'd seen advertised or the improved version of an old standard. Not me. I knew where everything was located and I'd be in and out in ten minutes. At least, as long as I didn't run into anyone who wanted to stop to gossip.

So, when I spotted Mrs. Geary pondering the selection of paper towels, I headed down the pet food aisle. My supply of treats for Piper, the landlords' dog, was getting low.

The brand he liked filled the bottom shelf. I leaned over to grab a box when I saw a pair of scruffy tennis shoes much too close. Close enough the wearer might kick me if he wasn't careful. While pretending to read the package, I studied the guilty party.

His jeans matched the shoes. The rips in the knees didn't appear to be a designer feature. The zipped-up jacket, although clean, showed signs of wear. His five o'clock shadow looked like it was seven o'clock. The outfit didn't go along with the selections in his cart, all top brands, and expensive meat.

He glared at a can of cat food. "Stupid cat," he muttered and I almost giggled. Had his wife sent him out on this errand? He put that can down and chose another. "Can't eat the cheap stuff, can ya'?"

Although his agony was entertaining, my knees ached from kneeling on the hard tile floor. With one hand on the handle of the cart, I pulled myself up. At the same time, he reached for yet another brand of cat food and we ended up bumping into each other. Not hard but enough to annoy me. Had he even known I was there?

"Do you mind?" I snapped, not feeling the least bit charitable.

"Watch out!" he barked in the same moment.

A second glance told me I could take him—he didn't seem to have much in the way of muscles—but, more importantly, he wasn't a threat. I dropped Piper's snacks in the cart, stuck my nose in the air, swiveled on one foot, and marched away. I had more important things to worry about.

Monday dawned clear and dry, with enough snow still covering lawns and trees to make Oak Grove picture perfect. In fact, I snapped a few on the short walk I took halfway through the morning. Truth is, I was having trouble concentrating on paperwork. I'd received one call from Eli with a bad connection—I could hear him, but he couldn't hear me—and one missed call with no message. I still didn't know where he was but at least he was alive.

Around lunchtime, my cell phone buzzed again. Not Eli, but Chief Sorenson. I wondered if he wanted a non-existent update.

"Hello, Chief," I said.

"Ms. Duprie," he answered formally, "I'm calling to see if you are available to drop by during your meal break. There are people here I'd like you to meet."

He didn't sound happy. Red flags waved all over the place. What had I done wrong? The quick answer was nothing. I assumed the people he referred to sat in his office listening to the conversation, so I didn't ask the dozen questions that popped into my head.

A second glance at the clock assured me it was close enough to my usual time that I could leave without anyone commenting on it. Then I had a moment of panic about settling into a pattern, making me an easier target. But no one was after me anymore.

I took a silent deep breath and reached up to smooth my bun. Good thing I'd worn one of my better work outfits. "Let me finish reviewing this order, then I'll be on my way. It will only take a few minutes. Can your guests wait that long?"

It was a pure power play. Make them wait. Show them I wasn't at their beck and call. I would have loved to see the expression on their faces. Whoever they were. I placed a bet on representatives of the FBI or another three-letter agency.

I was wrong. Chief Hinds I recognized from pictures in the paper. The man with her I'd met in the grocery store. Yeah, him. He was the expert Chief Hinds brought in to help with her side of the investigation. Of course, he'd ditched his ratty jeans for a suit and tie.

Chief Sorenson made the introductions. Carlton Fiesker. No wonder I didn't like him. When we shook hands, he gripped mine too hard as if exerting dominance. I stared him in the eyes, planted my heels, squeezed tighter, and pulled. Not too hard, but enough to throw him off balance. The trick would only work once, but once was enough. He scowled, and I widened my eyes and blinked at him as I released my clasp.

Chief Sorenson coughed. As I turned to take my seat, I winked at him.

"I'm so grateful you came. I've been reviewing the research you've done." Thankfully, Chief Hinds sat in the chair between me and Fiesker, so I didn't have to look past him to talk to her. "Your statistics are impressive."

"But they don't show any trends or patterns. Unless you see something I've missed."

She shook her head. Her short, graying hair moved against the collar of her pale-yellow shirt. "No, but I've asked Carlton to check them for me."

I hated he'd have access to my work, but that was the reality of life. "I'll be glad to answer any questions that come up, Chief Hinds."

"Please call me Claire. I'm not a stickler for my title." She glanced towards Chief Sorenson and I wondered if this was a point of contention between the two of them. Not my concern.

"There's additional information I haven't added to my data." I didn't know if Chief Sorenson had clued her into the videos or not, and I didn't want to put him in a bad position. I'd spent most of my Sunday correlating the videos to the incidents and hadn't come up with any new insights.

"Chief-Claire and I discussed the website," Chief Sorenson said. "Have you been able to get in touch with your expert?"

"We made initial contact but he hasn't given me an update."

Chief Sorenson gave me a puzzled glance, but I wasn't about to give him the details until we were in private.

"I'll use my own experts," Fiesker said. I'd wondered when he'd get around to adding his penny's worth.

Chief Sorenson arched an eyebrow and Claire sighed. "As we discussed, this is a joint investigation.

You'll keep me and whoever Chief Sorenson designates as his contact updated and vice versa. While I value your expertise, our local resources have proven themselves more than competent."

Fiesker frowned but didn't object. "Who is my contact? I'd like to meet him and get to work."

Of course, he assumed it would be a man.

Sorenson grinned and leaned back in his chair. "Since Ms. Duprie has declined the opportunity, I've assigned Detective Thomason to the case. He and Ms. Duprie have worked together before and I'm sure if she gets one of her brainstorms she'll tell him. Right, Ms. Duprie?"

"Naturally." But I didn't look the chief in the eye. I was already hiding information from him.

My plan was to leave the meeting early and go back to the library without having to talk to Fiesker. But I needed an excuse, so I didn't appear impolite. I got lucky when my phone vibrated, and I left to answer it. And no, it wasn't Eli, just a random telemarketer. Even after I hung up on her, I continued to pretend to carry on a conversation for a minute. It was the cover I needed.

Once I killed enough time and 'hung up' for pretend, I popped my head back into the chief's office. The three of them were discussing the absence of a video for the last fire. "I need to run," I said. "Work calls."

"It's been a pleasure meeting you finally," Claire said. "I've heard so much about you. Based on what

I've seen so far, I don't think the stories do you justice."

Which stories? The one about me taking down a whole gang of moonshiners single-handedly? Or the time I hacked into the FBI computer system? Hopefully neither, and Chief Sorenson was the source of her information instead of the Oak Grove rumor mill. He'd tell her the truth.

"It's been nice to meet you, too," I said. "But don't believe everything. There are some wild stories floating around."

Claire laughed. "A lady at my church tried to convince me you worked for the CIA. Don't worry, I know better."

Over her shoulder, I saw Fiesker's lips draw into a thin line. Oh well, he didn't have to like me. As long as it didn't interfere with the investigation, I didn't care.

❊ ❊ ❊

The black panel wagon marked 'Mohawk Enterprises.' parked on the street in front of the library should have been my first clue, but I didn't give it a second glance. The grins on the faces of the staff when I walked in the door should have been my second. I assumed it was because of the group of kindergartners who walked out the front door as I walked in. Their cheerful chatter and laughter made me smile, too. I missed doing story hour for the little ones.

The dead giveaway came in the form of a large bouquet of mixed color roses on my desk. Their sweet fragrance filled the small space and I took a deep breath before twirling around, sure I'd catch Eli hiding behind the door. There wasn't any other place he could be.

Or not. Maybe he'd had the flowers delivered. The card would hopefully reveal all.

The message was cryptic. *John D. Rockefeller.* What did it mean? Sure, I knew who Rockefeller was, but he'd been dead a long time. The flowers didn't come from him.

But this was a library and Rockefeller lived on in bibliographies. Giggling followed me as I meandered out onto the main floor and headed towards that section. I was being watched, but I paid no attention. If Eli waited for me among the shelves, that's what counted.

When I turned down the right aisle, my heart sank. He wasn't there. I spotted a sticky note attached to one of the books. *Try again.*

He wanted to play, did he? Where else would he be? I'd look silly running past every aisle on every floor trying to find him.

A memory tickled the back of my brain. Where else to go for information about Rockefeller? The Gilded Era history section, of course, but I'd passed by there on my way to bibliographies.

The tickle turned into an itch. Something about parties. And menus.

I hurried up the stairs to the second floor. Once upon a time, in the housekeeping arts section, I'd found a book that described the meal served at one of Rockefeller's parties. When I looked for it the first time, I'd also found the palest blue eyes I'd ever seen. Eli's.

A faint earth scent greeted me at the top of the stairs. His aftershave. He always wore the same brand. I was getting close. My pulse picked up speed and I fought the urge to skip the short distance to the correct aisle.

I turned the corner and sighed. No Eli. I was so sure I was right. But no sticky note on the shelf taunted me either. A dead end.

Through the shelf, I caught a glimpse of someone in the next row. I sniffed. It certainly smelled like Eli. Then I remembered. We'd rearranged the shelves a few months ago. If he went by his recollection of where we first met, he was right.

I considered committing a cardinal sin and shoving a few books off the shelf on the other side to startle him. But that might damage the books and I didn't want to set a bad example. I'd do this the boring way. Tiptoe to the end of the aisle and surprise him.

It didn't work out according to my plan. It went better. I got to the end of the row and ran into a hard body. Before I had a chance to react, my feet were off the ground, Eli's arms wrapped around me and his lips pressed against mine.

"Miss me?" I murmured when we finally stopped to catch our breath and he put me down.

"Remind me to never catch a ride with Lando again. 'Take the back roads,' he said. 'We'll get to see the real America,' he said. I thought he meant two-lane highways, not dirt roads!"

And out of range of cell phone towers, I guessed. "Then it snowed."

"And both Lando and Scotty are Florida born and bred. They never drove in snow before. We had to stop and let them build a snowman. Then there were the snowball fights. Not just one, but every time we stopped for gas or food." Eli stroked my cheek. "I thought we'd never get here!"

"Me too," I said, snuggling against his chest. "I'm glad you made it. But you could have waited in my office. Although this is more fun."

"I wanted to be alone with you for a minute or two. With the guys here, I don't know how much privacy we'll have. But there's a brand-new bed we need to break in. I'll have to find a way to get Lando and Scotty out of the house for a bit. Send them to Pittsburgh on an errand or something."

I'd seen the bed. Jake had called me when it was delivered. The king-sized bed with its intricately carved headboard and footboard dominated the room and suited Eli perfectly. Jake had teased me about when I was going to move in, because there were two matching dressers as well.

"We only have a few days," Eli continued. "And this is a good opportunity to wire the house for conference and video calls. It will make it easier to keep things going when I'm here, and I'll be able to spend more time with you."

Exactly what I hoped for. "They can stay at the house while you stay with me."

He pulled me in tighter. "I'd love to do that, Buttercup, but we'll be pulling late nights this trip. I was hoping you'd bunk with me." He leaned over and whispered roughly, "I've been having fantasies of coming up the stairs and finding you in my bed."

His words sent a delicious shiver down my spine. We were heading into marvelously dangerous territory, and I liked it. I had a few visions of my own and they involved me, him, and lots of books. But I was at work, the library was open, and no privacy anywhere.

"Hold that thought," I said, resting my hand on his chest. "Someone is coming." I'd heard the giveaway squeak of the third step from the top.

Chapter 8

It was only Dorai Weston looking for a needlepoint book. After helping her choose and spending a minute talking about her littlest one's new tooth, the moment between Eli and I vanished. I needed to get back to my duties and Lando and Scotty waited for Eli at the house. They'd sent him with a shopping list and he had several stores to visit to pick up everything they needed.

To get a quick kiss, I followed him out to the van—Lando had replaced his old one for the newer black one. "Mama D's for supper?" I asked. "Just you and me?"

He shook his head. "Mama D's sounds good, but for takeout. That way you can catch up with Lando and Scotty too. The entire trip they were figuring out how to get you to go to a ComicCon with them."

"Did you remind them I have a steady job now? That I can't hang out with them?"

"Several times. Then they started with the sexy librarian jokes."

I've heard them all. From the wrong people. The one about having fine written all over me the most. "Warn them that if they start spouting them I'll fight fire with fire. There are a ton of geek jokes. And I'm a librarian. I bought the books."

The edges of Eli's mouth quivered like he was trying to hold back laughter. "I'll pass along the message. See you at six?"

❊ ❊ ❊

We ate supper picnic style, sitting on the floor of the front room. The rest of the first floor was stacked with equipment—computers, wires, stuff I didn't recognize. Eli managed a miracle and got internet access turned on. That was the one utility the house was set up for but I hadn't activated.

Lando made a big show out of trying to sit next to me but eventually relinquished the spot to Eli. I teased him about his hair—it was a bright blue. He'd dyed it after losing a bet, decided he liked it, and had kept it the same color for three months, a new record.

Eli had filled the guys in on the situation. Except for the part about the stalking emails. I wanted to discuss those privately with him.

Lando played with his tablet while we ate, but I couldn't tell what he was doing. I didn't ask either, because the resulting explanation might take ten minutes or more and end in a raging headache. And I didn't want anything to interfere with the first night in the new bed and what I hoped would happen there.

As I plated the cheesecake Eli bought for dessert, Lando let out a whoop. "Finally! Took them long enough."

"Pass it over here," Scotty held out a hand.

He seemed quieter than I remembered. I hadn't been able to get him to loosen up all evening.

Lando passed him the tablet and he swiped the screen. "Good for now," he said. "How long until they post another copy?"

"What are you guys talking about?" I asked as I handed Eli a slice of cheesecake.

"The video of your friend. It's down for now." Lando grinned. "We did it the old-fashioned way."

"Which is?"

"DMCA takedown."

I'd learned lots of their technical jargon, but this one was new. "I don't have a clue what you are talking about."

Eli swallowed. A third of his cheesecake was already gone. "Copyright violation. When we couldn't hack the website, we filed paperwork claiming the video is owned by us and the poster didn't have the rights to it. The claim won't stand up to legal scrutiny but hopefully, it'll be a few days before it gets re-posted."

"Won't you get in trouble when the request comes back as a fake?"

Lando's smile stretched across his face. "We didn't fill the paperwork out as us. We used a fake identity. If they trace it back, it will look like it came from one of our competitors. Not exactly, but close enough at first glance."

"At the same time, we made the changes so obvious that when someone finally sees them, they won't know how they missed them." Eli seemed unconcerned as he took another bite of his dessert.

I leaned my back against the wall, chewed my bite of cheesecake and pondered the ethics of what they had done. It amounted to little more than a white lie and didn't hurt anyone while at the same time helping Jake. If I threw in the idea that the person who posted the video was potentially responsible for the fires, things more than evened out. I could live with it. "What's the next step?"

"Tracking down who is posting the videos," Lando answered. "We've started the process. The account is set up with a fake name, so it could take some time."

Time that we might not have.

The scream of sirens woke me the second time. The first time was when Eli carried me upstairs to his bed. I'd fallen asleep as he and the guys discussed varying strategies for tracking the culprit. Eli's room was on the side of the house away from the street and the sound faded as I pulled myself away from his warmth.

I fumbled for my phone, trying not to wake him. A few weeks earlier, I'd installed an app that worked like a police scanner. I planned to sneak off to the bathroom and find out what was going on without waking him.

It didn't work because as I pulled on my robe he

rolled over and asked, "You aren't leaving, are you?"

Not a chance. "Just headed to the bathroom," I whispered. That was the one improvement we hadn't been able to fit in—a separate bathroom for the master bedroom. To make up for it, we'd made the main one bigger by taking over an adjoining closet. And added a half-bath on the third floor.

"With your phone?"

He'd caught me. "I heard sirens. I wanted to make sure it wasn't a fire."

"That'll wait. Come back to bed."

But now that I was all the way awake, I realized the trip was a necessity. "I'll be right back. Promise."

He held out his hand. "Give it here."

He knew me too well. With an exaggerated sigh, I gave him the phone. "Now can I go?"

"Don't stay away too long," he chuckled. "Or I'll have to come looking for you."

Hmm. Strip hide-and-go-seek. I knew of several good spots to hide. I'd save the idea for later. Sometime when Lando and Scotty weren't around.

I almost didn't make it to work on time. It was hard waking up when the alarm went off, harder to shut it off without waking Eli up because my phone was on his side of the bed. And when he woke just as I picked up the phone, it took a while to say our 'good mornings.' I didn't even have a chance to check for any new police reports before leaving.

While waiting for my cup of coffee to brew, I brought up the website. The video of Jake directing traffic still didn't show up on the list and I wondered if Eli had contacted him yet. There weren't any new videos and I hoped that meant the sirens last night had nothing to do with a fire. The newspaper didn't run an article about one either. No surprise, they were typically a day behind.

I settled into my daily routine. Run the reports to find out how many people visited the library the previous day and how many books got checked out. See which books topped the best-seller lists and make sure they were in our inventory. Listen to the voicemail and make sure no one had called in sick. Enjoy the scent of the flowers sitting on my desk. It was shaping up to be a wonderfully normal day.

I was busy shelving books that got returned overnight. I didn't need to do it, the volunteers were more than capable of the task, but I liked to do it once in a while. Handling the books connected me to the basics of the job, and there is something magical about the feel of the covers that had passed through dozens of hands. Then, *he* walked in the door.

"We need to talk," Fiesker said, planting himself in front of my now almost-empty cart.

I considered pushing the cart into his knees, but that would be a bad idea.

"Good morning to you, too." I pointedly turned away from him to put the last two books where they belonged. Job completed, I leaned against the cart. "Will this take long?"

As usual, a patron wandered by and stopped, pretending to look for a book, while actually hoping to overhear our conversation. He noticed. "Is there somewhere private?"

I hated the idea of him tainting my office, but it was the best option. I pushed the cart forward, forcing him to back up a step. "If you move out of the way, I'll take you to my office."

Accompanied by the stares of most of the staff members, I led the way, not watching to see if he followed. But his loud footsteps trailed behind. Once inside, I topped off my cup of coffee to warm it up and settled into my chair behind the large wooden desk. It was a sturdy piece of oak furniture used by head librarians since the day the library first opened.

I sipped my coffee and waited while he decided where to sit. With only two chairs to choose from, it shouldn't have been a hard decision. Neither suited his purposes, so he just stood, crossed his arms and glared at me.

"You need to understand something," he said. "I'm in charge of this investigation. I don't need amateurs running around and getting in my way."

"Did you review the spreadsheet Chief Sorenson provided yet?" I asked, leaning back in my chair, trying not to let my anger rise to the surface.

"It's good but doesn't tell me anything."

"How long would it have taken you to put all that information together?"

He scrunched his eyebrows. "Why?"

"Because you should thank me. I've saved you hours of work. And don't try to pretend the report isn't thorough. I doubt there's a speck of data missing except the events that have come to light since it was last updated. I have no intentions of getting in your way, but I answer to Chief Sorenson. If he asks for my input, he'll get it. Oak Grove may be a small town, but he's a brilliant man and could easily work for any major city. I suggest you bring your ego down a level or three and figure out we are on the same side. We all want to stop the fires."

"That's *my* job, and I'll thank you to remember it."

"From my research, you are good, but you aren't the best." His eyes flared. "You're in a running feud with George Akosti. Last year he won the state award for the top arson investigator by only a couple of votes. I'm guessing that since then, he gets the high-profile cases while you get stuck with ones in podunk little towns that don't even make the news. You resent being sent here to chase down brush fires when you're itching to hit the headlines. Am I close? If you want to solve this case quickly and get out of here, I suggest you take what help you can get." While Eli and the guys were plotting their strategy, I'd been doing my own searches.

His mouth opened and closed and opened again. I prepared myself for a wave of criticism to pour out. When no words were forthcoming, I slid my phone across the desk to him.

"Take a look at that," I said. It was a picture of one of the brooches. "Have you seen this before?"

My sudden switch in topics shook him from his stupor. "No. What's that got to do with anything?"

"It's one of two identical items. One was found at the fire behind a property I renovated, the second at the fire last week."

"They aren't in your report. And how did you get your hands on them? Did you just 'happen' to find them?" His lips narrowed.

Chapter 9

I let Fiesker's accusation roll off me. "Firefighters located the brooches at the scenes. The first pin was found by someone who used to volunteer here at the library and knew I owned the property. He thought I'd lost it. The second one was picked up by a different guy who showed it to his coworkers. They are now in the hands of the police who are planning to search for more once the snow melts. My expert believes they are replicas. Decent quality, but nothing of any value."

His mouth curled downward at the mention of my expert, and I was glad I hadn't mentioned Jake's name. "Why didn't you include them in your report?" he asked.

I also hadn't included the reports of stalking. My oath of secrecy remained unbroken.

"Lack of time and the fact that my initial computations indicated they didn't add any significant data. If more of the pins show up, it'll be easy enough to adjust the spreadsheet to factor them in. If you want an electronic version of my calculations, I'll be glad to provide one. That way you don't have to start from scratch."

"I'd prefer to do my own analysis."

I caught the unspoken inference that mine was wrong. Although seething inside, I kept my face expressionless. If he wanted to waste his time, so be it.

"I'm sure Freddie—Detective Thomason—will give you copies of the files. Now, if you don't mind, I have work to do." I indicated a stack of paperwork with my hand. "Do you need someone to show you the way out?"

The path to the front door was almost a straight line, with only one right-hand turn. Although I'd phrased my question in the politest of terms, I meant it as an insult. I think he knew it because his cheeks reddened.

"Don't worry about it. Just stay out of my way. If you interfere with my investigation, I'll have you arrested."

Fiesker's threat held no merit. He was a civil investigator working for the fire department, not a law enforcement official. And with Chief Sorenson as my ally and unofficial boss, no one on the Oak Grove Police Force would touch me unless he told them to. Still, it was a relief to watch him walk out of the library.

After work, I headed home. Not to Eli's place, but my apartment. I needed a change of clothes and a few minutes of alone time. Since Eli hadn't shown up to take me to lunch—we hadn't planned it but I'd hoped—I didn't feel bad about not rushing to his house. My African violet needed watering, anyway.

My conversation with Fiesker reminded me of the research I'd gotten distracted from. Was it possible Jake was wrong about the age of the pins and they were recent replications made to look old? That was the only theory I'd come up with that could explain why there were two of them.

Piper met me at the base of the stairs, barking and bouncing on his side of the fence. I felt bad that I didn't have a doggy-treat to give to him, since I'd missed giving him one in the morning. He didn't care and happily settled for several minutes' worth of petting.

Counting the stairs on my way up helped me relax. The numbers never changed, of course, but the ritual is what mattered. Then, as always, the moment of tension when I checked to make sure my door remained locked. It was protected by the best lock Jake could recommend.

I hung my coat up before sinking into the cocoon of my easy chair and listened to the quiet. As much as I loved my job, putting on a happy face no matter how many problems I dealt with wore me out. There'd be no privacy at Eli's either.

But I couldn't hide out forever, and I had things to do. A cup of hot Earl Grey sounded perfect to go with some digging on the internet. So, with a kettle of water on its way to boiling, I turned on my laptop.

A reverse image search was the best bet. Experience showed I'd get a ton of close but not close enough results that took forever to wade through, no results at all, or, the rarity, an exact match. I hoped the quality of my phone's photo would be good enough to work.

As I waited for the program to analyze the picture, the electricity blinked. My laptop didn't turn off of course, but my modem did and I got kicked out of my connection. As I waited for the system to reset, I leaned back, sipped my tea, and wondered what Eli was up to, and what he wanted to do for supper. Maybe Dairy Barn, if they had electricity. I doubted he'd made a trip to the store to buy pots and pans and all the basics needed to stock the cupboards.

Then the electric cut off for a second time. By the dim light of the laptop's monitor, I fished my flashlight, emergency candles, and matches out of the junk drawer. I didn't care about the lights being out, but staying warm was another issue.

I spotted lights twinkling in the distance as I closed the curtains on my kitchen window. So, at least part of Oak Grove had electricity. If my calculations were correct, Eli's house was in the wrong direction. Jake's little apartment, however, might be unaffected by the outage. I didn't need to reach out to him yet, but at least I had the possibility of staying someplace warm. If Eli and the guys went to Jake's too, it would be a tight fit, but we could make it work. Luke and Joe had a small gas heater in their bedroom, so they'd be okay.

I carried one of the candles into my bedroom and set it on my dresser. It cast enough light for me to re-pack my overnight bag with a fresh change of clothes. I'd need clean ones no matter where I ended up. It bothered me that I hadn't heard from Eli, but if he was in one of his programming comas, time became meaningless to him.

But before I called him, the phone came to life with the open bars of Johnny Cash's 'Goin' by the Book,' my ringtone for the library. That meant trouble, bad enough that our evening staff couldn't handle it. It was a good thing I hadn't changed. My work clothes carried more authority than a pair of jeans and sweatshirt. I switched back into professional mode.

"Harmony Duprie," I answered.

"Sorry to bother you, Harmony," Mabel said. "The electricity is out, and we can't get an estimate of when it'll be back on. Can I close early? We have a few stubborn patrons who are trying to read their books by flashlight."

"You've got my permission to kick them out. And I'll be there in a few minutes in case any of them give you a hard time." With the electricity out, we might have to lock up the library the old-fashioned way—with a key—and Mabel didn't have a copy. There was one stashed in my office, but it was easier to go in than talk her through finding it in the dark. Besides, if any of the people put up a fuss, I had no problem calling the police for a little backup. Mabel was too nice to do that. I'd also call the cleaning service to let them know they didn't need to come in.

I made sure the candles were out before I headed down the stairs with a silent prayer that everyone else in town would be careful, too. My shiver wasn't from the cold, but at the thought of a house catching on fire.

Dolores grumbled when I turned the key to start her engine, but I patted her dashboard and she settled into her normal purr. "I know it's cold and dark," I told her, "but this won't take long." As I pulled onto the street, I plotted a course down side streets and away from the main roads. With the traffic lights out, they were accidents waiting to happen.

Or they had already started. In the distance, I caught the scream of sirens although I didn't spot any flashing lights. At each stop sign, I waited an extra second to make sure no emergency vehicles were approaching.

With little traffic on any of the streets, I got to the library in near record time. Several of the parking spots out front were empty, and I slid Dolores into the one closest to the stairs. Mabel waited for me at the top, bundled up in her heavy winter parka.

"Everyone's gone," she said. "I convinced them they needed to save their batteries for when they get home. I called the electric company to find out how soon the power would be back on, and they wouldn't even give me an estimate. It looks like this will be a long one."

That was quick thinking on her part. I'd make sure she got recognized at the next employee meeting. "Do you have someplace warm to go?"

"We've got a fireplace and the hubby's got a fire going. I'm more worried about our freezer thawing. What about you?"

"It looks as if the west side still has power and I can stay with a friend. Are the other doors locked?" I asked as I pulled the keychain from my purse.

"Tight as a drum. The alarm system is down, of course."

True, I'd have to call the non-emergency line for the police and ask them to send extra patrols until the power came back. I yanked on the now-locked door to double-check my work. It barely budged.

"Have a good night and drive safe on the way home," I said as I gave the door one final tug for good luck.

"You too!" Mabel was already halfway down the stairs. She always parked in the same spot at the end of the block, and I waited until she pulled out to climb into Dolores. While letting her engine run, I placed the call to the police station.

My next call was to Eli but first I plugged in my cell phone, so it could charge as I talked. Before I could press the button to dial him, a police car roared down the cross street, followed by a second one. Then two fire trucks and the small red pickup used by the on-duty captain. Whatever it was, it didn't look good. So, I followed them.

Chapter 10

The emergency vehicles traveled faster than the speed limit and soon were out of eyesight. It didn't matter because the red glow in the sky led me to the fire's location, a residential area on Broad Street.

I parked a block away. Close enough for my purposes. I knew the house because I thought about buying it to fix up before I started working at the library. Built in the '50s, it wasn't anything fancy, just a solid little house that had seen better days. No one lived there when Sarah, my real estate expert, took me on a walk-thru, and I prayed no one had moved in since then.

I couldn't resist getting out and walking a little closer but staying well back from the police lines. I wanted a better view, not of the fire, but the people in the crowd. Was one of them the mystery videographer? With all the cell phones aimed at the incident, it would be impossible to isolate any one person as the guilty party. Unless they did something that made them stick out, like sneaking in under the police tape. I eliminated the ones in pajamas, rousted from the neighboring homes as a safety precaution. But everyone was behaving themselves.

The water brigade made their appearance, with cheerful smiles and those silly purple vests they wore. They stood as close as possible to the fire lines. It was like those water stations they use along the routes of marathons. Every now and then, a firefighter grabbed a bottle from them and emptied it before returning to work. The volunteers always cleaned up after themselves, so they were tolerated.

With a loud crash, the roof caved in. The shower of sparks fell as far as the police lines, and the people in front forced their way backward. Torrents of water from every available firehose streamed through the sky to quell the hotspot. Steam and ash from the fire drifted throughout the neighborhood. The stench of smoke and over-heated chemicals burned my nose and I sneezed several times.

Engrossed in the scene, I didn't pay attention to my personal 'bubble.' My self-defense coach taught me better. I wished I had listened to him when Fiesker appeared only inches in front of me. How did I miss him in the crowd? My first instinct was to push him away but stopped myself. He hadn't touched me.

"You shouldn't be here. You're interfering with my investigation."

His frown and narrowed eyes would scare most people. Not me.

"And you should be over there," I waved my

hand towards the fire, deliberately almost touching the tip of his nose. "Instead of hassling me. I'm standing well away from the area, minding my own business. Go find out what caused the fire."

Which he couldn't do until it was out and had cooled. But his presence irritated me and I wanted him to go away. After I got in one last dig.

"Just stay out of the way of the real firemen."

That was low of me, I'll admit. When I researched his background, I found out his dream career had been to become a firefighter. At least, according to his high school yearbook. I didn't know what had changed but he'd never achieved that goal.

His scowl deepened and he clenched his fists. I shifted my weight so that if he tried to hit me I could block the blow. Instead, he abruptly turned and marched away.

Goal accomplished. I tracked him as he pushed his way through the small crowd, bent to scramble under the police tape, and stood by a fire truck. He stopped to talk to a man with his back turned towards me. It didn't appear to be anyone connected to the fire department, which I found curious.

The street lights flickered but didn't stay on. A good sign progress was being made. I'd done enough damage for one night. Time to go home and figure out what came next. I needed to get out of my bad mood before talking to Eli.

As I reached to open the car door, my name was called. I plastered a smile on my face before I turned to greet Freddie. He didn't deserve to be a recipient of my anger. In fact, I might get some useful information out of him.

"It's a bad one," I said jerking my head towards the fire. "Do they know if it was deliberate or accidental?"

He shook his head. "Too soon to tell. Neighbors said someone's been working on the house, but it'll be up to Fiesker to figure out whether that had something to do with it."

All the house had needed were simple renovations. "Any sign of one of those pins?"

"It's too dark to see. And there are more important things to worry about." He glanced up as the street lights flickered again. "By the way, Fiesker asked me to warn you away from any future fires. I shut him down, of course. You have as much right as anyone to be here as long as you aren't putting yourself in danger or impeding the work of the fire department. Which you aren't."

"He's worried I'll steal his glory."

Freddie raised an eyebrow. "I wondered what his problem is. I'm struggling to be civil with him. He doesn't make it easy."

"He stands too close to people for them to be comfortable with him. I don't know whether it's a lack of social awareness or a power move. Look."

As we talked, Fiesker stopped one of the fire officials. We couldn't hear the conversation, but it was the body language I cared about. Fiesker stood, arms crossed, within a foot of the official and each time the man eased a few inches back Fiesker shuffled forward. It looked like two awkward preteens at their first dance. Except these were full-size adults. If I hadn't been the recipient of Fiesker's habit, I might have found the situation comical.

"It's obvious now that you pointed it out," Freddie said. "How do we fix it?"

"*We* don't. He and I are on bad terms and he's only been in town a few days. And I have my doubts you can fix it either. My suggestion is to have Claire approach him. He answers to her, and if it's a power thing it's better coming from his chain of command."

"That makes sense."

We stood in silence as the fire found a new source of fuel and fresh flames shot into the air. It would be a long night for the firemen.

"Well, I should get back to work," Freddie said.

"And I need to figure out where I'm going to spend the night. My apartment will be too cold to sleep in if the electricity stays off."

"There's been discussions about opening a school to use as a shelter. They are waiting for more information from the electric company."

I was glad the city was thinking ahead but hoped it wouldn't come to that. Lots of elderly people would be reluctant to leave their homes or didn't have transportation. The community buses wouldn't be able to handle everyone at once. A few years earlier, the city received funding to plan for evacuations after the remnants of a hurricane passed through. Hopefully, those plans were up-to-date.

"If there's anything I can do to help, call me. My

cell phone should have enough battery to last through the night," I told him.

"Will do. Stay out of trouble, Harmony."

Driving home, I realized he didn't ask what I was doing at the scene. A slip on his part or deliberate? And I'd forgotten to ask him the rookie's name.

Lights flared on as I pulled into an empty spot on my street. I wouldn't be staying long, and it didn't make sense to put Dolores in the garage for the few minutes it would take to run upstairs and grab my overnight bag. As I climbed the now-lit stairs, my phone rang. I didn't recognize the number, but it was a Florida area code so, I answered.

"Hello?"

I heard laughter in the background and almost hung up. Then someone said, "Pipe down, she answered." Then directly into the phone, "Harmony, it's me, Lando. Your boyfriend asked me to call because he can't pry his fingers from the keyboard right now." There was more laughter.

Were they drunk?

"Anywho," Lando went on, "the bossman figures no restaurant in town will be open after the blackout, and wonders what you want to do for supper."

Maybe it was sleep deprivation. I cataloged what my freezer held that was microwavable. I packaged everything for one serving and it wouldn't be enough to go around. I'd witnessed Lando wolf down what I considered three servings for a bedtime snack.

"The fast food joints out by the interstate didn't lose power," I said. "If you want, we can head out there."

Lando must have covered his phone because the background conversation was muffled. Then he came back. "Can you pick up burgers and fries and bring them here? That way we don't have to stop what we're doing."

How had they continued to work with no power? Were they playing a trick on me?

Eli's faint voice said, "Where're your manners? Say please!"

"Will you *please* pick us up some burgers, Harmony?" Lando asked. "We haven't eaten all day,"

That explained it. They were starving. But I wasn't above giving Lando a hard time. "So, four small burgers," I said. "One for each of us."

"No. The big ones. Two for each of us. And large fries. And chocolate shakes. Please?"

Another muffled conversation. "Scotty says he wants a strawberry shake. I don't know what's wrong with that guy," Lando said. "Oh, and Eli says get some brownies or cookies."

If I didn't know better, I would have thought they'd been smoking weed.

"Anything else?" I asked, laughing.

"That should do it. Just hurry, please? Your boyfriend is hungry enough to start chewing on the wallpaper in the kitchen. The stuff that is covered in pictures of fruit."

I despised that wallpaper. It was the one bad decision I'd made in redecorating. Jake insisted it would be fine once the new owners hung pots and pans on the rack in front of it. It wouldn't hurt my feelings at all if it got damaged because Eli wasn't the fancy pots kind of guy.

"Tell him to hold off. He doesn't want to ruin his supper." The burgers might taste like cardboard, but at least they wouldn't smell like glue.

"Help us, Harmony, you're our only hope," Lando said gravely.

I caught the geeky reference, but I wasn't going to play into his hands. "You'd better hope the restaurant's supplies haven't been wiped out by hordes of hungry villagers without electricity. See you soon." I didn't give him the chance to respond before ending the call.

Chapter 11

"Generator," Eli explained. "Big enough to run all the equipment, but not big enough to power the whole house. It's a business expense, so I can write it off. Bought it yesterday," he added before he took another bite of burger.

That's how they kept working during the electricity outage. We sprawled out on the floor again, leaning against the walls, and I wished he'd bought chairs, too.

"Make any progress?" I asked.

"Progress, yes. Have we solved the mystery? No," Scotty said.

"But that's some kick-ass new video up on the site from the fire tonight. Unfortunately, we weren't able to trace where it originated. It didn't come through the local cable provider." Lando stuffed several french fries in his mouth.

"Anyone get hurt?" Scotty asked between swallows of his shake. He acted more like I remembered him. Maybe the previous day he'd been tired because he'd done most of the driving, although Lando played navigator.

I shook my head. "No, the house was empty and being renovated for flipping."

"That opens up a whole ton of possibilities," Eli said. "Was there a spark that caused the fire? An electrical fault? A jealous competitor? Burned down for the insurance money?"

"Or just kids playing around in an empty house who started it?" Lando suggested.

My voice hardened. "That will be up to the fire investigator to determine."

"Is there a problem?" Eli put down the remnants of his burger and rested his hand on my knee.

I sighed. "He's an egotistical, overbearing know-it-all who doesn't have the foggiest inkling about how to treat people so they'll want to cooperate. I'm afraid he'll hoard information and not share it so he comes out looking like a hero on the back of the hard work other people did. And give them no credit."

The three men glanced at each other. "So not a nice guy," Eli said.

"But smart." I grimaced. "One of the top investigators in the state. Just not people-smart."

Their faces were grim. The frivolous mood vanished. "Do you still want us to chase down the owner of the website?" Scotty asked. "Or let him solve it on his own or fail? What's his name anyway?"

"Carlton Fiesker." It didn't take much for me to decide the answer to the first question. "And if you can find who's responsible for the videos, it won't be for him. It'll be for Chief Sorenson and Freddie and my friends and all of Oak Grove."

My fervent speech drew an unexpected chuckle from Eli. "You've been reading too many superhero fantasies, Buttercup. You should go back to biographies. Either that or you're tired and need to go to bed and get some sleep."

Lando hooted and winked at me. "Bed. Sleep. Good one, Eli. If we keep you down here for a few more hours, she'll get some rest."

I crunched my burger wrapper into a ball and threw it at him, well aware of the heat in my cheeks. "So, how are the Magic doing?" I asked, changing the topic to something safer.

The rumor mill was on full alert, floating a variety of explanations. The fire had caused the electric outage or conversely, the outage had caused it. A lightning strike on a transformer started it. The outage covered the tracks of whoever set the fire. One man in line, as I waited for coffee, speculated it was a terrorist attack but was shushed by his friends.

Even the cleaning crew hazarded guesses about the cause as they emptied garbage cans and swept the floor, readying the library for opening. I'd arrived extra early to let them in, leaving Eli asleep in his bed. Their favorite theory involved the fire being set to claim the insurance, and it had burned the overhead electric lines causing the outage.

Logical but incorrect. Since I didn't know the real cause, I didn't bother to tell them differently.

While they cleaned, I gathered the abandoned books and piled them on a cart to be shelved. Then I restarted the computers to get rid of the errors displayed on their screens. Finally, I took a few pens and one notebook people left behind and put them in the lost and found.

By eight thirty the first of the staff showed up. By nine we were ready for customers. The first one walked in the door five minutes later, and everything was back to normal. At least, in my favorite little corner of the world.

So why couldn't I shake the feeling that something was wrong?

Eli called at lunchtime to tell me he wouldn't be coming. He needed to deal with a problem back in Florida. I knew that might happen, so I wasn't too disappointed. At least that's what I told myself. Still, the feeling persisted.

Jake stopped by to say hi later. He hadn't heard back from the job interview yet. I suggested he call the guy and try for an update. Or the waitress he'd flirted with could give him the low-down. But the feeling didn't go away.

It almost disappeared while I talked to Mrs. McCartney about her baby goats. She showed me a video of them bouncing around a few days after birth. I had to stifle my giggles, so I didn't disturb the other patrons. But a niggle of worry teased me.

I ignored the phone the first time it vibrated while I sorted through the mail. The caller could leave a message if it was important. When it vibrated again after only a few seconds, I deigned to look over and check the screen. Caller ID displayed the name and my heart sank.

"Hey, Janine," I answered with fake cheerfulness.

"Harmony," she sniffed, and the line went silent. We were still connected, so I assumed she'd muted her end.

It didn't take words for me to get the message. I had to be the strong one. "Do you need me to come?" I didn't know what to do about the library, but Janine was my priority. Her mother became my safety net when my parents died, and I'd do whatever it took to help Janine now. Including facing my fear of getting on a plane.

The line was unmuted, and her soft sobs pulled tears from my eyes. So much for being strong. Thank heavens a fresh box of tissues sat on my desk.

"I'm so sorry. When did she pass?" I managed to ask.

"This morning. I visited her earlier and when she fell asleep, I left to get coffee. She never woke up. I wasn't there for her when she died."

I wanted to reach through the phone to hug her. "Janine, you've been there for her for weeks. Maybe she chose to leave while you stepped away to spare you from the pain. It was her way of showing you how much she loved you one last time."

Janine's sobs got louder, and I was afraid I'd said the wrong thing. "Listen. You did everything you could for her and she appreciated it. She told me so, remember?" I'd talked to her mother a few weeks earlier during one of Janine's calls.

"But it's hard," Janine wailed.

I wouldn't argue with that. I tossed my tissue in the wastebasket and grabbed two more. "Let me call around and find a flight. I'll text you when I'm coming in."

She sniffed. "No. There's nothing you can do here. Mom made all the arrangements before she died. I'll come back after she is cremated. She wanted a memorial service in Oak Grove, so her friends could come."

I needed a to-do list. The first item was calling the church she'd attended while she lived here. "Do you want me to make the phone calls?"

"Please?"

"Of course." I added the newspaper to my list. The obituary was already written and stored on my laptop along with her mother's requests for her service. She'd planned it all out when she accepted there'd be no miracle to save her life. If I concentrated on what needed done, I'd get through this without breaking down. Janine didn't have the same option.

"I have to go," she said. "I need to find a flight back."

"Leave it to me." If Janine bought her own ticket, she'd get the cheapest one available when she deserved to fly first class. "What day do you want it for?"

She didn't protest, a testament to how drained

she was. "They said the cremation would need to wait for two days. Some sort of weird regulation. So, Friday, I guess. I'll need to come back later to handle the final bills and close up the condo, but that will wait." Her voice caught.

Condo management was added to the list. And the post office, to forward the mail. And a local cleaning service to do a deep clean of Janine's apartment before she returned. I'd been keeping it halfway clean when I watered her plants, but it needed more than a good airing out.

"We'll help you. Anything you need. Me and all your friends here." I'd find time to cry later. Sarah's name got put at the top of the piece of paper. She needed to be told before anyone else.

"I have to go now." Janine sniffed. "They need me to sign paperwork."

"You take care of yourself. If you don't, I'll… I'll… I'll think of something to make you regret it!"

That earned an almost-laugh. "I'll see you in a few days."

I gathered my thoughts for a few minutes after ending the call. It gave me time to wipe away my tears and pretend everything was okay. First reach out to Sarah and Merrilee, then an emergency staff meeting. No, that was wrong. First the call to Sarah, then a second to Margo Windler, the head of the Board of Directors, then the staff meeting. The Board of Directors needed to be informed that Janine would be back soon.

I shoved the worry that followed out of my brain to deal with later. Much later.

Naturally, I wasn't in the mood to hang out with the guys even after I got done with as much as possible. All I wanted to do was go home, drink a glass or two of wine, and ugly cry. I didn't even feel bad when I told Eli he'd have to do supper on his own.

I was on my third glass when someone knocked. I decided to ignore it. My eyes were swollen, my throat hoarse and my nose red from blowing it. No way I wanted company.

But the knocker was determined. And had a key. So, when Eli opened the door and held his arms out, I let him wrap them around me while I cried more.

Chapter 12

For the time being, I was cried out. Eli convinced me to eat something, and made scrambled eggs and toast for the both of us. After we ate, I snuggled in his arms on the loveseat, half asleep, when there was another knock on the door. I glanced at the clock. It couldn't be good news, not this late at night.

"Do you want to ignore it?" Eli asked.

I was in no shape for company. But my conscience and curiosity wouldn't let me. "I suppose I should see who it is." I pried his arm off my shoulders and started to get up.

But he grabbed me and pulled me down. "You sit," he said sternly, "I'll check."

It was a fight I wouldn't win so, I let him be the one to answer the door. As I put on my glasses, my tired brain registered the action when he pulled his gun from his coat pocket and tucked it in his waistband. I wasn't expecting *that* kind of trouble.

From the loveseat, the angle was wrong to see

who was at the door when Eli opened it. "Can I help you?" Eli asked.

"Is Miss Duprie home?" There was a moment's hesitation.

I guessed Eli had his scary face on—the one where he scowls and squishes his eyebrows together.

Pete! I nodded to Eli as I got off the loveseat. "Let him in, Eli. What's going on, Pete?"

He stepped inside. "Sorry to bother you, but we figured this was important. I mean, the guys down at the firehouse. We talked about it and thought you should know." He looked at Eli. "Should I come back?"

"This is Eli Hennessey, my computer expert." And lover, but that remained unspoken. "I haven't had time to fill him in on your emails yet. Did you get more?"

Pete's eyes scanned my face and his lips tightened. "Can we talk in private?"

"I trust Eli. Whatever you want to say, he'll keep it a secret."

"Please. It's urgent."

I rubbed my forehead. A massive headache was heading my way and Pete's odd request added to it. I didn't see a way around it. "Eli, would you step into the bedroom for a minute?"

Pete watched as Eli shut the bedroom door, then grabbed my hand. "Come on, let's get you somewhere safe."

I pulled away from him. "Whoa, there, what do you think is going on?"

"You've been crying. Your nose is red, your eyes are swollen, and your hair is a disaster. There's a man with a gun deciding who is allowed in your apartment. You're a smart woman, what does it sound like to you?"

He thought Eli was abusing me? Oh dear. In spite of everything I laughed. "Pete, that's sweet of you, but you have it wrong. A dear friend died today, and I've been crying. Eli came to comfort me. The gun is a safety precaution based on my history. I carry one, too, did you know that? I've got a concealed carry permit and everything."

Pete's eyes widened. "You carry?"

I would have said the same thing a few years ago. "It's funny the way life plays tricks on you. But you don't have to worry, Eli is one of the good ones." I raised my voice. "Eli, you can come out now."

I met him in the hallway. He tipped his head and mouthed "What?"

"I'll explain later," I whispered.

Pete hovered anxiously in my front room. No one ever can figure out where to sit in my apartment until I tell them. Not enough choices, I guess.

"Take the chair. Eli and I will share the loveseat. Do you want something to drink?" My hostess skills had been slipping.

"No, I'm good. I don't want to take up too much of your time." He glanced at Eli. My explanation hadn't convinced him.

"You didn't come at this time of the night for something unimportant. Is it to do with the emails?"

I leaned back and placed my hand on Eli's knee, trying to show Pete I trusted him.

"Yes and no." Pete cracked a knuckle.

I remembered him doing that as a volunteer when he was nervous.

"I didn't work the fire last night, so I didn't get anything new like a few of the other guys. What's different is that two of the guys got texts on their personal cell phones."

Eli leaned forward. "Did they come from a local number?"

Pete shook his head. "The numbers are weird. It's the right area code but not the right exchange. I tried searching for them online and drew a blank."

"You said numbers. As in plural."

"Yeah. Three of them between the four texts. Another strange thing is neither guy heard a notification when the messages reached their phones. Antonio noticed the light flashing on his and that's when he realized he had an unread text."

"What did they say? Anything different than the emails?" I asked.

"No, they were pretty much the same as the latest ones. The creepy ones."

"I've got a few samples," I told Eli. "I'll forward them to you. With your permission," I added, looking at Pete.

"Do what you have to do."

"Does that mean I've got your approval to discuss this with my police contacts?"

"We talked about that too. The guys were divided. When Antonio mentioned he had a new phone with a new number, we figured it was time. He was tired of his mother calling so much, even when he's at work. It's not like she never sees him, he lives a few blocks from her house."

"Will you send Harmony a list of those numbers so she can share them with me? And have the texts forwarded to her?" Eli used one finger to draw imaginary lines on the top of the coffee table. Or he was playing with water droplets that I couldn't see?

"I'll give you my number," I said, "but please don't share it with anyone."

Pete nodded. I wandered into the kitchen and pulled off the top sheet of the pad I keep on my refrigerator for making grocery lists. A pen hung alongside, so I didn't need to search for one. I jotted down my number and returned to the front room.

"Here you go," I said, handing the note to Pete. "And speaking of the fire, what's the current theory on what started it?"

"That fire investigator they brought in isn't saying." Pete frowned. "I had the 'pleasure' of meeting him yesterday. I hope he doesn't stick around long."

So, I wasn't the only one who didn't like him.

"But it looks accidental. A spark got into a pile of sawdust and took forever to develop a flame. There were plenty of flammable chemicals around to it going. With no one in the house to put out the fire when it started, there wasn't any way to save the place. It went 'poof' like the magic dragon."

If I remembered the song correctly that was 'Puff' but I kept my correction to myself.

"How long until Fiesker releases his official results?" Eli asked.

"Days? Weeks?" Pete shrugged. "Depends on how long it takes to get results back from the lab. Word is he took a bunch of samples after the house cooled down, so it might take forever. You would think he could make a determination from the pattern of the fire, even if we don't know the point of origin."

My fingers itched for my laptop to do some investigating of my own to find out what Pete was talking about, but it would wait.

"Did anyone find one of those pins?" I asked.

"Nope. Doesn't surprise me though, with all the equipment and guys trampling around in the dark. One of them could have stepped on it and never noticed."

If Fiesker was good, he'd find it, anyway. Would he tell Freddie?

Pete left soon after that, saying he had an early shift, but I suspected he had a late date. I walked him to the bottom of the stairs, reassuring him I was in no danger from Eli. He tried to give me the number to the battered woman's hotline, just in case. It took me mentioning that Freddie had met and liked Eli to get Pete to back down.

When I got back upstairs, explaining what happened to Eli without hurting his feelings was a challenge. "I didn't think I looked *that* bad," I protested. "Or I wouldn't have let him come in."

He held me at arm's length to study me. "Your eyes are pretty red," he said, but a small smile touched his lips. "And your hair is a mess. And you know what? You're still beautiful."

"You make me feel that way."

He drew me in for a hug. "And I'm glad you have friends who look after you."

We stood like that for a while, my head against his shoulder and his arms wrapped around me. Slowly, he started swaying, rocking us back and forth. When he started shuffling his feet, it turned into a slow dance to unheard music. Or the music of our hearts beating in rhythm. I didn't want it to ever end.

Reality stepped in when Eli's phone rang. As one, we sighed. He planted a soft kiss on my forehead before releasing me to retrieve the phone from his coat pocket. He glanced at the screen and shook his head.

"What's up, Lando?"

If Eli was going to talk business, there were better things I could do with my time beside wait for him. Like splash cold water on my face to try to get the swelling down and brush out my hair. I hoped he would stick around and not have to rush back to his place.

Five minutes later, he was still on the phone in a mostly one-sided conversation, pacing the apartment with the phone to his ear and his left hand tucked under his right arm. Lando was doing all the talking and Eli grunted once in a while. I used the time to wash our dishes and put away the seasonings Eli left on the counter.

Then it was his turn to talk, and I understood about half of what came out of his mouth. The rest was technical jargon that was way over my head. Something about restful web servers and dot net and java. And they weren't talking about the island. They could go on all night. And I was exhausted.

So, I went to the bedroom and laid down, fully clothed, on top of my bed. I'd stay out of his way and rest my eyes at the same time. At least, that's what I intended. Of course, it didn't work out that way.

I remember cracking my eyes open at Eli's chuckle. And when he pulled a spare blanket out of my closet and spread it out on the bed, covering me. And I remember his warmth when he crawled under the blanket and lay next to me.

"Go back to sleep, Buttercup," he whispered, and I did.

Chapter 13

Only Eli's arm draped over my body made it worth waking up too early. That way my first—and second—thoughts were of him and nothing else. But he couldn't stave off the problems of the day forever.

As I made coffee, I considered calling in sick. Take a day to hide from reality. Go for a long drive to nowhere and back. But I had responsibilities and commitments I couldn't escape, not even for a day. For the first time in my life, I dreaded going to the library.

I hoped to arrive early enough to get some time for myself before unlocking the front doors. The last morning kiss from Eli delayed me, so I made it to the library two minutes before nine. Enough time to get the front door unlocked without upsetting the waiting patrons.

I spent most of the morning cloistered in my—Janine's—office, making and receiving phone calls. Freddie got sent a text message, asking him to drop by when convenient, preferably without Fiesker.

Most of my time was spent texting back and forth with Janine as she made arrangements on her end. I'd moved her reservation to Saturday to get a better flight.

Sarah volunteered to pick her up from the Pittsburgh airport because her car had more trunk space for Janine's suitcases. The church secretary offered to contact everyone needed for the memorial service on Monday and the lunch following it. In a meeting held by phone, the Board of Directors agreed to close the library for half the day so the staff and volunteers who wanted to attend the service were able to. The maid service found an opening and was cleaning Janine's apartment. Everything was falling into place.

And that made me nervous. What was I missing? The last time I'd done this, it was Janine's mother who helped me through it. I wanted—no, I *needed*—to make sure everything was perfect.

It was almost a relief when Freddie knocked on the office door. I gestured to him to take a seat while I finished my conversation with the florist. Janine's mother had requested donations to a cancer charity instead of flowers, but I couldn't stand the thought of there not being at least one bouquet at the service.

When I hung up, a few tears escaped my eyes and I grabbed a tissue to wipe them away. I didn't even care if Freddie saw.

He cleared his throat. "Sarah told me about Mrs. Janson. Do you want to put this off for now?"

"No. I've sat on this information for too long." He opened his mouth and I held up one hand to stop him. "Whatever you were going to say, don't. My source didn't give me permission to share this until last night."

He closed his mouth and I continued. "Some of the firemen are getting strange emails. They started off like something you'd expect a young teen girl to send to a star she had a crush on, and that didn't bother them. Then they got more stalker-ish. That's when they came to me but made me promise not to tell anyone.

"After the house fire, two of them got texts sent to their personal cells. One a brand-new number." I slid a folder containing copies of the printed-out emails across the desk to Freddie. "I don't have all of them. This is a sample. Eli is working on tracing them."

I'd arranged them in chronological order. Freddie's face was a perfect blank as he read through them, barely twitching an eyebrow. Not the reaction I'd expected.

He closed the folder, leaned back in his chair, and crossed his arms. "What else do you know? What's your theory?"

They were fair questions. Normally I'd have a good answer for him. Not this time. "I've had other things on my mind," I said, with more of a bite to my voice than he deserved.

"I'm sorry, Harmony," he said, his voice soft. "But the people sending these emails are escalating. If they are the same people responsible for setting the fires and the website, who's to say they didn't set that fire the other night? We're lucky no one got hurt. Even if a civilian doesn't get hurt, firemen get injured all the time on the job. How would you feel about that?"

Talk about a guilt trip. "Isn't that your job?" I snapped. "You and that jerk Fiesker? You and Chief Sorenson keep reminding me I'm a civilian and to stay out of your way. I've given you the information, now go be a detective and figure it out."

I regretted the words as soon as they left my mouth. Freddie didn't deserve them, but it was too late to take them back.

We sat and stared at each other for a few seconds. "I'm sorry," I said.

"I'm sorry," he said at the same time.

We stared at each other some more.

"I shouldn't have pushed." Freddie gave me a half-hearted attempt at a smile. "This is a bad time for you and you've done more than anyone should expect." He took a deep breath. "And we're all on edge because our investigations are going nowhere."

"It's only been a couple of weeks."

"Feels like longer than that. The City Council is doing their typical job of screaming at Chief Sorenson, so they can tell the citizens of Oak Grove they're doing everything they can."

And making sure they look good for the elections. Politics.

"At least the chief can throw Fiesker at them. He's got to be good for something, right? Proof that the fire department and police force are cooperating and doing everything they can," I said.

Freddie shrugged. "So far he's been nothing but smoke and mirrors."

I couldn't help myself. I grinned.

"What?" he asked.

"A fire investigator. You said he was smoke and mirrors. That's a good one."

The tightness of the muscles in his neck eased. "That is a little bit funny, isn't it?"

My grin turned into a smile and Freddie smiled back.

"Smoke and mirrors. I'll remember that one."

I'd created a monster. He had to be stopped. "Be careful. If a certain someone hears you say it, he'll be offended."

Freddie snorted. "He takes offense at everything. But you're right. I'll keep it to myself."

Emergency avoided. Time to change the subject. "Has anyone found any more of those pins?"

"No, but we haven't done a sweep of all the locations yet. I'm hoping we don't get another storm before the last batch melts."

"I was trying to track them down the night the electricity went out."

"Don't worry about it. Unless we find more, I'm ready to mark it up to coincidence."

That seemed like a mistake, but I wasn't going to say anything. Returning to the search would wait until I had free time. That would be all too soon. I quickly shoved the thought to the back of my mind to deal with later. A new worry replaced it. I'd forgotten to ask Freddie the name of the rookie.

Eli, Lando and Scotty showed up before lunchtime. We traipsed to the diner down the street, beating the lunchtime rush, and took over a booth. They spent the hour clowning around and joking about trivial things, trying to cheer me up. It worked, mostly. How long it would last was a different question.

As they tackled their desserts, Eli put his hand on my knee. "Want some good news?"

Of course, I did.

He didn't wait for an answer. "We made progress on tracking down who is loading videos to that website. They're definitely local, but it will take a search warrant to get an exact name. The Oak Grove ISP won't release the information unless ordered to do so. I'll contact Freddie this afternoon, but we wanted you to know first."

"It's possible to get the names by retrieving the data from the cable company," Scotty added, "But the information wouldn't hold up in court."

They talked like hacking the records was as easy as breathing. "How about the emails?"

"We'll tackle them next," Lando said. "The sites they're using aren't in the US and my Croatian is rusty."

The three of them thought his statement was hilarious, but I didn't see the humor in it at all. I figured it wouldn't be funny once they explained it either, so I let it slide.

"The even better news," Eli said after gulping down about half of his soda, "Is that the video starring Jake hasn't reappeared. Either the site's lawyers are overwhelmed, or they don't care enough to deal with it."

"Have you talked to Jake?" It was strange that he hadn't popped in to say hi all week.

"I called him the day after we got here. Invited him over, but he said he was busy and couldn't make any promises. I wonder what he's up to."

Me too.

"I'm sure he'll drop by when he has time." Eli snagged a forkful of the chocolate cake I wasn't eating.

I pushed my plate his direction. "You finish it. I hate for good cake to go to waste." If I ate it, I might fall asleep at my desk.

He tackled it like he hadn't already eaten an over-sized sandwich and his own dessert.

I didn't want to watch him devour the whole thing and needed to get back to work. "Time for me to go," I said and pushed him, so he'd let me out of the booth.

"So soon?" Lando asked. "If you leave, he'll make us go back to work." He smiled broadly as he indicated Eli with a jerk of his head.

Eli swallowed. "Isn't that what I'm paying you for? You got to get away from the office, get your food and housing paid for, and you're complaining?"

"Don't forget the bonus you promised us if we tracked down the perps," Scotty added.

Not once had I ever heard Freddie use the word 'perps' for perpetrators, but I didn't want to ruin Scotty's fun.

"You bribed them to come?" I asked Eli.

"No bribe," Lando said. "Just a little something to make the trip worth our while."

I winked at him. "Call it what you will, but I'm upset that the opportunity to see me wasn't enough to get you here."

He laughed. "We would have come no matter what, but it's good to get one over on the boss."

I'd bet the last dollar in my wallet that Eli knew exactly what the guys' game was, and he let them 'win' for his own reasons. I pecked him on the cheek as I slid by him. "Will you be working tonight or can I come by?"

His eyes turned a darker shade of pale. He caught me, pulled me close, and whispered into my ear, "How many times do you want to come?" then released me with a lecherous grin.

Blood rushed to my cheeks. I'd get him back for that. It might take me all afternoon to figure out how, but when I did, it would be good.

As I stepped onto the sidewalk, I clutched my coat closed and glanced at the sky. Dark clouds rolled overhead, holding the threat of more snow. Better now than Saturday when Janine was scheduled to fly in. Would it also slow down the person responsible for the fires? Bad weather for one day and no more fires was a tradeoff I could support.

Chapter 14

The blizzard hit fast and hard. At least I made it to the store first, because I wasn't taking Dolores back out into the weather, not even to go to Eli's. She wasn't built to handle streets covered in ice and snow. The city put out warnings to avoid unnecessary travel, so I resigned myself to staying home. As long as the electricity didn't go out again, I'd be fine. There was a list of things to do to keep me entertained—after I called Eli and told him about the change in plans. Anything to keep from thinking about Janine's mother.

The first item on the list was more research on the brooches. I wasn't ready to write them off as a coincidence. After tuning my radio to a classic rock station, I made myself a cup of tea and went to work.

I uploaded the image to my favorite website and prepared to wait. In the blink of an eye, the search came back with hundreds of images. None were an exact match but I spent a few minutes scrolling through the results, hoping to get lucky.

After the third page, I gave up. It was unlikely I'd find anything beyond that. But another website might give me different results. I wasn't ready to throw in the towel.

The lights flickered and I held my breath, but they stayed on. I mumbled as the picture took forever to load the second time and hoped the results would come back faster. Mere moments after I hit the 'Search' button, the pounding of footsteps on my outside stairs alerted me to company. My heart fluttered. Had Eli braved the storm to come stay with me?

Despite the swirling snow, I recognized the man at my door as I peered through the peephole. Freddie. Why wasn't he home staying warm?

I opened the door and yanked him inside, slamming the door behind him. Of course, some snow came in and I knocked what I could out of his hair. "What the heck are you up to?" I asked.

He unbuttoned his coat but didn't take it off. "I was out patrolling, and I saw your kitchen light on, so I decided to stop by and apologize again."

Something didn't compute. He was a detective and didn't run patrols. Plus, his Mustang wouldn't handle the streets any better than Dolores.

"How did you get here?"

"City works pickup. The Chief sent as many guys as possible home, but I volunteered to stay so Madigan could leave. He's got a month-old baby and both he and his wife are sleep deprived. The truck is a four-wheel drive and I'm not concerned about getting stuck."

I knew there was a reason I liked him. Most of the time. "While you're here, do you want something hot to drink? I'll put on a pot of coffee."

"No, but thanks. I have to hit the streets again. People get stupid and think the weather warnings don't apply to them. I've already had to pull two cars out of drifts. But like I said, I've been worrying about what happened earlier and wanted to say I'm sorry again. And check to make sure you were safe while I was at it."

That was sweet of him. "Thanks. I'm sorry too."

He shuffled his feet and snow fell onto the tile in the entrance way. "Well, I'd better get back out there. I'll see you around."

"Drive safe."

Freddie buttoned his coat and as he looked back up something caught his eye and he stiffened. "What's that, Harmony?"

"What?"

He pointed towards my laptop. I swiveled to see the results of my search. And there it was. The perfect match.

"Holy crap. Check it out."

"What is it?"

"Reverse image search. I was checking if anything on the internet looked like the picture of the brooch. And voila." I sat in the recliner pulled the laptop closer. "We have a match. Let's see what's on the original page."

He shucked off his coat and hung it on the rack before leaning over my shoulder. "Sure looks the same. But I'm still not convinced the pins have anything to do with the fires."

I ignored his doubts, excited by the find. "It's an online store. Says it's dedicated to the needs of the worldwide steampunk community, whatever that is. The brooch itself is a replica of a piece from the nineteenth century." So Jake was wrong in his assessment. Was he losing his touch?

"What can you find out about steampunk?"

I opened a new tab and started a search. Thousands of results flooded back. I started with the definition. "Oversimplified explanation. You know about the people who dress up as superheroes and cartoon characters, right?"

"Yes, several of the younger officers are into it. I've overheard them talking about it."

"This is similar, but more science fiction. And based on nineteenth century technology and clothing. Here are some pictures." I unplugged the laptop and handed it to him.

He used the back of the chair as support as he juggled the laptop and scrolled through the images. "Huh. They put a lot of effort into these outfits. How can we find out if anyone local is involved?"

"I'd start with asking the guys you work with." I took my laptop back. "And I'll start by looking on the internet. I wonder if Lando and Scotty know anything about it."

"Who?"

"Did Eli talk to you this afternoon?"

"No. But there's a message on my office line I haven't listened to yet."

I frowned. "You know he's in town, right?"

Freddie sat on the loveseat, resting his elbows on his knees and his chin on his hands. "No. He comes and goes so much I've stopped keeping track."

That was fair. "You remember the guys who came with him when I was kidnapped?"

"Vaguely."

"They're here. In Oak Grove. All three. And they are pretty sure they've got a line on who's uploading the fire videos. That's why Eli called you. He figures you'll need a warrant to get the final piece of information to make it admissible in court. In case they are tied to the person setting the fires."

It was Freddie's turn to frown. "I can't ask him to head over to the shop in this weather. And I can't ask a judge to come in to sign a warrant when it's not an emergency."

True. No one had been hurt. Yet.

"You should call him."

"Can you give me his number? That way I don't have to go back to the office to retrieve it."

Eli shared his business phone with everyone, but his personal cell was another story. He'd changed it a few months ago due to prank calls. I hesitated, not knowing which number he'd left in his message. "Why don't you use mine?" I asked.

His lips tightened. "Really, Harmony?"

The area rug under my feet was fascinating. "I can't give it out without his say-so. Just like I wouldn't hand out your number without your permission."

He tilted his head. "That's fair."

As a bonus, it gave me another opportunity to

talk to Eli. I tapped my right foot on the floor as the phone rang at his end. Three rings and he didn't pick up. Five rings and it switched to voice mail. Either he was asleep or, more likely, busy playing computer games with Lando and Scotty.

"Voice mail," I told Freddie while the message played and I waited for the beep. "Hey Eli," I said when the moment arose, "I've got Freddie here and he wanted to talk to you. Give me a holler or expect a call from him tomorrow. Love you." I ended the call and asked, "Will that do?"

Freddie stood and stretched. "It'll have to. Now, I'd better get back out there before the truck cools down. It takes forever to get it to a comfortable temperature."

I wished I had a thermos of coffee or hot chocolate or something to give to him. "Be careful."

He slipped his coat on and pulled the collar up around his neck. "Pay attention to the weather in the morning. Don't go to work if it isn't safe. I don't want to pull your car out of a ditch."

"I promise."

With his hand on the doorknob, he hunched his shoulders and took a deep breath. "Good night," he said, before opening the door, stepping outside, and pushing it shut. Even in that short span of time, a gust of wind sneaked in, bringing snow with it. I locked the door, shook a few flakes of snow off my shirt and stared at the now-quiet room. Suddenly, I was lonely.

My normal way of dealing with these moods involved Dolores and a long drive on country roads leading nowhere. That wouldn't be happening. I could head downstairs and hang out with Joe and Luke, but chances were, they were tucked in for the night. Besides, that involved putting on shoes and a coat, and I didn't feel like exerting the minimal effort.

I also didn't want to play detective anymore. I'd gathered the experts, and everything was up to them. Fiesker took the joy out of it anyway.

Looking for a distraction, I scanned the room. Nothing was out of place, except for a few books in my to-be-read pile. A smile played on my lips as I found my answer. It had been too long since I'd enjoyed a drugstore romance. I'd let someone else's imaginary woes be my salvation. And if the descriptions of the lusty, well-built hero entertained me for one night, it didn't count as cheating, because it was all make-believe. Would I choose the vengeful pirate or the spymaster viscount to keep me company?

I chose the pirate, hoping he plundered in the warm waters of the Caribbean. A blast of wind rattled my front window, so I grabbed an afghan to drape around my shoulders before settling onto the loveseat. With a pillow crunched behind my back, I leaned against one armrest, dangled my feet over the other, and propped the paperback on my knees.

By the time the dangerously handsome Captain Jacque released shy Lady Amelia from the cabin in which he held her captive, I was half asleep. It seemed like too much work to go to bed. I was just getting to the good part anyway. A few more pages, then I'd call it a night.

"You need to go to bed, Angel."

I tried to sit up, but Jake was lifting me from the loveseat. What was it with the Hennessey men, thinking I couldn't walk on my own? "Put me down, Jake. How did you get in?"

He chuckled and lowered me so my feet touched the floor. "How do you think? You left the door unlocked."

I knew better but wouldn't waste my breath arguing. "Why aren't you at home and out of the weather?"

"I was working. There's always someone looking for a place to get a drink, even when it's storming. We stayed busier tonight than we've been for a few weeks because other bars in town closed."

Drinking and driving is a bad mix on a good day, but on a night like tonight? "I hope everyone got home safe."

"We stopped serving alcohol and started serving free coffee an hour before we closed. Only a couple of the customers made a fuss about it, and they were close to being cut off anyway. The money the boss lost doing that was more than made up for by increased sales earlier in the night."

That would only happen in a small town. "You haven't said why you're here." I realized Jake still had his arms around me and pushed him away.

"You finally woke up all the way," he laughed, erasing my fears he'd take offense. He took off his thick, fake glasses and tucked them in his shirt pocket. "I'm here because I overheard something you'll be interested in."

Maybe I wasn't tired of playing detective. "About the fires?"

"Yes. About the fire. The next one."

Chapter 13

Where did my cell phone get to? Freddie needed in on this conversation. "When? Where?" I asked, running my hand between the cushions of the loveseat.

Jake put his hand on my shoulder. "Settle down. Not tonight. I would have called someone if that was the case."

"Still, I should call Freddie so he can ask the zillion questions I forget to ask."

"You can convey the message. If someone spots both his car and mine parked out on the street, it will look suspicious. Well, that's the wrong word, but I have to keep a low profile if there's a chance to get more information."

He was right. Both cars were distinctive. Although Freddie might still be out in the truck. I didn't know what time it was and gave up wearing watches a long time ago. I started searching for my phone again and bent over to check under the coffee table.

"What are you doing?" Jake asked.

"I can't find my phone."

"I'm trying to tell you about the fire and you're worried about your phone. Focus, Angel! And it's on the table, in plain sight."

It hadn't been there a minute ago. Or I was still half-asleep. I scooped it up and punched the button to bring it back to life. It was after three. That explained why I was having a hard time staying on track.

"Okay, I'm with you. Tell me what you heard." I blinked, hard, to clear sleep from the corner of my eye.

He made me wait while he sank into my recliner. And wait some more until I sat on the loveseat. "First off," he said, "I didn't recognize these guys. They weren't regulars. They didn't fit in with the rest of the crowd but weren't standoffish either. More like they tried to blend in but weren't very good at it."

I understood. Sometimes I felt that way.

"They started drinking at the bar," Jake continued. "Watching the game. Atlanta against Dallas. They made conversation with the folks sitting by them and weren't loud or obnoxious. The kind of customer you can mostly ignore.

"When a table in the back opened up, they moved. No biggie. When I had a chance, I cleared the empty glasses off the table and brought them a new round. They stopped talking when I got there, but that's normal."

I wished he'd get to the point.

"Then they stopped talking when I cleaned the nearby tables. And that's not normal. So, every time things slowed down at the bar, I made a point of being in their general vicinity. Not checking on them or anything, just cleaning around them.

"After a while, they began ignoring me. That's when I overheard them talking about fires. Didn't catch much because I had customers at the bar. And everything they said was public knowledge."

So why had he come to me?

"I guess they drank enough to loosen up. That's when they started talking about a house on Green Street. I didn't hear most of the conversation because I got busy. I thought they were talking about the fire from a few nights ago."

That fire wasn't on Green Street.

"But the fire wasn't on Green Street," Jake said, echoing my thoughts. "It was Broad. I don't think any of the fires happened on Green."

In my head, I reviewed the latest edition of my spreadsheet. No, Green Street wasn't on it. A surprise, because part of it traveled through a run-down area of town.

"Did you get a name?" I asked, fighting my excitement. This could be the break Freddie needed.

He shook his head. "No. And they paid in cash, so I couldn't check the credit card slip. Tipped crummy, too. I got one picture but it's bad."

Was he going to show it to me or did he want me to beg? I crossed my arms and stared at him, refraining from tapping one foot.

The corners of his mouth twitched. "The lighting in the bar is awful to begin with. And I turned off my flash so, they wouldn't realize what I did."

I hoped my stare burned a hole in his conscience.

"Do you want to see it?" He winked, and his trademark smile lit his face.

I played it cool. "Oh, I guess so. Maybe I'll recognize them."

He dug his phone out of his pocket and ran his finger across the screen, sighed, and frowned. "I'm not sure it's worth showing you."

"Uh-huh. Hand the phone over, Jake."

He slid it across the coffee table. I felt his eyes on me as I picked it up and tapped the screen. He was right. It was a terrible picture, the two faces lit only by a dim overhead bulb. It reminded me of childhood pictures where the only light came from birthday candles on the cake. Photo manipulation software might fix the picture enough to make the faces clear, but that was beyond my skill level. And I didn't know if that fell within Eli's magical skills either.

"I don't recognize them. How about forwarding me the picture so I can share it with Freddie?" A second glance didn't provide me with any new insight and I gave the phone back.

"Sorry I couldn't get a better picture." He fiddled with his phone for a few seconds. "It's on its way to you."

My phone pinged and the screen went dark, the battery dead. "That figures," I said. "I better go plug it in. I have to get up for work in a few hours."

"Have you checked the weather? I don't think you'll be going anywhere. Even if it stops snowing, the roads won't be clear."

Which meant another day with the library closed. I didn't like it. Especially if the schools closed, too. Another gust of wind rattled the front window as I tried to see outside. The light from the room behind me created a mirror effect and all I saw was my reflection.

"I'll still have to get up and find out whether the city plans to open their offices," I said. "We might have a delayed start but work part of the day." In the end, it would be my decision. One of the last I'd make in the position.

"You can see better from here," Jake called, breaking my reverie. He'd turned off the kitchen light and was looking out the window by the sink. "In fact, I'd better get going or I'll be stuck here all night." He wiggled his eyebrows. "Or would you like me to stick around?"

And there was the Jake I knew so well. I'd wondered where he was hiding. Peering over his shoulder revealed the storm had slowed down although heavy flakes still whirled in the wind.

"You made it here. You should be able to make it back to your place."

"Oh well, you can't blame me for trying." He covered his mouth and yawned so, of course, I yawned, too.

"Go home, Jake," I said.

I expected a snarky response, but instead, he dropped a peck on my forehead. "I'll do that. And you go to bed. No staying up and trying to match those guys to other pictures on the internet. You hear me?"

I'd considered doing just that but wouldn't admit to it. "Loud and clear."

I considered it again after he left, reminding me with a cocky grin to lock my door. But there was only enough time for a quick nap before I'd have to get up and decide what to do about the library. I needed all the sleep I could get.

We opened at eleven with a skeleton crew. By that, I mean me and Danielle, the children's librarian. And no, I didn't drive Dolores. Although the city workers were out early cleaning the major streets, the neighborhoods remained a disaster. My ride came in the form of a black van with three knights in shining dark armor. Eli, Lando, and Scotty showed up with breakfast, sporting new winter wear.

It was all Jake's doing. He'd left Eli a message ratting out my plans to open the library and worrying about me driving Dolores. So, the three of them decided to practice driving in inclement weather, found an empty parking lot, and put the van through its paces. Once they got comfortable with how the van handled, they hit up a convenience store for fresh coffee and day-old donuts.

After we'd finished off the coffee, I put them to work shoveling the sidewalks while I cleaned off my steps. Figured I'd give Joe and Luke a break. Lando and Scotty made a race out of it and cleaned the entire length of the block. They played it off like it was nothing big, but I placed a bet their arms would be sore by supper.

Especially as I requested they clean off the steps and sidewalks of the library, too. Just Lando and Scotty. I conscripted Eli into helping to shelve books. For some reason, people decided the middle of a snowstorm was the perfect time to use the overnight drop box. Danielle and I barely kept up with the phone calls asking if we were open. Half of the callers wouldn't show up anyway.

By noon, several volunteers arrived, and I retreated to my office. Eli and the guys disappeared at some point but came back with enough pizza for the staff and volunteers. Eli and I ate in the privacy of my—Janine's—office. Everyone else took turns between the break room and the front desk. Even Lando and Scotty played at being librarians. Mostly, I suspected, so they could flirt with Danielle.

Between the confusion, excitement, and lack of sleep, I forgot to call Freddie until mid-afternoon. With Lando and Scotty back at the house doing whatever they were doing, and Eli ensconced in a back corner of the library working, I finally had a quiet moment. As I listened to the phone ring at the other end, I hoped I didn't wake him. And that Fiesker wasn't with him.

It was no surprise when I ended up with his voicemail. The message I left contained few details in case someone else overheard it. *Sending you a picture. Call me and I'll explain.*

Freddie showed up in twenty minutes flat. Without Fiesker. He plunked himself into an empty chair and said, "So?"

"Do you recognize them?"

He snorted. "Not from the picture you sent. Who are they?"

"I don't know. Neither did the person who took the picture."

"Are you deliberately trying to annoy me, Harmony?"

"No, just trying to not get your hopes up." I got up and closed the office door. "They may or may not have something to do with the fires. All we have to go on is snippets of an overheard conversation. No names, no nothing. The picture may not be useful without more information."

"Where were you when you heard them talking?"

"Not me. Jake. And he was working so, he only got bits and pieces. He doesn't recognize them either."

Freddie rubbed his forehead. "How does this tie into the fires?"

"What do you remember about the fire on Green Street?"

"What fire on Green Street?"

"Exactly my point. So, how could these two know about it?"

Chapter 16

The good news was that Green Street wasn't the longest street in town. The bad news was it had a lot of old, run-down houses along its route, some of them empty and neglected, not worth salvaging. Any of them would be the perfect target for an arsonist.

The good news was that the police could set up extra patrols in the area. All it took was one phone call to Chief Sorenson. And the bad news? The alley that ran behind the houses was barely passable on a good day, and after the storm, it wasn't a good day.

At least it was a new lead. And according to Freddie, Fiesker had received the preliminary lab results and it looked like the house fire a few days earlier was an accident and not deliberately set. So, the arsonist hadn't escalated his targets.

Of course, the picture would be circulated to the ranks of the police. If the two men were locals, someone would recognize them.

At least, that's how Freddie explained it, and that's what I shared with Eli and the guys as we ate supper that night. At my place, because I wanted to sit in a real chair and at a real table. And have something besides takeout, even though I loved Mama D's food. I whipped up a double recipe of meatloaf to make sure there would be enough to fill several bottomless stomachs and hopefully have leftovers. It always tasted better the second day.

Scotty tried to explain how to trace down the owners of the email accounts used to stalk the firemen. And how, this time, it didn't work. Usually, people use the same name for email as they used for something else on the internet, but not this person. Not that they could find, anyway. But they hadn't given up. Not yet. They wrote a script to crawl the internet searching for matches. Whatever that meant.

Truth is, my mind wandered elsewhere as he rambled. What had I missed while getting things ready for Janine's arrival? I didn't want her to walk into a house with no food and I'd scheduled the task of buying groceries for the morning, so everything would be fresh. And I'd be able to check that the cleaning service hadn't missed something.

The later the evening got the more distracted I became until I didn't even try to follow the conversation. Eli sat at the kitchen table working on his laptop, taking care of business, only occasionally putting in his two cents worth. Any other night, I would have grabbed my laptop to do research of my own. But I couldn't start my job search without the possibility of being overseen. And I didn't want to talk to anyone about it yet.

The job hunt was complicated by the fact that Eli had bought the house. Chances of me finding my dream job in Oak Grove were zero. But how could I leave town when he'd bought the house to give us more time together?

The footsteps on the stairs followed by the pounding on the door provided a welcome distraction from my thoughts.

"Are you expecting someone?" Eli asked as he shoved back his chair and stuck his handgun into his waistband.

I tried very hard not to roll my eyes. As much as I loved him, at times his over-protectiveness made me feel smothered. No one was after me. Not anymore. But late-night visits always seemed to bring bad news, so I was glad he was there.

A quick peek through my peephole and I yanked opened the door to greet Sarah and Freddie. Despite numerous phone conversations with Sarah, I hadn't seen her in person since the news of Mrs. Janson's death. She opened her arms as she stepped inside, and I fell apart as she wrapped them around me.

Sarah and I ended up in my bedroom so we could cry without making it awkward for everyone else. She hadn't been as close to Janine's mother as me, but spent plenty of time at the Janson's house as a teenager. That was back in the day when people mistook us for sisters. The resemblance lessened as we got older but, in my heart, I still thought of her as one.

When we returned to the front room—after a stop in the bathroom to wash our faces—Freddie and Eli were deep in a discussion about the fires. Scotty and Lando were nowhere to be seen. I wondered if they'd gone for a beer and snacks run.

Freddie and Eli exchanged glances. "No, they received an alert about activity on an account they've been tracking," Eli said. "They headed back to the house to check it out."

His eyes didn't meet mine. He was hiding something. And that meant Freddie was in on it.

"Will they be coming back?" Sarah asked as she sat next to Freddie on the loveseat.

I wiggled into a comfortable spot in Eli's lap. It was better than making him sit on a kitchen chair. "You don't know the guys very well," I said. "Once they get deep into figuring out an issue, they won't stop until it's solved. Like someone else I know." The kiss I planted on Eli's cheek made it clear who that someone was.

Sarah grinned. "Pot, meet kettle."

"I didn't say it was a bad thing," I pointed out. "Just one of the things I love about him."

Freddie grimaced and shook his head. "Before things get mushy, can we talk about the reason I'm here?"

So, it wasn't an impromptu visit among friends. I should have known.

"I figured you'd be interested in an update on the warrant."

That got my attention. I sat up so fast I accidentally poked Eli in the ribs with my elbow. He groaned and clutched his side, but I ignored his theatrics.

"How did they react down at the cable office when you served it?"

"I didn't. The request got denied."

"What?" I screeched.

"Judge Turner decided we didn't have evidence the person or persons posting the videos are the same people setting the fires. He said the couple of recordings with a fire starting looked like campfires to him. And he believes if the corporate office's lawyers challenged the validity of the warrant, they'd win. There's nothing illegal about filming firefighters at work in a public area."

The judge was right, of course, but that didn't make the news any easier to accept.

I didn't push Eli until after Sarah and Freddie had left. "Can you track down the users without a warrant?"

"Legally, no. The only way to do it is to hack into the cable company's records. And that may not be possible, even illegally. I won't ask Scotty and Lando to try."

"I hate this. You got us so close. It seems wrong to have to stop now."

He grinned as he helped me to carry the dirty glasses to the kitchen. "Who said anything about stopping? There are a couple of other ways to track down who's posting the videos. We're still working on it."

I wrapped my arms around him and snuggled against his back. "You know how much I appreciate you doing this? But you should stop now. I don't want you to risk your reputation by doing anything that's against the law."

He chuckled. "I haven't been caught yet." He suddenly swung around so we stood face to face, chest to chest. "But," he said as he leaned in to gently touch his lips to mine, "I promise I'll stick to strictly legal means of tracking the culprit, even if it's harder that way."

Something else was harder, too. But he'd have to wait. We had more kissing to do. I didn't have to worry about anyone overhearing us, and I planned to make the night worth our while.

We moved from breathtaking kisses to territory a little lower when my home phone rang. I stopped long enough to let out a deep sigh. Eli shook his head and I decided to ignore it. If it was important, the caller would leave a message.

A minute or two later, my cell phone buzzed. I forgot to turn it off before accosting Eli. With a grimace, I reached into my pocket and pulled it out. Keeping my eyes locked on Eli's, I turned down the volume and tossed it onto the counter behind us.

My reward came in the form of Eli paying additional attention to that particular spot on my neck. Things were moving along nicely when his phone rang.

I started to worry. It didn't feel like a coincidence. But he didn't let it interrupt the moment. His phone ended up silenced next to mine.

We were in the slow process of heading towards the bedroom, with frequent stops along the way, when a loud knock distracted us. In unison, we groaned. "If we pretend that we aren't here, will they go away?" I whispered into Eli's ear.

He didn't have time to answer before they knocked again. Louder this time. "Miss Duprie, open the door," then in a muffled voice, "Get the key from her landlords."

"I'll answer it," Eli said, reaching for his gun where he'd dropped it in the recliner. I hastily buttoned my blouse as he strode towards the door. "Who is it?" he called.

"Fire department. You need to evacuate the premises."

Eli peered through the peephole and yanked open the door. "What's going on?"

I darted back to the kitchen where I'd left my shoes, hoping whoever was at the door wouldn't see me.

"Didn't you hear the sirens? There's a house fire across the street," the man explained. "The Axcel place. With the wind, we're concerned about sparks spreading to nearby roofs. We're evacuating the neighbors as a precaution.

The only window I had facing that direction was in the bedroom and we hadn't made it there yet. I slipped my cell phone into my pocket and picked up Eli's phone and shirt.

"We're trying to get a shelter opened at the school a few blocks away," the firefighter continued, "but most folks are going to stay with friends and relatives."

"We've got a place to go," Eli said. "But we need a few minutes to get ready."

"Don't take too long. We'll be closing the street soon. Now I've got to go wake up a few more people."

I grabbed a garbage bag from under the sink. It would be faster to toss the few clothes and personal items I needed in one of those than retrieve my suitcases from storage in the basement. What I really wanted was to pack up everything I owned and take it to safety, but there wasn't room in Dolores.

"Thank you. We'll be out in a jiffy."

By the time Eli closed the door, I'd put his shoes by the recliner along with the rest of his things. I added my laptop to the pile. He had less to carry than me.

"Anything I can do to help?" he asked, pulling on his shirt.

I put my purse on the top of the stack. "Get Dolores out of the garage and warm her up. Take the laptop with you. I'll be down in a flash."

"Are you trying to get me out of your way?"

Is that what I was doing? "No, I just don't want to get into a cold car."

He grabbed my hands. "Why are you shaking?"

I looked at them in surprise. Then looked back up at him. "I don't know."

All it took was the slightest tug and I fell into his chest. He wrapped his arms around me and kissed the top of my head. "It's going to be okay, Buttercup."

I wanted to believe him. Really, I did.

Chapter 17

I was shaking again, from the cold. Or was it Fiesker's frosty glare? His crossed arms and puffed up chest told me everything I needed to know about his opinion of me. Even Eli's arms wrapped around me weren't enough to warm me up. We stood on the street corner and watched as another fire truck rolled onto the scene.

Of course, Fiesker and Freddie had been summoned when the call came in to 911. They'd been on the scene almost since the first fire trucks arrived. It was Freddie who tried reaching Eli and me on our phones when the decision was made to evacuate nearby houses.

"At least Mrs. Axcel saved a few of her mementos," Freddie said as firemen directed a spray of water towards the back corner of the roof. "That and the feral cat living under her back porch. I'm hoping her clothes will only need a good washing to get out the smoke."

"It's too bad they weren't able to confine the damage to the front room where it started," Eli said.

"I don't understand how she got it into her head it was a good idea to have a fire. She's what, pushing ninety? The fireplace hasn't been used for years and she'd never made one before. She told us her late husband was the expert."

"And he's been dead for three years." I'd gone to his funeral, along with many of the neighbors. "Maybe now Mrs. Axcel will listen to her kids."

"What do you mean?" Freddie asked.

"They've been trying to get her to move in with one of them or into assisted living," I explained. "And she keeps refusing. Now she won't have a choice."

"How do you know about that?" Fiesker asked, stepping into my personal space.

I didn't budge an inch. His intimidation tactics wouldn't work on me. "Mrs. Axcel told me so, last fall, when I spent an afternoon raking leaves for her. Lots of folks in the neighborhood tried to help her keep the place up. She fed me milk and cookies too because she was just happy to have someone to talk to. She told me she wanted to stay in the house as long as possible. It's the house she and her husband bought when they were newlyweds and they raised all three of their kids in it." There was a lot more to our conversation, but nothing that mattered to Fiesker and his investigation.

"At least she's going to be okay," Eli said, switching the topic. The paramedics had taken her to the hospital to get checked out as a precaution.

Her oldest daughter had been called and was on her way to take charge of all the arrangements needed. Like temporary housing and a new home for the cat. And the insurance paperwork.

Fiesker didn't get the hint. "Did she set the fire on purpose for the attention?"

Did he really believe that or was he searching for a way to justify his continued stay in Oak Grove? I shook my head. "Not a chance. Between her church and the senior citizen's group, she has plenty of friends." He didn't need to know I thought she'd been slipping mentally the last few months. I talked to her every time the senior group made a trip to the library, and the last few times she forgot my name. I didn't want Fiesker to write a report that would cheat her out of her insurance money.

Eli and I hung around to observe the cleanup after Fiesker and Freddie left to go bug some other unlucky souls. As interesting as watching the firefighters at work was, the small crowd captured my attention. Almost everyone had a cell phone aimed at the action and I bet the social media sites would be flooded by videos in the next day or two. With the fire being an accident, our person of interest was no more than another spectator. I recognized most of the faces, if not the names, and didn't believe any of the neighbors could be the arsonist. No one stood out as not belonging. The water brigade was out in full force and I recognized many of them, too.

"Ready to go?" Eli asked. "We have unfinished business."

Is that all he ever thought of? Of course, he still smelled like sex, and it was sending my hormones into overdrive despite the circumstances. "Your place or mine?" Mine was safe even though a sheet of ice covered the roof. It had been sprayed with water as a precaution to protect it from wind-driven sparks.

"Yours is closer, but we can't get to it right now. Too many fire trucks and hoses in the way. Besides, people will try to find us there. So mine."

It sounded like a good plan.

He dangled my keys in front of my face. I reached for them and he pulled them away. "First one back to Dolores gets to drive."

He wanted to play, did he? I pulled myself out of his arms and swiveled. "Go," I said as I darted down the sidewalk.

He laughed but his footsteps followed close behind me. It would be a tight race. Unless I figured out how to cheat.

As I dashed by a pile of snow, put there by a neighbor after shoveling their sidewalk, I leaned down and picked up a handful. Without first packing it into a snowball, I tossed it over my shoulder. He sputtered, and his footsteps faltered. It must have been a lucky shot. I wished I could have seen his face, but if I turned to look I'd lose the slight advantage I'd earned. My best bet was to keep running. Dolores was only a few feet ahead.

As I reached out to touch her trunk, I was grabbed from behind. "That was sneaky," Eli said as he swung me around. I expected a kiss but got showered by snow instead. I shivered and giggled as I shook it out of my hair.

"Now we're even," he added.

Maybe, but neither of us had officially reached Dolores yet. With one hand, I pulled his head down as if drawing him in for a kiss, while with the other hand, I tapped Dolores' rear fender. With my lips a breath away from his, I whispered, "I win. Give me my keys."

"You might get to drive, but I still win." Eli gently stroked my cheek before closing the gap between our lips. The heat of the kiss we exchanged may have accelerated global warming.

Yes, I let him drive.

It was nice, waking up next to Eli and knowing it didn't matter if we slept in. I didn't need to go to work, and Janine wouldn't arrive until early afternoon. It was even better because he didn't seem to be in a hurry to get his first cup of coffee and get to work on whatever project demanded his attention.

"I could get used to this," he murmured, running his fingers through my hair.

I rested a hand on his thigh. "You and me both," I agreed.

His hand stopped moving, he closed his eyes and his breath evened out. I stayed still, thinking he was falling back to sleep. That was okay, I'd give him a few minutes before I slipped out of bed to go take a shower. Or go back to sleep myself.

Then his hand resumed its movements. "I'd like mornings like this more often. When are you going to move in with me?"

My eyes jerked open. "What?"

"You're aware of my plans to hold business meetings here. They'll be on the first floor. We can make the third floor our oasis. No one needs to go up there except us. One room can be your office, another one mine, and in the rest of the space, we can do whatever we want. We'll keep our bedroom here, of course. If we add a sink and a fridge, we'll never have to go downstairs if we don't want to."

"You've been thinking a lot about this."

"About setting up the third floor? No, but it seemed obvious once the idea popped into my head a few minutes ago." He drew in a deep breath and blew it out. "About living with you? Ever since you made the trip to visit me and I realized how much I liked having you around and how much I missed you after you left. When I figured out I'd never convince you to move to Florida, I had to come up with another way to make it happen. Buying this house seemed like the perfect solution. Your place is too small for both of us."

Small, yes, but it was my home. And I wasn't ready to give it up, not even for Eli. But how could I tell him that without hurting his feelings?

"That's why I only bought furniture for the bedrooms," he went on. "I wanted us to pick it out together."

145

For a man of few words, Eli was talking up a storm. Was he that nervous?

"You haven't said anything, Buttercup. Especially not the one word I want to hear. Yes."

I needed to choose my words carefully. "I love spending time with you. But this house is too big for me to rattle around in when you're gone."

He rolled over and stared at the ceiling. "And my business takes me away a lot."

"And I knew that before I fell in love with you, and I don't expect you to change. And there's another complication." Now it was my turn to stare at the ceiling. "I'm going to be out of a job in a few days. My research business is gone, and if I want to be a librarian, I'll have to look out of town for a position."

He raised himself up on one elbow. "What do you mean? I figured your research was put on the back burner while you helped out Janine."

I shook my head and closed my eyes, so he wouldn't spot the tears forming. "The grant the authors' group used to pay me ran out. Janine will want her position back. I'm going to be jobless."

"I don't understand the problem. You have plenty of money. You don't need to work."

That was true. But I *liked* working. And I didn't like dipping into my funds.

"You have plenty of money, too," I pointed out. "And I don't see you sitting back and letting someone else do all the work."

"It's my business. And my passion. I can't hand it off to anyone else."

"My point exactly. The passion part, at least." Although I didn't own the library, I cared for it like it was my business. "I've thought about going back to school and getting a second Masters or trying for a Ph.D. That still won't get me a job here in town."

"That complicates things. I wish I had known before I bought this place. I might not have spent the money." He rolled over, his back toward me, shutting me out.

I got the unspoken message. The plans for a perfect morning dashed, I rolled over in the opposite direction and got out of bed. The compromise I'd concocted for our living arrangements never even made it into the discussion.

Chapter 18

"Exhibit C," Freddie said, pulling a plastic sandwich bag out of his pocket and plopping it on my coffee table. The dark circles under his eyes made me wonder if he stayed up all night writing reports.

I escaped the uncomfortable atmosphere at Eli's with the excuse I needed to head over to Janine's to make sure everything was perfect for her arrival. Which I'd done twice, but I was over Eli's brooding. The small talk we made after he got up did nothing to ease the strain between us.

I don't like lying, so I stopped at her place. Everything was as good as I could get it. I resisted the temptation to replace those ugly floral curtains in her bedroom. No matter how much I hated them, Janine picked them out, making them untouchable.

Freddie showed up a few minutes after I got home. I'd put the last cup from the previous night away and was ready to tackle my normal Saturday cleaning when he knocked. I half expected Eli with a bouquet, but I'd take whatever interruption life would send me.

This disruption took the form of another brooch. Or was Freddie testing me? "Looks like Exhibit B," I said. "Are you sure you don't have your letters wrong? After all, last night's fire wasn't deliberately set. There'd be no reason for a brooch to be left at the scene if my theory is correct."

Freddie's lips formed a thin line. "It didn't come from across the street."

"So, where did it come from?"

His lips all but disappeared. "The other fire. The one across town. A fireman found it sitting on a post where it could be easily seen."

"This is the first I've heard about it."

"Wasn't much." He shrugged. "Basically a pile of pallets and cardboard. Like homeless people use to keep themselves warm. It was in the hardware store parking lot, and everything had to be carried there. One of the overnight staff stocking shelves called it in."

"Does the store have security cameras?"

"Not covering the whole parking lot."

"Whoever this is knows exactly what they are doing. They picked a relatively safe spot for their bonfire, chose a time when most people's attention would be somewhere else, and left their calling card so there'd be no question about it."

"Sounds as if you read my report. And Fiesker agrees."

That didn't bring me any comfort. "Does he

believe that means one of our local firefighters is responsible?"

Freddie nodded. "You nailed it."

"Are there any new messages or emails to the firemen? New videos on the site?"

"There are videos of both fires on the internet. Haven't heard of new emails. Of course, most of the guys on duty last night are probably still sleeping."

They deserved every minute of sleep they could get. "Did Fiesker find any clues?"

Freddie hesitated. "Not that he shared. I thought I saw him slip something into his pocket, but when I asked he denied it. He claimed his hands were cold. It's not like I could search him, but I wasn't convinced. And before you ask, I haven't discussed it with Chief Sorenson. I figured he deserved to have the rest of his weekend uninterrupted."

My gut told me that wouldn't happen.

❊ ❊ ❊

Janine didn't look like someone who spent the last couple of months in Florida. The only color in her face came from the little bit of makeup remaining after being washed off by her tears. Sarah looked as if she did her share of crying, too. It would have been too easy for me to dissolve into tears as well, but I fought them back. One of us had to be strong.

All bets were off once Merrilee showed up. I hadn't seen her since she took the assistant principal's job in Pittsburgh after the holidays. She'd only be in town for one day and wouldn't be able to attend the memorial service because of her new duties. We had to do our catching up and mourning at the same time.

A pot of beef stew simmered on the top of the stove and a batch of cornbread was cooking in the oven. The scents of home—onions and garlic and warm bread—drifted from the kitchen to the living room. I'd filled Janine's fridge with a case of beer, and an assortment of wine graced the kitchen counter. The freezer was stocked with ice cream. We planned on spending the night and there'd be no need for any of us to go out so we didn't need a designated driver. Sarah had Freddie on speed dial in case of a snack emergency.

Oh, and I strategically placed a case of tissues under the coffee table. Sarah and I made a side bet about how many boxes we'd need. I thought four, one for each of us, and Sarah guessed six. Sue us, we needed something to lighten our moods and help us make it through the night.

At first, we talked about everything and anything but Janine's mother. How bad the high school football team was doing. How Merrilee's new job was going. How much snow we'd gotten this year.

"Mom confessed to missing the snow," Janine said as she emptied her second beer. "She liked the warm weather, but said it got boring after a while."

And that was all that it took.

"I always suspected she secretly loved the snow," I said. "Even when she complained about it. Remember when we were home from college on winter break and built a flock of snowmen in the front yard? She was right there with us."

"Didn't she start the snowball fight that day?" Sarah asked.

"I wanted to be mad at her because she was hanging out with us," Janine said. "Then one of you guys pointed out Dad was away on a work trip and maybe she was lonely." She popped the top of another beer and took a swig. "Whoever suggested it, thank you. She mentioned that day and how much it meant that we let her join in the fun."

That did it. Four hands reached for the tissues.

Janine gave up first and went to bed. Which I expected. She'd had a long day. Hell, she'd had a long week. Merrilee passed out on the couch not long after that. Sarah and I stayed up, talking in whispers, making sure nothing had been forgotten for the service on Monday.

I made the switch to water early in the evening, deciding one of us needed to be almost sober in case of an emergency. Like if a tree fell on the roof or a drunk driver crashed his car through the front door. Not that I expected anything, but life threw surprises at me all too often.

I was half-asleep in one of Janine's easy chairs, covered with an afghan, when the sounds of trouble brought me back to wakefulness. Tires screeched on the street and a horn honked. An engine revved several times. Then another screech of tires as the vehicle roared away. I didn't bother peeking out the curtains. Probably a teenager dropping off his date and trying to impress her with his noisy car. Nothing to worry about. I drew the afghan around my shoulders, wiggled my butt to find a comfortable position, and closed my eyes again.

Sunday was a day of rest and recuperation and visitors. An endless stream of old movies ran on the TV but no one watched. People dropped by to pay their respects and leave their specialties—Janine wouldn't need to cook for a week. Sarah, Merrilee and I stayed to keep the tissues handy and the trays of cookies stocked. Merrilee left first to drive back to Pittsburgh before dark, and Sarah and I left soon afterward to give Janine some time alone.

Although they didn't fill the church, enough people showed up for the memorial to do Mrs. Janson justice. Almost every staff person and many of the volunteers came, more for Janine than her mother. Janine's brother made it into town from whatever far-flung post the Navy assigned him to, looking dashing but somber in his white uniform.

But my eyes were drawn to Eli. He shed his normal college professor look for a tailored black suit. My heart flipped as he made his way through a group of volunteers to offer Janine a hug and his condolences. After she introduced him to her brother, he sat beside me where Sarah had been and casually placed a hand on my knee. I'd been so busy watching him I didn't even realize she had moved.

I didn't know how to react. Was this his way of apologizing? I couldn't ask because the minister requested everyone to take their seats.

It wasn't like any funeral I'd ever attended because that's what Mrs. Janson wanted. Instead of solemn funeral dirges, classic rock played softly in the background. Other than a welcoming blessing, there were no prayers. Stories of her life replaced the eulogy. Janine and her brother didn't have to speak at all. I managed to recite my little story of how she helped when my mother died without breaking into sobs.

His hand on the small of my back, Eli stuck with me when we moved to the church hall for lunch, his presence both comforting and puzzling. I opted to let him stay. Even if we were at odds with one another, I needed his support.

It came as no surprise when his phone buzzed as lunch was wrapping up, or that he excused himself and stepped outside. But it came as a shock when he returned and breathed into my ear, "We need to go. Now. Tell Janine goodbye."

I opened my mouth to ask why and he shook his head before I got the word out. His right cheek twitched, a sure sign he was nervous, unusual for him, so I didn't push.

The original plan was for us to head to Janine's place after the official service finished. But with her brother's arrival, Sarah, Merrilee and I decided to give them some time alone. In fact, Janine was so busy chatting with her brother, she barely noticed when I told her I was leaving, but I'd talk to her soon. I didn't even need the excuse I'd prepared about a minor emergency at the library.

Once we were outside, I didn't restrain myself. "What's so important that you dragged me away from Mrs. Janson's funeral?"

"Check your phone," Eli said. "Can I hitch a ride with you? I really hate not having my own car. Remind me never to ride with Lando and Scotty again."

I had a sudden vision of Eli, in his immaculate black suit, crawling out of the back of the Mohawk Inc. van. In spite of myself, I giggled as I reached into my purse to retrieve my phone. I'd shut it off before the service started.

"Of course you can ride with me," I answered as we walked towards Dolores. Strode might be a better word because he walked fast enough I had a hard time keeping up in my heels. "Where are we going?"

He stopped abruptly and I almost ran into him. "The police station," he said, "We've been summoned."

Chapter 19

"By whom?" I asked as I unlocked Dolores. "What's so important we needed to leave the funeral?"

"Chief Sorenson. And he doesn't say why. At least, he didn't tell me." Eli buckled his seat belt. "Check your voice mail and texts to see if he left you any information. I bet he used me as a messenger when he couldn't reach you."

My three messages held no clues, only requests in Chief Sorenson's somber tone to come see him as soon as possible. The underlying meaning came through clearly. He wanted to talk to me immediately. And it was important enough he couldn't leave his office to find me.

The trip to the police station seemed to take longer than normal although traffic was minimal. I hit each and every light as it turned red and that didn't help. I drove around the block twice before finding a parking spot that would minimize any damage to Dolores from someone opening their doors without paying attention.

I nodded to the rookie at the front desk—I still didn't know his name—as Eli and I pushed through the gate to the duty room. The rookie rose to intercept us, but one of the senior patrolmen, Officer Kinchloe, stopped him and waved us through.

"Chief's expecting you," he said.

I didn't dare ask him what was going on. He wouldn't be able to tell me anyway.

We paused outside the chief's office because agitated voices came from inside and we didn't want to interrupt his meeting. Someone must have alerted him to our arrival because Freddie opened the door. "Come on in," he said, jerking his head.

I didn't anticipate seeing Claire and Fiesker in the office. Whatever it was, it had to be bad.

There was only one empty chair in the room and, with a swipe of his hand, Freddie offered it to me. I didn't protest. Freddie leaned against the wall and Eli stood behind me, his hands resting on my shoulders. The small space barely had room for all of us.

Chief Sorenson looked up from his paperwork. "You two looked like you're going to a funeral."

I caught my breath and Eli cleared his throat. "We just left one," he said.

Freddie covered his mouth and coughed. Chief Sorenson rubbed his temple. Claire gasped and Fiesker's stone face didn't change at all.

"I'm sorry," Claire said. "This is my fault. I insisted Chief Sorenson ask you to come. Although

I don't believe I've met your companion."

Companion was a good term. I reached up and laid my hand on top of his. "This is Eli Hennessey. He's the computer expert I brought in to help track the people posting the videos and sending the emails." And, I hoped, still my lover. "Eli, this is Chief Claire Hinds of the Oak Grove Fire Department."

Fiesker straightened. "Another amateur to interfere with the investigation."

"Actually, Hennessey is the owner of a computer security firm that specializes in software for law enforcement. We've been using his product for several years now," Sorenson said. "He and two members of his staff are here for other business and agreed to help with this investigation as a personal favor to Miss Duprie."

I didn't realize he knew about Lando and Scotty. Freddie must have filled him in.

"Do you sell software for fire departments?" Claire asked. "I swear, the program we use gets worse every time they update it."

"We don't, but that could change." I heard the smile in Eli's voice. "Since I'm going to spend a lot more time in town, perhaps we could discuss a collaborative project. Once we get past this crisis, of course."

No one had told us what the crisis was yet. "What *is* going on?" I asked.

"I may be overreacting," Claire said. "But one of the men is missing. His captain assures me he's never done this before—not show up for a shift.

The last time anyone from the department talked to him was two days ago. His mother called the station looking for him because she hasn't talked to him either."

Sorenson leaned forward with his arms on his desk. "We checked his apartment. His car is in the complex's parking lot, and the landlord let us in to look around. No sign of a break-in and nothing appeared to be out of place."

"He's not answering his phone," Claire added. "And his records don't list any medical conditions."

"We asked the hospital," Freddie added, "They don't have a record of him coming in recently. That's all they were willing to tell us without a warrant. There have been no major accidents either in town or the county where he might have been taken to another facility."

"The cell phone company is trying to locate his phone," Sorenson said, "I expect it will take a while until they get back to us."

"He doesn't appear to have a steady girlfriend, but we're tracking down the last few women he dated." Freddie rubbed the back of his neck. "It's hard because he didn't tell his coworkers anything but first names. Two of the women had unusual names and if they live here, we should be able to find them."

Sorenson stood and stared out his window. "We could use your help to check his emails, Hennessey."

Eli's hands gripped my shoulders. "What makes you believe any of this is needed? Maybe he just took off for a few days to relieve stress and forgot to call in? There's a first time for everyone."

Fiesker nodded in agreement.

Sorenson turned to face us and grimaced. "That was my first reaction. But as a favor to Chief Hinds. I sent a patrolman to his apartment complex to do a wellness check. You know, knock on the door, ask if he's okay, peer in the windows if no one answers, that sort of thing. Everything seemed fine until he checked out the parking spot assigned to the unit and the car sitting there." Sorenson shoved a sandwich bag across his desk. "That's where he found this."

I didn't need to pick up the bag. I already knew what it held.

"Is it a match to the others?" From where I sat, I spotted the familiar shape of a brooch.

"Yes. Same pattern and size," Sorenson confirmed.

"What is it?" Eli asked.

"A replica Celtic brooch. That makes four found so far," Freddie said. "Three at places where there were fires, and now this one. Harmony identified them as something sold to the steampunk community."

"I'm familiar with it," Eli said.

"I've asked around and there doesn't seem to be an active group in Oak Grove. That doesn't eliminate the possibility locals aren't going to Cleveland or Pittsburgh or somewhere to do whatever it is they do when they get together."

"Were there more brooches in this guy's apartment?" I asked. "And who is missing? I know a few of the firefighters."

"Antonio Galas," Claire answered.

Was it bad that I was glad it wasn't someone I'd met?

"He's the guy who got messages to his new cell phone, right?" Eli asked.

He was right unless there was more than one Antonio working for the fire department. It wasn't an unusual name.

"I hadn't heard about that," Claire said.

"Withholding information?" Fiesker snarled.

"She told me about it,' Freddie snapped. "And I told Chief Sorenson. It's a police matter and not part of your investigation. So, pipe down. We're including you in this discussion as a courtesy but if you don't have anything constructive to contribute you might as well leave." He crossed his arms and glared. "You can show yourself out."

Whoa. I didn't anticipate that. Fiesker must be pushing Freddie too far. In the awkward silence that followed, I checked my phone for the messages that had been forwarded. They didn't reveal a last name either.

Fiesker didn't move. Chief Sorenson ignored him. "Do you have more than one Antonio on your force, Chief Hinds?"

"Not that I'm aware of."

He nodded. "Will you ask your HR department to verify?"

She typed a short message on her cell phone. "Done."

"Hennessey?"

Eli had removed his hands from my shoulders a few minutes earlier. His reflection in the window revealed he was doing something on his phone. "We've had no luck tracking those email accounts to a real person. Did Galas have a computer or tablet in his apartment?"

Freddie shrugged. "The officer didn't check."

"Can you get a warrant allowing a search of any electronic devices? If Galas is your standard user, there's a good chance we can access his accounts."

"Hack, you mean?" Fiesker's mouth scrunched up as if he was saying a dirty word.

Eli looked up from his phone. "All three of us are certified ethical hackers. But chances are, we won't need to put our skills to work. Most people leave their social media and email logged in on their personal machines. And if they don't, they keep a notepad with their passwords somewhere on their desk or a sticky under their keyboard."

Claire's cheeks reddened but I didn't point it out. I was willing to bet later she'd ask Eli for suggestions on how to change her computer setup.

"I'll ask the judge to include you on the search as an expert consultant," Freddie said.

Eli nodded. "You have my number. Call me when the paperwork is in order."

"What did you need me for, Chief?" I asked.

"I hoped you'd take another look at those spreadsheets of yours and see if anything new pops up. Maybe cross-reference with the work Fiesker has done. He's shared it with you, right?"

There it was, my chance to throw Fiesker under the bus.

"I haven't given it to her yet," Fiesker rushed to say. "It needs revising."

I didn't believe a single word. From the scowl on his face, neither did Sorenson. Claire cocked her head. "We can't wait. Can you send her an email?"

From my purse, I retrieved a flash drive and waved it in the air. "If you have your laptop in your car, you can drop your documents on here. That will speed up the process." And leave him with no easy way out.

Eli patted my shoulder. In approval, I hoped.

"Well?" Sorenson asked.

"I'll be back." Fiesker shuffled out of the office.

I took a deep breath and relaxed. I hadn't realized how much his presence put me on edge.

"What's the real reason you wanted Harmony here, Chief?" Eli asked when Fiesker was gone.

"I want her to check his work, although I don't expect any new revelations." Chief Sorenson leaned forward. "Miss Duprie, I hoped you would give us some time and research if there are previous cases of a firebug turned kidnapper."

The tension that descended on the office needed a chain saw to cut through it. I crunched my hand around the flash drive, trying to choose words that wouldn't insult the chief. "You didn't mention signs of a struggle when the officer checked Antonio's apartment. Is it a stretch to think he's been kidnapped?"

"Perhaps abducted would be a better choice of words. I was considering a scenario similar to what you went through."

Twice, actually, but who was counting?

The chief flipped through a manila file folder. "It's the text messages that led me to consider the possibility. They remind me of a stalker I tracked early in my career. A young schoolteacher found notes on her desk and shared them with other teachers but didn't think too much about them. When notes showed up on her car and at her home, she got worried and mentioned it to the retired police officer in charge of security for the school. He treated it as a prank and told her it was likely kids horsing around."

He closed the folder.

"What happened? I asked.

"He called my sergeant when she didn't show up for work one day, although her car was in the school parking lot. I was assigned to the case." He stopped. "Do you really want to know the rest?"

Bumps rose on my arms. Had she been murdered? Locked in a basement and raped? Better knowing the truth than leaving it to my imagination. I gulped. "Sure, go ahead."

"This was before everyone had a cell phone and debit card. We got permission to tap her mother's landline in case someone called her childhood home. Five days after the teacher disappeared, the call came in. I caught a break and was there when the phone rang." Chief Sorenson leaned back, his hands clasped behind his head.

And?

"Turned out she ran off and married one of the janitors. He only worked weekends, and no one missed him. The notes were from a high school boy who had a crush on her and had nothing to do with her disappearance. She'd left a letter for the principal, but his secretary lost it in a stack of paperwork.

His voice softened, and he fixed his eyes on me. "The point is, Miss Duprie, is that it could have ended much differently. I'll never forget the terror her family felt and how helpless I was to make it go away. And I've vowed to never make the mistake of brushing off early warning signs."

Is that why he wasn't as gruff with me as he was with most people? Guilt for not protecting me?

"That reminds me," Sorenson said, straightening his back and reverting to his command presence. "Detective Thomason, make sure those warrants include Galas' bank records and accounts. We need to know if anyone is using his cards and where. Throw in a request for his medical records. Let's cover everything in one swoop instead of annoying the judge by bothering him two or three times."

Chapter 20

"I can give you the rest of the day," I said. "That should give me enough time to do the research and review Fiesker's documents. But tomorrow I go back to the library. I don't expect Janine to start work until next week, and I'll cover until then."

A deep line formed on Chief Sorenson's forehead. "What am I missing here? I thought you were the head librarian now."

I wouldn't get through the story without tears, so I was thankful when Freddie jumped in. "Harmony's assignment as Chief Librarian was temporary. She filled in for Janine, who was taking care of her mother during a long illness. That's whose memorial service she and Hennessey were at today. The mother's, not Janine's."

"Again, I apologize, Miss Duprie." He tapped his fingers on his desktop. "Did Fiesker get lost? It shouldn't take this long to get to his car and back."

Unless Fiesker was hiding documents on his laptop he didn't want anyone else to see.

"I'll go look for him," Freddie offered.

"Let's give him a minute or two more," Claire suggested. "I'm sure he'll show up. So, Harmony, what are your plans when you aren't our librarian anymore?"

She had to ask. I swallowed, trying to come up with an answer that wouldn't reveal my utter lack of a future.

"That will give you more time to work with me," Sorenson said. "I'll create a position and make our arrangement official. That will help free up our street officers and make me look good to the City Council."

"I've got first claims to her time, Chief," Eli said. "With my company expanding operations in the area, I need someone local to respond to prospective customers. Harmony will be perfect for the position."

That was the first I'd heard of it, but I wouldn't call Eli out on it in front of everyone. I was saved from having to commit to either man by Fiesker's arrival. He made a show of placing his laptop onto the chief's desk so it didn't disturb any of the stacks of paper covering the surface.

"For the record," he said as he opened the lid. "I object to sharing this information with non-law enforcement personnel who aren't security cleared."

"Miss Duprie has been cleared by me and I vouch for her," Sorenson said. "As for Hennessey, he has a higher security clearance than anyone in the room. Including me. Probably higher than anyone in town."

I knew Eli ran in some interesting circles, but I hadn't realized how interesting. He'd never told me, and I hadn't asked. How had the chief found out?

Fiesker frowned. Was that his last attempt at withholding the information? He held out an open hand. "Is your flash drive protected?"

"256-bit encryption," I said as I handed it to him. I might not understand the coding behind it, but I knew it was good. Eli had given me the device. But I could play tit-for-tat. "Are you running a current antivirus solution?"

Someone chuckled. I think it was Eli. Fiesker ignored it and rattled off the name of a common company. The one I used until Eli switched me to a better program.

The prompt popped up and I turned the laptop so Fiesker couldn't see as I entered my password. It took longer for all the preliminaries than it did for him to move a solitary folder to my drive. He removed it and handed it back. "If you don't understand something, you can send a message through Detective Thomason."

That would be a cold day in hell. The glare I shot him could have burned off the ends of his uneven sideburns.

"Thank you," Chief Sorenson said. "Now, unless you or Chief Hinds have anything to add, may I suggest we break up this meeting? There's work to be done."

Eli and I stared at each other over the roof of Dolores. "I guess I'm riding with you," he said.

There didn't seem to be another solution unless I made him call a taxi. Which I didn't want to do. One side of me wanted to take him to the Pittsburgh airport and make him go back to Florida until he forgot about me, the other part of me wanted to take him back to my apartment and strip that gorgeous suit off him and have my way with him. Neither choice would work because we'd promised Chief Sorenson our help.

"Where am I taking you?" I asked.

He swallowed, hard. "I hoped we'd go someplace together. We need to talk."

"You're right. But there's a man missing, potentially in serious trouble, and we need to find him. That comes first."

"We can do both."

"I know how you get when you concentrate. You shut the world out." And so did I.

"But I can always sense when you're in the same room, and it makes me happy even if I'm busy and it seems like I'm ignoring you."

He was crumbling my resistance bit by bit.

"I can't think straight when you're not around." The corners of his mouth lifted and he shook his head. "Hell, I can't think straight when you are around, but for a totally different reason."

That did it. "All right, we can work side-by-side. Your place or mine?"

"My place *is* your place, Buttercup. At least, that's what I'm hoping."

169

"You're pushing your luck."

He laughed. "Okay, so we examine this logically. Your apartment offers more privacy, which is a huge plus. On the other hand, the house offers the fastest internet access you've ever seen and two assistants at our beck and call to help with research and keep us supplied with our choice of beverage. Plus, a wood burning fireplace to sit by while we work. There are even chairs to sit in now."

The chairs were not what I'd imagined—deep brown leather armchairs to sink into that you needed help to get out of. What I got was folding camp chairs with a side table. Still, better than sitting on the floor.

We swung by my place first, so I could grab different clothes and my laptop, but the plan was to change at the house. Which sounded fine, until I realized that Eli and I would be changing in the same room at the same time. Which would lead to serious temptation for both of us. I should have used a room on the third floor, but they weren't furnished yet.

"Nice suit, by the way," I said as he waltzed into the bedroom behind me. I'd tried to make an unnoticed escape while he talked to Lando and Scotty, but it hadn't worked. "Did you bring it from Florida?"

"No. I made a rush trip to Pittsburgh to buy it." He took his tie off and tossed it on the bed. "I don't remember seeing that dress before. It's nice. I don't know if black is your color, but you are beautiful no matter what you wear."

"Laying it on a bit thick, aren't you?" I asked as I sat on the bed to unbuckle my shoes. It gave me an excuse to bend over so he couldn't see me blush.

He peeled off his suit coat to reveal an immaculate pale blue cotton shirt, only slightly wrinkled. I considered the best place to start to add more wrinkles to it. But I was enjoying the game and didn't want to rush things.

I wiggled out of the light black sweater I'd worn, one shoulder, and then one sleeve at a time. Eli's eyes darkened, and he leaned over to plant a kiss on my neck, simultaneously unbuttoning the top buttons on his shirt. I ignored the small voice of guilt telling me we needed to stop and get to work as I stood to unzip my dress.

"Do you need help?" Eli asked, his voice husky with desire.

Of course I didn't, but I wasn't going to stop him. I turned to give him easier access.

He lowered the zipper slowly, his lips tracing the line with soft kisses. He gathered the hem in his hands, ready to lift the dress up and over my raised arms.

And his phone rang. Of course.

In unison, we groaned.

"Maybe it's a spam call," Eli said. He took his phone out of his pockets, glanced at the screen, and shook his head. He punched the button and held it to his face. "Hey, Freddie,' he said, sitting on the bed and pulling off his dress shoes.

Game over. I slipped out of my dress and hung it in the closet.

"That soon? The judge must have rubber-stamped the paperwork."

I occupied myself with putting on the jeans and t-shirt I'd brought.

"Can you pick me up? I don't have a car."

I pulled a pair of slacks and polo shirt off their hangers and laid them on the bed.

He blew me a kiss. "Five minutes? I'll be ready. I'm at the house, not Harmony's place." He hung up. "I need to do something about that."

"About what?"

"The no-car thing. I need one here and one in Florida, and I'd rather have one of my own instead of renting."

I couldn't help myself. "More money to spend tying you down when I may not be here."

He hesitated. "I deserved that." He closed the gap between us and put his hands on my cheeks, forcing me to look into his eyes. "I need to apologize, Buttercup. I took for granted that you'd always be here. For me, for your friends, for the whole town. I shouldn't have done that. Will you forgive me?"

It was a very nice apology, as apologies go, although a bit overdone. I scored him a nine out of ten. "I'll forgive you. But we still need to talk about this."

He tilted his head downward and I raised mine, anticipating one of his epic kisses. Our lips met, and offstage, the fireworks awaited their entrance.

And the doorbell rang. During the renovations, I'd installed a ringer on each floor so it could be heard no matter where someone was in the house I regretted that now.

"It hasn't been five minutes yet, has it?" Eli asked, not withdrawing his lips from mine.

"I don't think so."

"Good. If that's Freddie, he can wait."

We didn't make him wait too long. As soon as Eli and Freddie had pulled out of the driveway, I went to work. I opened my laptop to log in and Lando set a cup of freshly brewed coffee by my elbow. "You might need this," he said.

I was about to spend hours staring at crime statistics, exploring the dark corners of the internet, so I'd need more than one cup, but it was a good start. "Are you and Scotty having any luck?" I asked.

He slumped into the camp chair beside me. "No. It's totally illogical. There's got to be a trace of those email addresses somewhere. The good news is, we did penetration testing and can get into the cable company's databases if we get permission."

I doubted that would happen, but I didn't want to dash his dreams. "Maybe Eli will let you hack into the missing guy's computer."

Lando's face brightened. "Yeah, that would be cool. Wouldn't take long, but at least I'd accomplish something. We're doing nothing but spinning our wheels here."

I knew the feeling. "Do you want to help me while you're waiting?"

Scotty wanted in on the action, so I put him and Lando to work searching for a combination of firebug and kidnapping while I tackled the official crime databases. Everything I found dealt with fires used to destroy the evidence of a crime. If there was an incident of someone setting a fire to lure a victim in, I couldn't locate it among all the other statistics.

I leaned back in the chair and closed my eyes. They had dried out from the long minutes of staring at the even smaller print on my small laptop screen.

"You finding anything?" Lando asked.

"Nothing. If it happens, it's so rare the databases don't have a category for it. How about you?"

"No luck. And I'm tired of reading about bad guys torching a car with a dead body inside. Some nasty shit happens out there."

Which I avoided thinking about by concentrating solely on the numbers.

"You know," Scotty said, "I've been watching you work, and I can make it easier for you."

I thought I had a good system going.

"What you need," he said, "Is a bigger screen. We can set you up with a flat screen mounted to the wall. You won't strain your eyes as much and you can detach your laptop when you're done and still be mobile."

It sounded like a good idea. "How much does a setup like that cost?"

Lando laughed. "Like you need to worry about it. Don't worry, it won't even dent your pocketbook."

How did they know about my finances? Then I remembered who I was dealing with. "You guys checked me out online."

Scotty, at least, looked a little ashamed. Lando had a smirk on his face. "When we realized the boss was getting serious about you, sure, we scoped you out. We wanted to make sure you weren't playing him. The numbers we found for you were pretty damn impressive.

"But don't worry, we didn't tell anyone."

My heartbeat raced, and the blood drained from my face. I didn't like people knowing my secret. It made me vulnerable and I wanted people to like me for being me, not because I had money.

"And you won't, right? Please?"

Scotty slapped Lando on the back of his head. "I told you we shouldn't have done that, asshole. And that we should never tell her. Now you've gone and upset her."

I did a breathing exercise to calm myself. I trusted these guys, right?

Chapter 21

Eli trusted them, or they wouldn't be here. And I trusted Eli. Besides, they helped when Eli rescued me from my kidnapper. I drew in a breath and counted to ten before blowing it out.

"If you can find me, you can hide me, right?" I asked.

Lando shook his head. "It doesn't work that way. These are all public databases."

"You can't do that DMCA takedown stuff?"

"Not for this. Don't worry, you were next to impossible to find. Until we identified the shell corporation you hide behind, we wondered if you kept all your money under your bed or something."

"And it's not like you're in the top one hundred richest people in the country," Scotty said, "So no one is looking for you. You're safe."

It made me feel a little better. Besides, they'd only found one of my shell corporations.

"By the way, I researched a few of your investments." Lando smiled "Good, solid stuff. You shouldn't worry about losing everything in a stock market crash. It won't happen."

My father taught me everything I needed to know about finance, but I liked leaving it in the hands of an expert. "I've got a great financial adviser who takes care of my money. I prefer not to think about it."

"But anyway, back to the big screen..." Lando surveyed the room, "I'm thinking it can go on this wall." He pointed to the wall between the living room and dining room. "That way the boss can use it for business presentations."

"And at night you and Eli can use it to watch movies or play games," Scotty suggested.

There it was. I chuckled. "I suspected you two had an ulterior motive. You want me to buy it so you can use it for your games."

Scotty widened his eyes, fluttered his eyelashes, and put his hand to his chest. "Who, us? Naw, we've got your best interests at heart."

Lando chimed in. "That doesn't mean we aren't willing to take advantage of the situation."

"We should ask Eli before we mount anything on the wall," Scotty said. "This is his house."

"We can't do anything about it tonight, anyway. I doubt there's a store in Oak Grove that sells what we need." Lando grinned. "It'll give us a good excuse to make a trip to Pittsburgh tomorrow. That is if Eli doesn't need us for anything."

Which reminded me, where was Eli? It had been several hours since he and Freddie left. How long did it take to serve a search warrant? I checked my phone, but hadn't missed any calls or messages.

"I'll be back at the library tomorrow," I said. "In the meantime, I need to keep digging. Are you two having any luck?" Working would keep me from worrying.

"I don't think what you're looking for exists," Scotty said. "I found one case from ten years ago where a fireman set a fire to lure his ex out of her house, so he could snatch her, but that's not what you're looking for."

It was close, but not close enough. I was stumped, and I hated it when that happened. "We can try different search terms," I suggested.

Lando nodded. "That could help. But after we take a break and get supper. And believe it or not, I'm tired of delivery pizza. I'd like a change of scenery along with a change in my diet. Any suggestions, Harmony?"

I'd had enough of restaurants and was looking forward to a home-cooked meal one of these days. Not tonight. "We could hit up that little diner at the edge of town. Their food is basic, but at least they aren't a chain. And they're open twenty-four hours so we can wait for Eli."

"My stomach can't wait for him," Lando grumbled. "Why hasn't he called?"

"Maybe he had a stack of paperwork to fill out," Scotty said. "We can bring food back for him."

Or I could call him and get an ETA on his arrival. But when I dialed his number it went straight to voicemail. I didn't leave a message. If he was busy, he didn't need an interruption.

"Now what?" Scotty asked.

"I'll try Freddie. He *is* playing Eli's chauffeur." My call to him ended up at voicemail too, but it took a few rings.

Freddie always answered his calls. Even if it was just to tell the caller he'd get right back to them. My gut screamed something was wrong. But I had no proof.

"Why don't you guys go ahead and eat? I'll stay here in case Eli shows up. You can bring me back a meatloaf dinner. I'm not hungry right now anyway," I lied.

They exchanged glances. "Tell us what's up, Harmony," Lando demanded.

I shrugged. "It doesn't feel right. It shouldn't have taken this long. And Eli would have called if he got held up. I'm worried."

"Did they say where they were going?"

"Some guy's apartment. I didn't get an address."

"How about a name?"

That I remembered. "Antonio Galas. He lives in an apartment complex. I don't know which one."

Scotty had a map of Oak Grove pulled up on his monitor. Lando pulled up a different website and typed in the name.

"Only one person in town with that name," Lando said. "He's at 451 Anchor Way. Unless he's moved recently."

"Got a unit number?" Scotty asked.

"No. But how hard can it be? We drive around the parking lot until we spot a red Mustang. That's what Detective Thomason drives, right, Harmony?"

"Right."

Scotty grabbed my coat and tossed it at me before getting his own. "Let's load up. The game is afoot."

The apartment complex was on the other side of town, so I made them drive by the police station on the way. Actually, I made them drive *around* the station, in case Freddie didn't park in his normal spot. When that didn't produce any results, we headed for the apartments.

It turned out to be an older development of fifty or so single-story units, built in blocks of six. The narrow roads dead-ended into small parking lots and we frequently needed to turn around and start back at the beginning. After two trips through the complex, we still hadn't spotted the Mustang.

"One more trip through," I suggested. "But don't look at cars. Check out the apartments themselves. Look for crime scene tape or anything that looks out of place."

"It's worth a try," Scotty said from the driver's captain chair. I'd claimed the passenger seat and Lando leaned forward from the bench seat behind us. "Harmony, you take starboard. Lando, you have port."

"Dude, is that left or right?" Lando laughed.

"You're left, she's right."

It sounded correct after reading the pirate romance a few days ago. I peered out the window, hoping to find a clue, praying I didn't. For all I knew, Eli and Freddie were off celebrating, having a drink, after discovering evidence that led to locating Antonio stone cold drunk at his girlfriend's. If they were still hanging around the apartments, it translated to something being wrong. Very wrong.

Half the street lights were out, adding to the gloom of a winter night. Scattered ice flakes glittered in the headlights and I zipped up my coat, despite the van's heater running at full blast. I didn't understand why I was worried—both Freddie and Eli could take care of themselves.

Scotty patted me on the knee. "If you're cold, we have a blanket in the back."

I'd checked out the van when I got in. If there was a blanket hiding in the clutter of cardboard boxes stacked in the cargo area, it would take forever to unearth. "Thanks, but I'm good."

Lando tapped on Scotty's shoulder. "Stop. Back up. That's weird. Why would anyone have their front door open in the middle of winter? Unless they're carrying out the garbage or something."

Scotty slammed on the brakes and I put a hand on the dashboard to brace myself. Not that we were going fast, but it was a reflex action. He shifted into reverse and guided the van backward. I craned my head to confirm what Lando had spotted.

Only to see a man leaning against the door frame, smoking a cigarette and glaring our direction. We were suspicious looking, cruising the neighborhood, but Scotty had us covered. He rolled down his window and I wished for that blanket when the cold air struck me. He stuck his head out of the opening. "Do you know Antonio?" he called. "I can't find his place."

The man threw his cigarette to the ground, ground it out with one foot, turned and stomped inside, slamming his door behind him.

"I take it that was a no," Scotty said as he rolled up the window and shifted back into drive.

One more round through the complex and we found no evidence of Eli or Freddie. "What do we do now?" Scotty asked.

"I'm out of ideas," I admitted.

"I'm not." Lando waved his cell phone in the air. "Remember that tracking program Eli developed a few years back?"

I remembered. That's how Eli found me when I was abducted. "So?" I asked.

"I was one of his guinea pigs and I've got the program, too. If he can track me, I can track him as long as his phone is on."

"He replaced his phone a few months ago."

"And I'm the one who set it up for him." Lando grinned. "You don't think I'd let a teenager at one of those phone kiosks in the mall touch his phone, do you?"

Scotty glanced at Lando in the rearview mirror. "Does the boss know you added the tracker? Didn't he decide the program was a dead-end because of too many similar apps on the market?"

"His was the best," Lando grumbled.

We didn't have time for them to debate the issue. "Well, prove it," I said. "Find him."

Scotty pulled into the next empty parking spot to

wait as Lando fiddled with his phone and cursed. "Dammit, he blocked me."

"And you thought you were so sneaky," Scotty sneered.

"He wouldn't block me," I said as I dug my phone out of my purse and handed it to Lando. "Try mine."

"Is this the same phone you had back then?"

I nodded. "It works, so why replace it?"

"We've got to bring you into the modern world. Cell phones are so much better these days. In the meantime…"

Lando bit his lip as he swiped through the screens on my phone. "I don't see the app. He must have removed it."

Scotty held out his hand. "Or hid it hoping Harmony would forget about it. Hand over the phone and let me take a look."

I didn't care who got the glory, as long as one of them found a way to track Eli. Scotty navigated to the settings of the phone, territory I rarely wandered into.

"Found it," he said. "The program, that is. Now let's hope it will lead us to the boss." He played with the phone and I watched as a map filled the small screen. "Aaand contact." He handed the phone back to Lando. "Tell me where to go, bloodhound."

It felt like I imagined following a tracking dog would be. As Scotty drove, Lando gave directions. We stayed on major streets at first but eventually turned onto a side street. I kept my eye on the street signs, trying to guess where we were heading.

"Turn right in a block and a half," Lando announced. "It'll be a block down on the right-hand side."

I didn't recognize the area until Scotty made the turn and I spotted the street sign. I checked to make sure Betsy was in my purse. "Pull over," I ordered.

"We're not there yet," Lando protested.

"You're right. But guys, we have a problem."

Chapter 22

I checked to make sure a cartridge was loaded in Betsy's chamber. "You're sure the tracker is right?"

"When Eli creates an app, it's perfect," Lando said. "And the marker hasn't changed location since we started. What's weird is that the signal keeps bouncing in and out. One moment there's a dot on the screen, the next it's gone. But when it comes back, it's in the same spot. So, what's going on?"

"Do you see the Mustang?"

"Well, no," Scotty said. "But it could be parked on the side street. Or in the alley."

Or stolen, but I didn't say the words out loud. "Here's the deal. There are a bunch of boarded-up houses in this part of town. Especially on Green Street. And that's the street we're on."

"And?" asked Scotty.

I blew out a breath. "Jake overheard some guys talking about a fire on Green Street. There hasn't been a fire on Green Street. Not yet, anyway. What are Eli and Freddie doing here? And Jake didn't get a house number, so how would they end up here?"

"You want to call for backup?"

"And tell them what? That two men might be in a house including one of their detectives but we can't prove it, and they might be in trouble but we don't know for sure, and hey, we found them using a home-built app. That will go over real well."

"What's your plan, then?" Lando asked.

"We drive around the block once to see if we can locate the Mustang. Then we try calling them again. The third step will depend on the results of the first two."

❊ ❊ ❊

Scotty pointed down the street. "Is that it?"

I squinted into the darkness. "Sure looks like Freddie's car. It's not like him to leave it in this area." The Mustang was a restored mid-60's model.

"Just where I'd park," Lando said. "Far enough away from the house to not be obvious, close enough to get to it quickly."

"That means the two of them are nearby. Or were." I fiddled with my zipper pull. Up and down, down and up, until Scotty put a hand out to stop me.

"They're going to be okay," he said. "Next step is to call them, right?"

"Right. Lando, give me my phone."

"It won't make a difference," he grumbled. "If they could call, they would have done so already. If they're in trouble and still have their phones on them, isn't it better not to call? So, the bad guys don't hear the phones ringing?"

He had a point. I reconsidered my plan.

We parked behind the Mustang and sneaked through the alley on foot. With the front door boarded up, we needed a different entrance. My bet was on the neighborhood kids—or drug users—having removed the plywood blocking the back door.

Scotty had grabbed a flashlight from the van while Lando used the app on his phone to light our way. I'd expected more clutter and garbage in the alley, but our main obstacles were rusted bicycle frames and cardboard boxes. The cats whose territories we invaded barely stirred themselves to protest our passage with quiet meows.

I counted the houses as we passed by to make sure we ended up in the right spot. Several of the homes were still occupied, but I didn't worry about calls to 911. This didn't appear to be the kind of neighborhood that was friendly to cops.

The back door of the house indicated by Eli's tracker stood wide open. Even this close up, the signal dot on my phone faded in and out. From the interior, not a speck of light leaked out through the boards covering the windows.

As Lando started up the broken sidewalk, I grabbed his sleeve to stop him. "I'm the one with a gun," I said, easing Betsy out of my coat pocket, "I'll go first." The words were brave and the cool steel of the gun's handle gave me false courage. No one could see my stomach doing flip-flops.

I'd watched enough police dramas to follow procedure. Holding Betsy in front of me in my right hand and the flashlight in my left, I hugged the wall of the first room—the kitchen—before motioning Lando and Scotty to join me. It was a small house, with only three rooms on the first floor and not a soul in any of them. Now what? The steps going to the upstairs looked as if they would crumble under the smallest bit of weight. Several were cracked with pieces missing.

My nose itched, and I rubbed it to keep from sneezing. I handed the flashlight back to Scotty and readjusted my grip on Betsy. The air tasted like rot and mildew and I was helpless to stop the impulse. At least I was able to muffle the sound in the sleeve of my coat.

Scotty poked me in the ribs and aimed the flashlight towards a corner of the front room. Two beady eyes glared at us then skittered away. I shivered. Bad guys were one thing, but rats? I hated rats.

"Not the wildlife," Scotty hissed in my ear. "Check out the chair. They were here."

It took me a while to figure out what he was seeing. When I spotted it, it seemed so obvious I didn't know how I'd missed it. An old lawn chair was propped against the wall and from the lack of dust in the seat, it appeared someone had used it recently. Very recently, because small puddles of melted snow were on the floor by the legs. Still, that didn't prove it was Eli or Freddie.

"I wonder if this house has a basement," Lando whispered.

Most old houses in Oak Grove had one. "Do you remember the open door in the kitchen? I checked behind it but didn't look much farther."

The two men exchanged a glance. "There's one way to find out if they are down there," Scotty said. "Call the boss' phone and listen for the ring."

Lando nodded. "That will tell us if the phone is in the house."

Something was missing. "If Eli and Freddie are in the basement, why haven't they come out of hiding?" The floorboards squeaked with every step, reporting our presence.

"Because they don't know it's us? Or a bad guy is with them?" Scotty asked. Both made sense. So, back to the phone call.

We split up, one to each room. Lando took the front room and stood by the steps in case Eli and Freddie had gotten upstairs and couldn't get back down. Scotty took the small room between the kitchen and the front room, and I took the kitchen, positioning myself by the interior door. We'd peered through the opening, but it led to a dark abyss.

Scotty raised his hand and, moving one finger at a time, counted down from five. When the last finger folded and he clenched his fist, Lando pushed the button to dial Eli. I held my breath and listened. At first, all I heard was my heartbeat, then faintly, a musical tone.

In our prearranged signal, I waved my hand in the air. Scotty rushed to join me and Lando followed. "Do you hear it?" I asked.

"No. Lando, did he pick up?"

Lando frowned. "I thought so, but then the call dropped."

I stared at the unmoving dot on my phone. It flickered and disappeared, but two seconds later came back. "Call again. While Eli's phone still has a signal."

"Shit. She's right. That's what we've been missing this whole time." Lando hit redial. "His phone is blocked by something."

"Like thick concrete walls?" I asked.

Scotty shushed me. "Listen!"

I was tired of playing it safe. "Eli!" I screamed into the gaping blackness I assumed led to the basement.

"Harmony?" floated back up towards us.

"Eli! We're coming to get you."

"No! You can't!"

"Just try to stop me," I hollered, holding back my tears of relief.

"No. Listen. The stairs broke. They pulled away from the retaining bolts. You can't get down here."

"Are you safe? Is Freddie with you?"

His voice came clearer. He must have moved closer to the opening.

"We're okay. Go get help."

"She's got help, boss," Scotty yelled. "What can we do?"

"Unless you have a ladder tucked in your back pocket, I suggest you call 911."

It was good to know that Eli kept his sense of humor in spite of the circumstances. With no ladder handy, we left the rescue to the professionals, the fire department. And where the fire department goes, so do the paramedics. Which was good, because once they got Eli and Freddie out of the basement and into the ambulance, I saw both of them had scrapes and bruises.

"What were you doing in there?" a paramedic— his name tag read Lee—asked as he swiped at Eli's face with an antiseptic pad.

Eli winced and Freddie answered. "Following up on a disturbance call. Didn't find anything out of place, so it was probably kids hanging out who went home for supper." Freddie studied the floor of the ambulance. He was lying, and I wondered what he was hiding.

"Well, you won't have to worry about it too much longer. This house is scheduled for a controlled burn next month as part of the department's training."

Most of the town's paramedics were part-time employees for the fire department, so it didn't strike me as odd that Lee knew that.

Freddie raised his head. "Are you sure?"

"Yep. They've been quizzing us on how it'll burn if the fire is set in different places and what's used to start it. That Fiesker fellow has been handy to have around. He's a jerk but knows his stuff."

Lee pulled off his gloves. "All done. Since the pair of you won't let us take you to ER for a thorough check-up, I suggest you follow up with your own doctors tomorrow to make sure I didn't miss something."

I wouldn't hold my breath waiting for that to happen.

Eli grimaced as he shrugged on his shirt and buttoned it. The paramedic caught the look. "If you experience any soreness, try your normal over-the-counter pain relief. A heating pad might help, too."

A stop at the drugstore got added to my list of places to go. I doubted Eli had either of those things at the house. In fact, I might as well stock up on all the standard first aid supplies while I was there.

I stepped back to give Eli and Freddie room to climb out of the ambulance. Scotty had offered to act as a coat rack, and he helped them put on their jackets. I watched their movements with a critical eye, then held out my hand to Freddie. "Hand them over," I demanded.

"Hand what over?"

"Your keys. There's no way the two of you are walking back to the vehicles." In fact, I was still deciding if I'd let him drive home.

"It's only a block away."

I tapped my foot and attempted a 'mom' glare. Lee chuckled, and Freddie sighed and reached into his pocket. He pulled out the keys and dropped them into my hand. I closed my fist around them before he could change his mind.

"Lee," I said with a smile and pouring honey into my voice, "will you please stay with these two while we go get the vehicles? Make sure they don't wander off and get into trouble?"

He slammed the ambulance doors shut and leaned against them, a cocky grin lighting his face. "Sure, I can hang out for a few minutes as long as we don't get another call."

"I'll walk fast. Scotty, are you coming with me?"

Chapter 23

Despite their protests, we made Eli and Freddie take the lawn chairs while the guys and I sat on the floor to eat. Of course I took Eli aside and threatened to go home before he cooperated. It was a bluff, but he fell for it. Or, at least, played along.

"You guys would have been disappointed," Eli told Lando and Scotty. "Antonio's computer wasn't password protected and all his social media sites were logged in. I didn't get to hack anything." He took a bite of his club sandwich and rotated his head to crack his neck.

I'd hit up the Dairy Barn on the way home. We'd debated eating at the diner, but Freddie wanted privacy for our debriefing.

Scotty dangled a french fry in front of his mouth. "What did you find?"

"That he doesn't post much. He's got less personal information online than me."

Which said a lot. I'd searched, and except for his business postings, Eli didn't exist on the internet.

"You must have found something," Lando insisted. "Or do you need me to go back over the computer and check for hidden files?"

Eli raised an eyebrow. "Are you questioning my abilities? Who taught you most of what you know?"

Lando shook his head. "You're the best, bossman, but I'm a close second. No, I figured you were rushed for time."

"Truthfully, I got bored. While Freddie searched every nook and cranny for more of those brooches, I read Antonio's documents. They were mind-numbing. Who saves a paper they wrote for their freshman English class?" Eli grinned and fake-shuddered. "It was bad, too. An essay on what the common soldier in the Revolution carried in their backpacks. Stretched out to five thousand words."

The topic seemed interesting enough even if the length of the paper was too long for the subject.

"Freddie, I'm guessing you didn't find anything, either." I didn't want him to be excluded, although he seemed happy concentrating on his cheeseburger.

He swallowed. "The only thing that stuck out as abnormal were the pictures of his mother. They were everywhere. Even weirder, I found a bunch of them turned face-down. But no pictures of girlfriends or other women. Not even a girly poster in his bedroom."

I searched my memory. "Pete mentioned Antonio's mother is clingy. Maybe she gives him the pictures and guilt-trips him if he doesn't keep them."

"I was friends with a guy like that in college. We used to kid him that mom kept his balls locked in a drawer at home."

I imagined an old woman hovering over a steel box, waving a skeleton key in the air while a forlorn, awkward teenager lingered in the background. I couldn't help myself. It started as a giggle but turned into a full belly laugh. And damn, it felt good. All the stress of the last few hours melted away and I was helpless to stop.

Laughter can be infectious and Lando joined me. After that, no one fought it. The room resounded with guffaws and snorts.

Scotty sobered up first. "It wasn't that funny," he said, but I caught him wiping a tear from his eye. Then he chuckled again.

I caught my breath. Or at least tried to. "I'll never be able to look Antonio in the eye when we find him."

My words slammed us back into reality.

Eli frowned. "If we find him. The only clue either of us came across was a document on the computer discussing how the house on Green Street would burn. Now we know it was a training exercise."

Freddie stretched and groaned. The ibuprofen must not have cured his aches. "It was my fault, mostly. When Eli showed me the document, I came up with the theory that Antonio was involved with a group setting the fires. I figured he'd gone to the house to get things ready and we'd find him there.

"It was a good idea but wrong. When we found the back door unblocked, we thought we were on to something and sneaked in. We didn't find anything on the main floor, decided not to risk the second floor, but wanted to check the basement."

"The mistake we made," Eli interrupted, "was going down at the same time. It put too much weight on the supports. Freddie stayed a couple of steps behind me so, when the stairway disintegrated, he got the worst of it."

And, in my humble opinion, Eli was in better shape to begin with.

"Once we recovered from the shock and figured out we needed a different way to get out, we took our time looking around. But nothing's down there except broken metal shelves."

One corner of Freddie's mouth turned down. "And rats."

A shiver ran down my spine. Did I mention I hate rats?

"That's when we decided to call for help. And realized we had no signal. The walls of the cellar blocked our phones. We needed a Plan B." Freddie grinned. "We pretended we were acrobats and Eli tried standing on my shoulders to reach the landing but that didn't work, either."

"I'm glad there's no video," Eli said with a smile. "It wasn't pretty. Then my phone rang, but I lost signal right away. We tried holding our phones above our heads hoping to catch a stray airwave, but couldn't get a steady connection. So, how did you find us?"

Lando, Scotty and I exchanged glances. If we told Eli our secret, would he disable the app on his phone or remove it?

Lando scooted across the floor, not letting go of his over-sized cola. "Hand it over, boss."

Eli clutched his sandwich and chuckled. "You have your own. You don't get mine."

Lando sighed. "Your phone. Give me your phone."

Eli's eyebrows knotted, but he reached into his pocket, extracted the phone and gave it to Lando.

"Distract him, Harmony," Lando requested as he crawled over to his laptop.

The best way to accomplish that couldn't be done in present company. Or *any* company. "Why didn't you guys yell when you heard us moving around in the house?" I asked Eli instead, diverting his attention from whatever Lando was doing.

"You talked so quietly we could barely hear you and didn't recognize your voices. We didn't want to take the risk of making ourselves known to a couple of druggies who might not appreciate a cop being in their territory."

Fair enough.

"You still haven't told us how you found us."

"Can I tell him, Lando?" I asked.

He nodded. "I'm almost done."

I continued with our side of the story. "When neither of you answered my calls, I got worried. Lando tracked down the apartment complex Antonio lives in, but we didn't find you there. So, we let loose the bloodhound."

"Bloodhound?" Freddie asked.

"An app Eli built to track people's cell phones. He never released it, and only Lando, Eli, and I have it. Except he blocked Lando. Lando used my phone to find Eli's."

Lando rejoined us and gave the phone back to Eli. "I've unblocked my number. And put a password on it so you can't block me again." He winked at me. "Because we can't depend upon Harmony to keep you safe all the time."

Eli fiddled with his phone. "You realize it will take me no more than ten minutes to get through the password restrictions and block you again."

"But you won't," I said. "Because I'm asking you not to. I need a backup in an emergency." I widened my eyes and tilted my head.

"Aw, isn't that sweet," Scotty grinned.

One side of Eli's lips rose, then the other. "And darned effective. You win, I'll leave Lando unblocked."

Freddie left soon after we finished eating. There was still work to be done to find Antonio, and he was in for a sleepless night. I tried to convince him he'd think better after a good night's sleep, but he wouldn't listen, citing the statistics about finding someone within forty-eight hours.

Eli watched from the window as the Mustang's taillights disappeared down the street. "You guys ready to go to work?"

"I knew you were hiding something!" Scotty said. "What do you have for us?"

"Antonio's computer seemed too clean like someone went through it and cleared the recycle bin. So, I cloned it. I want a forensic analysis of the drive to see what I missed." He pulled a black square out of his back pocket. "Hopefully, the fall didn't damage the drive."

Lando's eyes sparkled. "I wondered if you were moving funny because you hurt your leg or what. Give it to me."

"Say please," Eli teased.

"Please and thank you and all that shit." Lando snatched the drive from Eli's hand. "Now go away and don't bother us. We'll tell you when we find something."

"I've got my own project. And it doesn't involve you two."

There was a silent exchange I couldn't translate. Lando nodded. "Right."

I felt like I didn't belong. "Well, I have to be at the library tomorrow. I guess I should go to bed."

Eli whirled to face me. "I've got a job for you, too, if you don't mind."

"Okay," I said tentatively. "What is it?"

"The brooch. It bothers me. I keep wondering if it's significant like there's a meaning behind it. I also want to know if it's been sold locally. Anything you can find out about it will help."

"On it." After I started a pot of coffee. It was going to be a long night.

At least I had a starting point, the website for the company that sold steampunk accessories. I'd bookmarked the main page with the intention of returning to browse their other merchandise. Not that I wanted to build a steampunk outfit, but their earrings caught my eye.

I glanced longingly at the selections while searching for the brooch and allowed myself to click on a pair that dangled to the model's shoulders. What came up in the description was not only the length but a delightful story of how they came to be.

These earrings are inspired by the tale of a princess and the airship captain who loved her. When she was promised to the king of a far-off country to secure a trade treaty, the captain gave her the earrings after swapping out the main stones for a tracking device. He followed her to the distant land and after fighting off the king's army, kidnapped her and took her to his home on top of a mountain, accessible only by airship.

Our earrings don't include a tracking device but will give the wearer many happy ever afters.

Did they write these tales for all their products? I swiped through the website, eager to track down the brooch and its background.

It was a harmless flirtation that ended up breaking Aislinn Byrne's heart. A simple governess and the Conte di Sesta could never have a future together. She had no money and no title, and he had wealth beyond her imagination and duty to his family. But she treasured the brooch he'd given her; a Celtic design to remind her of her homeland.

Several years passed, and her tears dried up, although she never got over him. Gossip told of a wife and she wished him the happiness she'd never have. The brooch was hidden away and never worn.

But true love conquers all, and the widowed Conte defied society's rules and traveled in search of his beloved governess. When he showed up at her employer's home in the steam-powered buggy they designed together, she had no idea of his intentions. She feared he'd demand she become his mistress, a request she was powerless to deny.

Have no fear. Instead, he dropped to one knee and presented her with a ring to match the brooch and requested Aislinn become his wife and Contessa. Which she did, and they spent many years together producing new inventions and a house full of children.

Our brooch was inspired by the Tara Brooch which resides in the National Museum of Ireland.

For a moment, I imagined myself on a Scottish highland, draped in a wool cloak, with the brooch on my shoulder. Eli, in a kilt, stood beside me, his arm wrapped around my waist. Then, with a gust of wind, reality swept in and I got back to work.

Chapter 24

I wondered if the company sold a ring to match the brooch. But before I checked, I wanted to find out more about the Tara Brooch. And Celtic jewelry in general. I dove into the rabbit hole and got lost. When Eli put his hand on my shoulder, I jerked and almost knocked my laptop off my lap.

"Finding anything?" he asked.

Sheepishly, I closed my browser. "Nothing useful. I'll try calling the company in the morning and see if they can give me any information about local orders."

He grinned. "Technically, it's morning already. If you plan to be at the library later, you better get some sleep. Me and the guys have at least another hour of work and will try to keep it quiet."

It had felt good to sink into my research and shut out the rest of the world, but Eli was right, I had other obligations. At least for a few more days.

He walked me upstairs to his room. To his bed. And left me there, after a tender kiss. I only felt a little cheated.

❋ ❋ ❋

The library bristled with the nervous energy of unfilled anticipation. I wasn't any help in calming it; in truth, I half-expected Janine to sweep through the front doors at any moment and reclaim her kingdom.

Instead, mid-morning I got Chief Sorenson, bringing a thundercloud with him. Which I assumed meant they hadn't located Antonio. I pushed the cart of books I was shelving into an alcove out of the path of traffic and made a beeline for my—Janine's—office.

He'd topped off my coffee cup and was filling a cup for himself when I walked in the door. "I understand you had a late night," he said.

How much of the story did Freddie tell him? "Not that it did any good. Now I'm waiting to hear back from the company that sells the brooches. Their call center wasn't much help but at least gave me a number for the main office."

Sorenson's lips drew into a tight line. "No one is having any luck. Galas' phone is turned off or destroyed, there're no security cameras at the apartment complex, and none of my officers have gotten anything from their usual informants. Even Hennessey has run into a dead-end according to Detective Thomason."

Or Eli wasn't sharing everything. I heard some jubilant yells shortly before he crawled into bed. Unless I dreamed them.

"I hate to admit defeat," Sorenson continued,

"But it's time to bring in the media. I've never had luck with the public giving me leads in a case like this, but it will get his mother off my back."

"Is she a problem?"

That earned me a one-sided smile. "Mrs. Galas holds the unique notion that, by law, her sons are required to call her daily. I can't convince her otherwise."

"Sounds like a good reason to disappear."

Sorenson's mouth opened, and he cocked his head. Then he shook it. "If I was going to disappear for any length of time, I'd take my car and clothes. And none of his cards have been used, so, unless he took a big wad of cash, he wouldn't get very far. We checked locally, and no one remembers him buying a new phone."

The last time I bought burner phones, I made the trip to Cleveland. "You won't mention Eli or me in your press conference, right?"

"Of course not. You aren't an official part of the investigation." He winked. "Be aware, I'm still going to try to change your mind."

It must have been a trick of the light or a figment of my imagination. The wink, that was. I pretended it hadn't happened. "Thanks, Chief, I'll keep it in mind." I didn't want to tell him no until I figured out my other options, including whatever Eli had in mind. We hadn't discussed it.

We didn't have time to talk about it at lunch, either, because the restaurant down the street from the library was packed with people discussing the news conference scheduled for the afternoon. Word had spread quickly about the missing man and Antonio's mother had scheduled her own news conference to plead for his return. Eli and I spent most of our time listening to other people's conversations to find out what the rumor mill knew. Which was mostly nothing.

He came back to the office with me to fill me in on what the cheering had been about and to take a box of my personal belongings home. I didn't want to wait to start the project until the last minute.

"We tracked down the IP address used to upload two of the videos," he said, helping me bubble wrap a picture of my parents. "After additional verification this morning, it turned out to belong to a coffee shop a few blocks away that offers free internet for its customers."

I waved my hand toward the public area only feet away. "The next address you latch onto will be from here," I predicted. "Not only do we offer free internet access, we allow a group to come in every week to teach a class on internet safety."

Eli rubbed his forehead. "I can't believe we've been defeated. And by a local. Lando's got his ear to the underground, and all he can find around here are script kiddies."

"Where does that leave us?"

He shrugged. "Change of tactics. To Plan B. Which I don't have yet."

The call came in around three. I almost didn't answer because I didn't recognize the area code and figured it was spam. But I took a chance and ended up talking to the owner of the steampunk supply company, Cornelia.

I explained my dilemma and the need for urgency. The unmistakable sound of her tapping away on a keyboard started before I finished talking.

"I'm sorry, Miss Duprie, but with all the events in your general vicinity, I'm afraid I can't be of much help. At least four vendors among our customers might go to shows in Pittsburgh or Cleveland. Three of them purchased the piece you are interested in over the last couple of years. I can give you their names and phone numbers, but I'm not sure the information will be useful."

Probably not. "How about other customers? People who bought one or two online?" Or four or more, but not at the same time, if I got lucky.

"That's beyond my limited skills," she said with a chuckle. "I'll ask one of my bookkeeping brainiacs to try. We're on the west coast, and the person I have in mind is at lunch. Can she call you at this number later?"

"Yes, and it doesn't matter how late. Even if it's the middle of the night. This is one of our few leads."

She sighed. "You don't know how much it bothers me that one of our products is tied to this. It's against everything we stand for as a company and part of the steampunk community. I promise, Miss Duprie, we'll do whatever we can to help."

"I appreciate it. By the way, I wanted to tell you how much I enjoyed reading your product descriptions. What a great way to sell things. It must take a lot of work to create those stories."

"Thank you! I never get tired of people telling me that. I used to write the fairy tales myself, but don't have time anymore. The work has been outsourced to a writing class at the community college as a contest and the students who win get paid internships with us. So far, it's worked out pretty good."

After hanging up, I scribbled a note to myself to find out if there was a way to donate to the effort. Or buy into the company. Anonymously, of course.

❊ ❊ ❊

On the way back to the house, I made three stops. Didn't even call Eli to tell him when—or if—to expect me. I didn't like the idea of being taken for granted, and this was my one little dig. All for a good cause.

I had a mission. I was tired of restaurant food and planned to make an easy supper. But I needed the right ingredients and the right equipment. It wouldn't put a dent into what Eli needed to stock his kitchen but would be a start.

The local hardware store was my first stop. They carried only a small assortment of kitchenware, but it was better quality than the offerings of the big box store down the road. Besides the family that ran the place had been in town for several generations.

Second stop was the grocery store. The main ingredients were easy, but I had to decide how many spices I wanted to buy and how many to bring from home. I didn't know how often they'd get used at Eli's place and didn't want to waste money on things that would get thrown out a year later. I ended up splurging and getting everything in the recipe as well as a few extra that were handy to have around.

Then I went home. I needed a change of clothes. Several, actually. I didn't know how to keep up this split living arrangement without expanding my wardrobe or nagging Eli until he bought a washer and dryer. He'd need them even if I didn't move in.

The van wasn't in the driveway, so I pulled up as close to the front door as possible. With as many bags as I'd stuffed into Dolores, it would take several trips to get everything inside without help. But the lights were on, so someone was home. I hoped.

As I put my key in the door, I caught the sounds of shots, grunts and screaming. Women's screams, mostly. And men yelling. Then Lando laughed. And Scotty cursed. It didn't take a genius to figure out what was happening.

I pushed open the unlocked door to see an oversized TV screen mounted to the wall of the front room. And when I say oversized, I mean it was so big I could read the fine print in a warranty from ten feet away, without my glasses. But the screen was filled with zombies and humans fighting.

"Hey guys," I said on my way to the kitchen with two of the shopping bags.

"Harmony!" they said in unison, keeping their eyes on the screen.

"I could use some help," I said, making sure I crossed between them and the screen on my way back to the car.

"Two minutes. We'll be there in two minutes," Scotty said.

More like ten. Or longer. "Do you want a home-cooked meal or not?"

"Home cooked? Like you throw a foil pan in the oven and heat it up?"

"No, from scratch. You know, where you buy the ingredients and put them together and cook them."

Lando hit the pause button and poked Scotty in the ribs. "You heard the lady. Let's go."

They didn't get away with only carrying in the bags. I made them chop the vegetables while I washed the pots. And while Scotty got bored, Lando was hooked. He browned the ground beef while I prepared the rest of the ingredients for hamburger soup. A deceptively simple sounding dish, but the recipe I used blended together a mouth-watering combination of flavors that got better when served as leftovers.

The task didn't distract me from wondering where Eli had gotten to. No matter how often I checked my phone, no new messages pinged me.

Lando noticed. "Eli told us he might run late. He went to Pittsburgh this afternoon to discuss a potential business deal and was worried he'd have to fight the traffic on the way back."

"It's a good thing I made soup then. If I planned steak for supper, his would be ruined." I presented a happy front, but why hadn't Eli mentioned the trip at lunch? Old insecurities rushed back to haunt me.

Lando waved his hand over the pot and sniffed deeply. "He'd better get back or there won't be any left for him. How much longer does it have?"

"Half an hour, give or take. Enough time for you to go kill more zombies."

"You want to join us?"

There wasn't anything else I needed to do in the kitchen. And the game looked like fun. Besides, I needed a distraction. Maybe killing zombies would allow my mind to work in the background and come up with an idea to help find Antonio. It was worth a shot. "Sure, I'm in."

Chapter 23

I strung Lando and Scotty along for as long as possible, pretending to know nothing about the gaming console controls during my practice round. They took pity on me and gave my character upper-level weapons from their stash so she wouldn't be killed. I leveled up, making it look painful, then limped my character through the next two mercifully short rounds, barely surviving, but gaining another level. The rust cleared from my veins, I was ready to play for real.

What I didn't tell them was that I belonged to a gaming club in college. As one of the few women in the group, I had to prove myself constantly. As a result, I got good. Real good.

When they placed bets on how long I'd last, I let my character go wild. At every new zombie we encountered, I was a step ahead of them. The carnage left behind was awesome. I picked up more than a few hits myself and finally had to take a break to heal. Besides, the aroma drifting from the kitchen told me the soup was ready, and my stomach was growling.

I stood and stretched. "Did I do okay?"

Lando dramatically placed his hand over his heart and fell to one knee. "I'll never find another girl like you. One who can cook *and* beat me at my games. Marry me, Harmony."

I laughed. "You're such a geek. Let's eat."

Fine china it wasn't, but foam bowls worked just as well for the hamburger soup. The soft rolls only needed warming up in the microwave and were perfect for dipping. After too many days of restaurant food, it tasted like a royal feast. But it was missing one thing—well, I was missing one thing— Eli still hadn't shown up.

The game set aside while we ate, Lando filled the screen with videos of cats. Cats climbing trees, rolling on the grass, chasing butterflies. In other words, cats being cats. The one of a cat interrupting a politician's press conference got me thinking. "I wonder how the chief's conference went today."

"Let's find out." Scotty put his soup bowl on the floor and picked up the laptop controlling the big screen. "There isn't a local news station, but will the Pittsburgh stations carry it?"

"If it's a slow day. The local paper will report on it tomorrow."

"Let's try their website."

My experiences with the paper's website were less than wonderful, but I kept my mouth shut. It seemed as if it only got updated once a day, and that was after the daily paper came out. Maybe we'd get lucky.

"Is their website always this slow?" Scotty grumbled.

"Always. One reason I'd rather read the paper."

"No video, but hey, they have the link to one. Cross your fingers it loads faster."

In no time at all, Chief Sorenson filled the screen, his command presence a stark contrast to the frazzled appearance of the older lady standing behind him, sniffing loudly and dabbing her eyes with a handkerchief. Mrs. Galas, I presumed.

In even tones, he explained the situation and asked for the public's help to locate the missing firefighter. Mrs. Galas cried loudly as he spoke, but only a minor flash of irritation crossed his face. The wails got louder the longer he talked until the police department's chaplain whispered something into her ear. Chief Sorenson ended his announcement with a number to call for new information. He left the room without taking questions, claiming he needed to get back to work.

Chicken, I thought, but I should have known better. He was avoiding the scene that followed.

Mrs. Galas raised her nose into the air and strolled up to the microphone. She gestured to someone behind the cameras and two young girls, dragging their feet, joined her on the elevated platform. She wrapped an arm around each one, pulling them to her side.

Then, with sobs between the barely intelligible

words, she began her speech. How her wonderful, heroic, dutiful, handsome son was missing, and how could she go on without him. How he always called her every day, and that's how she knew something was wrong. She'd felt it in her heart long before the police got involved. And how every mother out there knew her agony and wouldn't one of them help her find him. And on and on. A part of me thought she was enjoying the attention she was receiving.

"Holy shit," Lando said. "No wonder he disappeared."

I wanted to agree. But why hadn't he let his supervisor know he would be gone?

Scotty muted the playback. We'd all grown weary of listening to Mrs. Galas' overwrought crying. "We'll have to play it again for the boss," he said with a frown.

"Make Eli wear a headset," I suggested. "I should be more sympathetic, but I'm not sure I can take another minute of that lady."

Lando lifted his head. "Speaking of Eli…"

It took me a moment to hear it—a vehicle in the driveway. "What makes you think it's Eli?" I asked.

"Listen close. The van has a little miss in the motor. I haven't been able to track it down yet."

I listened but didn't hear anything unusual. The engine stopped, and I assumed Eli turned it off. I headed to the kitchen to turn up the heat under the soup, so he'd have a hot supper. As I twisted the knob, my phone buzzed, and I glanced at it to see a text notification from Freddie. He could wait. I wanted to greet Eli in the proper fashion when he walked in the door.

Which wasn't hard because when he strode into the front room he was still in business mode and all alpha. And, from the smile on his face, it had been a successful meeting. He swept me into his arms and leaned me backward for a lingering kiss, to catcalls from the cheap seats.

"Eli," I whispered into his mouth, "We have an audience."

"Yep," he whispered back between kisses, "I'm setting a good example for when they find their own women."

I would have laughed, except his mouth covered mine and my tongue was busy. Until both of our phones buzzed, and we broke apart.

"It's probably Freddie," Eli said, pulling out his phone. "He tried to reach me a few minutes ago."

My eyes widened. "Me too."

"Shit."

I agreed with the sentiment as I swiped the screen of my phone to wake it and read the message.

Galas checked in.

That was weird phrasing.

Come to the office for details.

Eli wouldn't get his hot soup.

Then our phones buzzed again.

Don't come. Too many reporters. I'll come to you.

I shared the messages with Lando and Scotty while Eli headed upstairs to change clothes. The deep brown business suit looked marvelous on him, but uncomfortable. I considered going along to 'help' him but if Freddie showed up we'd be interrupted. And it looked as if we were in for another long night.

How long would Freddie make us wait? With the kitchen spotless, and the guys busy discussing the finer points of the newest Java update, I felt about as useful as a vase of fresh flowers in a closed-up attic. I stared out the kitchen window, seeing only my reflection, trying to imagine how I could fit in, and coming up with nothing. Was this going to be my life, relegated to the kitchen or third floor like the servants of previous generations?

I blinked away the beginnings of tears when I spotted movement behind me. Eli slipped an arm around my waist and pressed his body against my back, peering at our reflections over my shoulder.

"What do you see out there?"

I needed a believable excuse. "I was looking to see if it was snowing. Light flurries are predicted."

He nuzzled my neck. "We didn't mean to scare you off. But talking programming helps me relieve the stress of running the business."

Which I'd never be part of. But it wasn't the right time to discuss it. "Waiting for Freddie to show up is stressing me."

"We should check the local news and see if there's an update."

I didn't want to burst his bubble explaining about the local paper's website. "Or run a search and see what comes up."

He flipped me around so we stood face to face. "If anyone can find it, you can. You're the best researcher I've ever met. If you bear with me, I'll figure out a way to leverage that brain of yours in a job with the company so we can work together."

I touched him on the cheek. "Thank you, but I'm a big girl and can find a job." Not in Oak Grove, but I'd find one.

He grabbed my hand and clung to it. "Buttercup, I've been plotting this back when I was keeping an eye on you for Jake. I watched you tackle the research jobs from the authors' group and you amazed me with what you found. I don't want you to feel obligated to take a job with my company, but I hope you will."

His words flattered and made me feel like a fraud at the same time. Then the realization hit me, and I pulled away. "Wait, you hacked my computer before we officially met?"

"I've never accessed your computer, no matter how tempting it was." Eli held his hands out towards me. "No, I'd look at your notes and check out what was on your screen, but never more than that."

That explained the times I'd come back from gathering books or taking a break to find that my paperwork wasn't in the same place I'd left it. The night was filled with unwelcome surprises and welcomed honesty. I took his hands in mine.

"I'm not sure how I feel about it, but I'm glad you told me. Is there anything else you should confess?"

He inched closer. "That I love you. But you know that."

I closed the gap. "I love you, too."

As we stared into each other's eyes, he chuckled.

"What?" I said.

"A soon as we start kissing, Freddie will show up."

Of course, he would. "That's a risk I'm willing to take." And I proved it.

Freddie did show up. Not right away, thankfully. And he brought unexpected news.

"So Galas never was missing. He was out camping with friends, staying at a cabin in the hills. Planned ahead of time and, according to him, he told his mother about it."

My mouth dropped open. "But…"

"That show she put on for the cameras? Evidently, she told him she expected him to call every day and wouldn't take no for an answer. But where he and his friends stayed, there wasn't a cell signal. Or electricity to keep his phone charged. He couldn't have called her if he wanted to. So, she convinced herself something terrible had happened after she didn't hear from him for two days. She got herself so worked up she believed her own lies."

"But his supervisor didn't know he was going to be gone either," Eli pointed out.

"We figured that out, too. He put in a request two weeks ago and got verbal approval. Then they switched around the lieutenants' schedules, and his new lieutenant never found the paperwork. His old lieutenant left for the West Coast for a funeral and the stations out there didn't carry the story."

"He's home now?" I asked. "And his mother has calmed down?"

Freddie grinned. "Actually, no. He and his friends had made a beer run and caught a snippet of the press conference on a TV at the store. He called to tell us he was safe but asked us not to tell his mother his location. He was worried she'd tried to go there and barge in on the camping trip."

Eli shook his head. "Just wait until he gets home."

"Between us?" With a nod, Freddie included Lando and Scotty, "He told us that he's fed up with his mother and is considering moving out of town. Far out of town. And not telling her where he goes."

"That bad?"

Lando grinned. "Wait until you see the news conference she gave. I don't blame him for wanting to get away from her."

"What happens to her now?" I asked, thinking of the wasted time and effort that had been put into the search.

Freddie frowned. "It's up to the DA. She could get off with a warning or be charged with a felony. In a high-profile case like this, it's not safe to make a prediction. Personally, I think she needs a psychiatric evaluation."

It was a bad situation all the way around. There'd be no happy endings for anyone.

"That's not the only reason I came over," Freddie said. "While all the excitement was going on, someone set three more fires."

Chapter 26

"Three?" I squeaked as I looked for my laptop. "All three fires at once or spread out? In the same part of town or different locations?"

Scotty and Lando grabbed their keyboards. "Have videos of the fires posted?" Scotty asked.

"I don't know about the videos," Freddie said. "But I've got a printout of the calls, Harmony." He pulled some quarter-folded papers from his coat pocket and handed them to me.

I unfolded them and smoothed them out on the side table of the chair. They weren't complete transcriptions of the calls, but summaries were all I needed. Eli handed me my laptop, which had been plugged in to charge. I squinted as I brought up my latest spreadsheet detailing the incidents.

"Put it on the big screen," Lando said. "That's why we got it."

Seeing the numbers in oversize print provided a different perspective on my work, but no new insights. The additional fires didn't supply any breakthrough information. The locations were seemingly random. "Did any of those pins show up?" I asked, hovering my mouse over that column.

"I haven't heard."

That toggled a different question. "Did Antonio say anything that would explain why one of those pins was by his car?"

Freddie scratched his head. "No one asked. He's supposed to check in with us tomorrow and I'll find out."

Another dead end. I scanned the spreadsheet again and created a new spider graph of the locations. One place created a dot out of average and I didn't recognize the street address. "Where was this one?" I asked, returning to the main spreadsheet and hovering over the entry.

"I'm not sure that one belongs," Freddie said, "I wanted to include it just in case. It was in the park, and a bunch of high school kids claimed they'd started a bonfire to keep warm when they finished tobogganing on the hill. They'd even stacked snow nearby so if the fire spread they could put it out."

"Who called it in?"

Freddie covered his mouth with his hand but I suspected he smiled. "I'll give you one guess."

"Fiesker."

"You got it. He happened to drive by on the way back from one of the other fires and stopped to give the kids grief about it. The call actually came in from an old lady walking her dog who was upset about the way Fiesker was yelling at the kids."

I hid the row so the information wouldn't show up on any of my graphs.

"Have you pinpointed the locations over a map of the city?" Eli asked.

I moved to a different tab of the spreadsheet. "Like this? No matter how I connect the dots, I can't create a word or draw a picture."

He stared at the screen and shook his head. "It looks like someone threw darts at a map and wherever a dart landed, they started a fire."

It was the best theory I'd heard.

Scotty stopped whatever he was doing on his computer and stood, arms crossed, staring at the screen. "There's something about that spread of dots that rings a bell but I can't place it. Can you hide the map and show only the dots?"

It was an odd request, but I was willing to try. I ended up with a splash of red spots on a white background—as if my computer had developed a case of measles.

"Does that help?"

Scotty shook his head. "Yes and no. I still feel like there's something to it, but I may be imagining things."

"We've all been working hard on this," Eli said. "And none of us got much sleep last night. We should hit the sack and try again in the morning."

Freddie yawned. "Sounds good."

Had they forgotten I needed to go to work? "If you solve the mystery, let me know. You'll find me where I always am." At least for a few more days.

"You should call in sick," Lando suggested.

Eli's lips twitched. "Do I need to start asking for a doctor's note when you take off?"

"When was the last time I called in, boss?"

Scotty butted in. "Three weeks ago when you had the sniffles?"

"I really did have a cold," Lando protested.

"That you got rid of by laying on the beach all day."

"It worked!"

I looked at them over the top of my glasses in my best school-marm style. "Mr. Hennessey, I believe you have a serious HR problem you need to address. Surely your employees can't be encouraged to bicker this way."

"You're right, Miss Duprie, I've been neglectful and spoiled them. Whatever shall I do?"

"You two need to knock it off," Lando grumbled. "Seriously. You're creeping me out. Both of you."

I batted my eyes at Freddie. "What do you think, Detective Thomason?"

He chuckled. "That it's time for me to leave. Have a good night."

❀ ❀ ❀

With the morning rounds behind me, I slipped into the office to spend a moment collecting my thoughts. Or trying not to think at all. I had a few more days in the position, but I felt like an imposter.

Everything was ready for Janine's return. I'd caught up on all the paperwork and completed the schedules for the next few weeks. I'd even finished the monthly report for the City Council. There was nothing more for me to do than be the figurehead.

But I was still getting paid so I needed to earn my money. Or look like it, anyway. I could browse through book catalogs and come up with a list of potential purchases for our collection. That never failed to garner my rapt attention, but today my heart wasn't into it.

My thoughts kept returning to the problem of the fires. All I'd found so far were dead-ends. Even the brainiac from the steampunk supply company hadn't gotten back to me, and I worried that meant she hadn't found any useful information. That reminded me I'd been wanting to do more research on steampunk in general. The conventions in Pittsburgh seemed as good of a place to start as any. No one would care if I took a few minutes to hunt down videos of them.

A few minutes turned into many more. The variety and complexity of the costumes astounded me. The best part—everyone appeared to be having fun. No wonder Lando and Scotty put so much time and energy into their costumes for the comic cons they attended.

But the videos didn't get me any closer to figuring out who was setting the fires. The one scan of a vendor hall I found was from a distance and didn't show the booths up close. I couldn't identify the items up for sale.

Another dead-end. No surprise. At least it killed

most of the morning. If I straightened the stacks, at least I'd look busy.

That's where Eli found me at lunchtime. On the floor, deep among the shelves on the third floor, the children's area, with a stack of kid's books in my lap. I'd forgotten how much fun it was to pick out books for the weekly story hour.

He held out his hand. "Need help getting up?"

I didn't but accepted it anyway. "How did your morning go? Any progress?" I asked as I brushed off my pants.

"Not much. But you were right. We tracked down the library's internet as a source for several of the videos."

I looked around to make sure no one was near. "Didn't you say you needed a warrant to get the information?"

He grinned. "I said that without a warrant the information wouldn't stand up in court. I never said we couldn't get to it."

"You hacked the cable company?" I whispered.

"Only the public side. We haven't touched customers' records. And we won't. From what we're seeing, most of the videos have been uploaded from business locations and not homes. That doesn't help the investigation at all. In fact, I'm thinking about sending the guys home. They aren't accomplishing anything, and I don't want them to get stuck here when the next storm rolls in. Besides, they're getting bored."

We'd been walking as we talked and reached the first floor. I checked in at the front desk to make sure there were no emergencies I needed to handle before leaving for lunch, but everything was quiet. Eli waited by the front door while I grabbed my purse and coat from my—Janine's—office.

He tucked his arm into the crook of mine and led me towards the van.

"You're staying?" I asked. I missed having Eli to myself.

"At least until I finish the deal in Pittsburgh. I have to go back this afternoon and discuss details, but it's looking good. It's possible I'll take the exec I'm talking to out for supper, so don't wait for me."

I could have supper at my place, enjoy the quiet and read. There were several books I'd been wanting to check out at the library.

We ended up at Mama D's. No surprise. I needed to expand Eli's vocabulary of restaurants. We avoided talking about the investigation and discussed everything else instead. His mother's health, the high school basketball team, the typhoon threatening the Philippines. Then we listened to the tables around us gossip about Antonio's mother. The odds were still even whether she'd be charged or not based on public opinion.

What we didn't talk about was the future. And I was okay with that. It wasn't the right time.

Eli pulled over to the curb as a fire truck screamed down the street. "Should we follow it?" he asked.

I wanted to. I really wanted to. But I was already fifteen minutes late. And Eli needed to get to Pittsburgh for his meeting. "No. There's nothing we can do to help. And only one truck means it's a small fire. Another dot to add to the map."

He waited until the traffic cleared to rejoin the flow. "How long does an arsonist normally take between the times they start with small fires until they move to bigger ones?"

I'd researched the answer. "From months to years. The unusual factor, in this case, is how close the fires are together. Fiesker might be able to give you more insight into the psychological factors that come into play." He should be good for something.

"If he'll talk to me. Remember, in his mind, I'm an amateur interfering with his investigation."

"As much progress as he's made, he's the one who looks like an amateur."

Eli pulled into a spot near the front door of the library. "Maybe that's the problem. We're looking for the trail an experienced firebug would leave— when this is the work of an amateur who gets lucky and doesn't get caught."

"And the emails?"

"Same concept. Someone who knows just enough to turn on a computer, read an article about hiding yourself on the internet, and enjoys the commotion they create."

"How do you track down someone like that?"

He shrugged. "You have to get luckier than they are. Wait for them to slip up—and they will—and jump before they realize their mistake. It takes time and patience."

Both were in short supply.

Chapter 27

When I pulled up to the house, the familiar sounds of screams and gunfire greeted me. Lando and Scotty were destroying zombies again. Or maybe it was aliens.

Eli had made me promise I'd be at the house when he returned. I made him promise to text me before he left Pittsburgh. He kept his end of the deal and I was keeping mine.

To fill the time until he drove in, I brought my laptop and the new James Caboodle book I'd checked out. The one Pete recommended. It would be a change of pace from my normal romances.

I didn't expect to need the laptop, but out of habit I took it with me everywhere. My sense of normal was badly off-kilter since I couldn't maintain my rituals, and I clung to each shred of my 'typical' to stay in balance. The laptop was one piece of my safety net.

The guys barely looked up when I opened the door. "Hey, Harmony," Lando said as he executed a perfect headshot on one of the living dead. "Do you want to play?"

"Another time. I've started a new book and want to get past the first couple of chapters."

Scotty chuckled. "Imagine that. A librarian who reads."

"I think it's sexy," Lando said. "Watch out! That one almost got you."

I thought about going upstairs, propping pillows against the headboard, and reading in bed. But I might fall asleep and wanted to keep my promise to Eli. So I got myself a bottle of water and settled into one of the camp chairs with the book.

I'd finished chapter two and flipped the page when I noticed the gunfire had ceased and Lando and Scotty were having a loud discussion. Something about which settlement to visit next. Curiosity got the best of me, and I looked up to see a map displayed on the big screen with a scattering of pins designating human colonies. The names were variations on existing cities although placed in unfamiliar territory. I took a moment to interpret some of the more fanciful names and connect them to real places.

Something clawed at the back of my brain. Without a word, I fired up my laptop and opened my spreadsheet to the tab with chickenpox or measles or whatever. I studied the big screen and the small screen, wishing I could get them side by side.

But Lando and Scotty had decided where they wanted to go next in the game and switched to a different view.

"Put it back."

"She's alive!" Lando quipped. "Put what back?"

"The map."

Scotty and Lando exchanged a glance, but Lando did what I'd asked. "What do you see, Harmony?"

I took control of the wall-mounted screen and displayed my dots. "Exhibit A. Now it's your turn."

Lando shrugged and displayed the game's map again. "What are you looking for?"

Scotty came and leaned over my shoulder, staring at my screen. He caught his breath. "That's what bugged me last night."

"It's not a perfect match, but close," I said.

"What?" Lando asked.

I pointed to the big screen. "Look at the spread of the cities in the game. Now, look at this," as I brought up my dots again. "Do you see it now?"

Lando's eyes shifted between the map on his computer screen and the non-map from my spreadsheet. He whistled softly. "Holy shit. The fires are recreating locations from the game."

This was beyond my paygrade. Time to call in the bigshots.

Freddie, remembering the lack of furniture, brought along two of his own camp chairs. Unfortunately, he also brought along Fiesker, but I'd prepared myself for his presence. The need to wait for Eli and the need to astound Freddie and

Fiesker with our revelation battled in my brain. I stretched out the introductions and hostess duties long enough for Eli to join in on the fun.

I'd texted him with the news while I was in the kitchen making coffee, not wanting him to be blindsided when he walked in the door. So, he was in full top-of-the food-chain business executive mode when he strode in the door to claim his kingdom and his throne. And his queen. Because he granted me one of his mind-blowing kisses before even putting down his briefcase.

"It appears we're in for an interesting conversation," he said, shucking his coat and glancing around the room. He nodded to Freddie and ignored Fiesker.

Fiesker's mouth grew taut. "It better be good. I have more important things to do than sit around and listen to nonsense."

Like yell at kids for lighting a campfire. He had different ideas of important than I did.

"It's better than good," Lando said. "And we appointed Harmony to be our spokesperson because most of the credit goes to her."

I turned on the big screen. "It was a joint effort. Sparked by the conversation we had last night about the spread of the events." I brought up the tab with the map and the dots. "Here are the locations of the fires."

"I still don't see a pattern," Freddie said.

"I didn't expect you to but wanted Mr. Fiesker to get caught up. Now here are all the points without the map."

From the corner of my eye, I watched Fiesker lean forward to study the slide, but his face remained stoic.

I switched to another file. "Here's a second one." Thanks to quick work by Scotty, the game map now lived as a file on my laptop. I studied each man's reaction. Puzzlement.

"I don't recognize that area," Eli said. "Where is it?"

"In a minute." I reduced the size of the map to only use half of the screen and brought up the Oak Grove map on the other half.

Eli leaned back and smiled. "Brilliant."

"What?" Freddie asked. "I don't get it."

I glanced at Fiesker. He stared at the screen and shook his head slightly.

I hid the Oak Grove map and brought up the screen dots again and resized the image, so the game map was displayed with the dots side-by-side. "I don't have the software or skills to overlay the two files and it's not an exact match. But, like in horseshoes, it's close enough."

Silence followed as Freddie and Fiesker stared at the images. "I'd say there's a strong correlation," Freddie said finally. "But I don't recognize the names of these cities."

As we'd discussed, Lando jumped in. "We didn't expect you too. It's not real. The map comes from a zombie quest computer game. Scotty and I play it when our programs are compiling."

Fiesker broke his silence. "How does that relate to the fires? I'm not here to play games."

Lando ignored his remark. "In this game, you choose to be either a human or a zombie. Most people pick humans because they are easier to play. Some like a challenge and play a zombie. I have one character of each.

"And just like you have teams of humans, you can team up with other zombies. Humans get together to save their colonies, zombies try to destroy them. Our theory is that a team of zombies based here in Oak Grove are celebrating their victories by setting fires in real-life spots that correspond to where the maps intersect."

Fiesker cleared his throat. "Theory? Sounds more like a shot in the dark. How are you going to prove it?"

"We're working on it. We're hitting up the game forums on various servers to find one where the zombies are in control. Then we'll need to identify if the players are local. It will take a day or two, but even if they've taken their forum private, someone will leak the information." Lando grinned. "And the bonus is that the boss won't be able to yell at us for playing games when we're supposed to be working." He and Scotty exchanged a high-five.

Freddie rubbed his chin. "There's one flaw in your theory. What about those pins that have been found at various locations? They don't relate to the game, do they?"

That bothered me, too. "No, they don't. And the fact that there are so few of them compared to the number of fires doesn't sit right. Did you ask Antonio about the one by his car?"

"He wondered what he'd done with that. A firefighter found it the night of the fire across the street from your place. He put it in his pocket and lost track of it. He figured it fell through a hole in the pocket of his jeans."

That didn't fit the theory at all. I hadn't even included the Axcel fire in my spreadsheet.

Fiesker stared at the screen where the game map and my dots were still displayed. "Zombies," he muttered.

My mouth twitched. I wanted to read his report when he wrote it up.

"What happens when the zombies take over every city on the map?" I asked Lando as he helped me to clean up the front room. The reusable cups were headed for the kitchen to be washed and put away, while everything else was trashed. I needed to hit up the second-hand store and get Eli some dishes to use until he bought his own. Scotty was off on a trip for munchies, and Freddie and Eli were outside having a private discussion. Fiesker had slunk off to wherever he was staying.

"The players move on to the next big game. Sure, a few will stick around, drop in once or twice a week to check out what's happening, but once the conquest is complete, the game loses its appeal."

I remembered that same behavior with the gamer group from college. "I guess what I'm really asking is if they'll stop setting fires."

"Sounds like a question for a psychiatrist. Or Fiesker. Based on his reaction tonight, I doubt his experience covers the situation."

If Fiesker played it right, he could turn this into an opportunity to become the premier expert on a whole new class of firebugs and earn the coveted award. All without mentioning any of us.

"So, the fires could stop and we'd never know who was responsible," I said, thinking out loud.

Lando shrugged. "Does it matter who set them if they stop?"

That was a good question. And one I didn't have an answer for.

I posed the same question to Eli as we snuggled in bed. He played with a strand of my hair as he thought it over.

"It depends on whose point of view you look at it from," he said. "Chief Hinds would say a lot of taxpayer money got wasted, besides the stress the fire department personnel went through, and the potential for the staff to get injured. Freddie and Chief Sorenson want to arrest someone for the crimes they committed as a matter of public safety. Fiesker wants to track them down for the glory. Someone else might say we need to find the culprits so they receive counseling to make sure they never set fires again. I'd like to find out who did it for personal satisfaction after all the time we put into the chase."

Did everything have to be so complicated? "Is it bad I hope it's just a bunch of high school kids and they never get caught?"

He kissed my forehead. "I wouldn't call it bad. I'd say it shows compassion. Everyone I listed, besides me, sees the analytical side of you. They don't see the soft-hearted woman underneath. And I love both sides."

"You say the nicest things. But the analytical side of me is worried. There are still pieces that don't fit the puzzle."

"The pins?"

"And the emails and texts. They have nothing to do with the game. At least, not as far as I can figure out."

"And we aren't spending much time on them because they stopped. At least no one's told us about any new ones."

He was right. For some reason, it didn't feel like a good thing.

Eli ran his fingers down my arm. "Don't stew about it all night."

I would. "I need a distraction. Can you help with that?"

He chuckled. And got right on it.

Chapter 28

I stood on a straight-backed wooden chair to adjust the position of the picture behind Janine's desk. Mrs. Amelia Schmidt, the first librarian of Oak Grove. At one time, her portrait watched over the front desk but had been removed from its spot sometime in the fifties. It languished in storage for many years before finding its new home above the chief librarian's desk. That was four librarians ago, and Janine didn't want to break the tradition.

"Need help?" asked a voice behind me.

I didn't even need to turn around. "Does it look straight now, Freddie?" I wanted everything to be as perfect as possible for Janine. She'd called to let me know she'd be dropping in to catch up on the current state of affairs.

"Looks fine. I wasn't sure I'd catch you here since your car's not around."

I gave the frame one last nudge to satisfy myself. "Eli took her to Pittsburgh. The guys needed the van to run errands and it was easier than making him rent a car." I reached for the back of the chair to step down, but Freddie came over, lifted me off and set me on the ground.

"What have you done to the place?" he asked. "It doesn't look like you at all."

I checked to make sure my bun hadn't got messy. "It's not supposed to. I'm returning it to how Janine left it." Minus the clutter and stray paperwork. And the photo of her mother I tucked in a drawer, so it wouldn't be the first thing she saw when she sat at her desk. "I took pictures of everything before I made changes."

"You're a good friend."

Heat rose in my cheeks. "Thanks. But you didn't come by to compliment me. What's up?"

"Thought you would like to know that Antonio Galas is back in town. And his mother is already causing him more grief. Officers have removed her from the apartment complex twice. She's been told if she goes back she'll be arrested for trespassing."

"Did she drag her younger kids with her to make him feel bad?"

"What kids?"

I crunched my eyebrows. "The ones at the press conference with her."

Freddie let go a short, harsh laugh. "Those weren't even her kids. They are her sister's. And boy, their mother was hopping mad when she saw the kids on TV. Mrs. Galas won't ever be allowed around them again."

"How crazy do you have to be to pull a stunt like that?"

He shrugged. "Or smart in a twisted way. It gained her a lot of extra sympathy."

I couldn't imagine thinking that way. "Has the DA decided to charge her?"

"Haven't heard. However, we'll pass along today's report. It might influence his decision."

"Well, at least Antonio's home. Maybe she'll settle down." But I didn't believe it. And from the frown on his face, neither did Freddie.

"At least we didn't have a new fire during the commotion," Freddie said. "That might be because we've increased patrols in the areas Lando and Scotty picked out as possible targets."

Or because school was in session. I needed to rework my spreadsheet to see if any of the fires were set during school hours. If my guess was correct and the zombies were high school kids, then the majority of fires would have occurred on weekends or after school.

Janine showed up after lunch, sneaking in through the back door so only a few people saw her. And half of them didn't recognize her with the large sunglasses and her hair tucked into a baseball cap. The sunglasses were a strange touch in the middle of winter, but they worked well as a disguise. Her camouflage reminded me I hadn't seen Jake for a while. Where had he gone?

But he could take care of himself. Janine, I wasn't so sure about. As she stood and looked around her office, she seemed fragile, as if she could fall to pieces at the drop of a pin.

A slow smile lit her face and I spotted moisture in her eyes. We'd promised each other there would be no tears and she was breaking our pact. She snatched a tissue from the box sitting on my-no, her-desk and dabbed them away. "Thank you, Harmony. It feels like home."

The only correct response seemed to be folding her into my arms. Which I did. And somehow, we both held back the tears.

After a long couple of minutes, we pulled apart. Janine shook herself, and I watched her transform back into the Chief Librarian. She pulled the guest chair up to the desk and sat in it, leaving me to sit behind the desk. "All right, fill me in on what I've missed."

❈ ❈ ❈

A police car drove down the street in front of the library for the third time in the last fifteen minutes. That's how long I'd been waiting for Scotty and Lando to pick me up. They'd messaged me they were running late, having spent too much time in a comic book store in Erie.

To occupy my time, I studied the sparse foot traffic in front of the library. Two waitresses from the restaurant hurrying home after work. A young couple, college kids I guessed, heading inside to study. A teenager boy strolling past, his hands in his coat pockets. Another teenage boy, carrying a shopping bag, heading the opposite direction. It didn't appear to be out of the ordinary when they stopped to chat. When they disappeared around the corner of the library, the back of my neck began to itch. There was no reason to cut through the alley. It wasn't a shortcut to anywhere.

I didn't make a conscious decision to follow them. I just found myself sneaking around the corner to see where they'd gone. Maybe they planned to hide behind the dumpster to sneak a cigarette. Or a beer or two. Or sell some weed.

Since the library was one of the spots Lando and Scotty had identified, I feared they planned to start a fire. But the garbage had been collected earlier in the day and the cleaning crew hadn't started their work yet. What would the boys use for fuel?

I slid against the wall of the library, staying in the building's shadow. It wasn't hard to hide because the only light back there filtered in from the street or from the library windows half a floor up. The boys talked quietly about school as they stood there, shuffling their feet and blowing on their hands to warm them.

It didn't add up. They weren't doing anything they couldn't have done on the sidewalk in front of the library. So, why were they hiding in the alley?

The answer arrived as I was about to give up and go back inside to wait for my ride. A third boy showed up, entering the alley from the other end. The original pair greeted him with an intricate series of hand movements and fist bumps. A secret handshake, I guessed. It seemed like a waste of time, but they got a kick out of it.

With the preliminaries completed, they got down to business. Or tried to. The last boy pulled himself up to peer into the dumpster. "Shit," he whispered. "It's empty. And there's no trash dumped on the ground. Now what?"

"There's got to be garbage behind the diner," the first boy hissed. "We go there."

"It's too far away," the third boy complained.

"Close enough to count," said the second boy. "Who cares, anyway? We're the only ones keeping track."

"Somebody does. The cops are involved now. At least, that's what my grandma told my parents," the third boy said.

"The cops are a joke," the first boy, the ringleader, said.

Little did they know. I debated my options. Whip out my cell phone and take pictures, call 911, or pull Betsy from my purse and order them to get on the ground and stay there until the police arrived. The last seemed a spectacularly bad idea. Especially as my hands shook as I reached for my purse, dangling from my shoulder. Not out of fear but from anger. How dare these waste of humanity trolls place my beloved library in danger?

The phone it was. I might not get good pictures in the dark alley, but it was worth a try. I'd only get one or two shots because the flash would alert them to my presence. They needed to count.

I took a deep breath and held it, trying to steady my nerves. With my back against the building, I raised the camera and aimed. I couldn't get a shot of all three boys facing me at the same time, so I settled for one and the side profile of another. As I pushed the button, a bright light illuminated the alley. Not my camera, but the spotlight on a police car.

The boys took off running. I wasn't going to follow them. There wasn't any chance I'd be able to keep up with them. Instead, I walked the opposite direction to make contact with whatever officer was on patrol.

It was the rookie. It had to be the rookie. And I still didn't know his name.

It was past time to put an end to that. With my hands high in the air, I marched over to where he stood by the car with his gun drawn. He frowned and put his gun away and I lowered my arms. "We haven't been introduced. I'm Harmony Duprie," I said as I stuck out my hand to shake his.

He ignored the gesture and didn't tell me his name. His coat covered his nametag. "What were you doing in the alley?"

How rude. If that's the way he wanted to play it, I'd make his life difficult. "Trying to get pictures of potential suspects in the arson cases. I'm assuming that's why you're here. Perhaps you should call Freddie for backup." I smiled sweetly to contradict the edge in my voice. Keep him confused.

"Freddie?"

My fake smile broadened. "Bless your heart, I mean Detective Thomason. Would you like me to call him?"

The radio on his shoulder cackled. Something crackle wait something pop backup crackle the way snap. I never learned to interpret those things. But the rookie got the message.

"10-4."

That I understood.

He turned off the spotlight and shut his door. I stared at him. He broke first.

"Detective Thomason will be here in a few minutes. He asks that you wait for him."

How he got all of that out of the garbled message I didn't know, but I wouldn't ask. "Okay. If it's all right with you. I'd like to go inside to wait. It's cold out here."

It was another test. He shouldn't let me out of his sight. But the air was getting chillier by the minute, now the sun had completely set.

He hesitated. "You can sit in the car."

He opened the back door and I stared at him again, shaking my head. A small bunch of onlookers stopped to watch the proceedings, with cell phones aimed our way, adding to the stress. For him. I was enjoying myself. I didn't have to worry about the library's board of directors disapproving of my extracurricular activities anymore.

He frowned, slammed the back door shut and opened the door on the front passenger's side. I smiled at him as I slid past him and into the car.

"Thank you so much!" I gushed. My lips twitched in amusement.

"Don't touch anything," he said before shutting the door.

I'd been in a police car a time or two, both front and back. I understood what was safe to touch. For now, all I cared about was directing the air vent to blow hot air on me. With the excitement at a standstill, I realized I really was cold. Or the adrenalin rush had worn off. Either way, the heat would stop my shivering.

Chapter 29

By the time Freddie arrived, I'd warmed up. And it made no sense to have our question and answer session on the street when I still had access to Janine's office, where I could make a pot of coffee and sit behind the desk and feel in control.

"These aren't very good pictures," Freddie said, flipping through the gallery on my phone.

I blew across the top of my coffee cup. "They ignored me when I asked them to pose."

The rookie coughed. He'd unzipped his coat, but his nametag was still covered.

"At least I can make out this one kid's face. You didn't recognize them?" Freddie asked.

"Nope, they don't use the library. Probably do their homework on one of those sites on the intranet that get everything wrong."

The rookie coughed again, nearly spitting out a mouthful of coffee. I tossed a box of tissues to him. He caught it one-handed and earned a point or two. I gave myself one for a good throw.

Freddie allowed himself to grin for only a second. "And you're sure they planned to start a fire?"

"No. They never mentioned the word 'fire.' But everything points that way." I'd already repeated their conversation for Freddie. And the rookie.

"I'm not sure how this will help the investigation."

I'd figured that out. "Easy. If they're dumb enough to use a picture of themselves as their gaming avatar, Lando and Scotty can track them down."

The rookie nodded in agreement.

Freddie rubbed his forehead. "You can explain that later. I haven't gamed since everything was text-based."

I wanted to ask him what he'd played but now wasn't the time. "And this strengthens the theory about zombies setting the fires."

"You realize how strange that sounds. I never thought chasing the living dead would be a highlight of my career."

"I can see it on your resume. Listed under accomplishments." I grinned and held an imaginary piece of paper in front of me. "Arrested the zombie arsonists."

The rookie couldn't control his chuckle. Which got me started. Freddie sighed and waited for us to control ourselves.

"Does it sound any better if I call them steampunk zombie arsonists?" he asked without a trace of laughter.

I admired his ability to keep a straight face.

"Steampunk?" the rookie asked. "Where did that come from?"

"The pins everyone is supposed to look for? Harmony traced them to a steampunk supply company, but they can't identify anyone local that bought the pins."

"My sister who lives in Pittsburgh is big into that. What do you need to know?"

"We can start with the names of people here in town who will work with us. We haven't established a connection between the fires and the pins and they might be able to help."

"Consider it done. I'll call her when I'm off shift."

"It's work. Call when you're on duty."

The rookie shook his head. "She'll ramble on for at least an hour before I even get to talk."

"I'll clear it with your sergeant and get him to assign someone else to patrol while you're tied up. I doubt those kids will try anything else tonight, but it won't hurt to have someone keep an eye out. You can use my office. We're done here and I'm heading home."

"Thank you, Detective." The rookie headed towards the door, but I was faster and jumped in his way.

"You're not leaving."

"Ma'am?" he asked, confused.

"Your name. Tell me your name." If I took him down with a leg sweep and sat on him until he told me, would Freddie bust me?

Freddie grinned. "You have to understand, Harmony has this thing about names. I'm surprised she hasn't invented one for you. So, tell her or you might get stuck with one you don't like."

The rookie raised his hands in surrender. "It can't be much worse than the one my parents gave me. It's Holt. Bo Holt."

Bo, huh. That wasn't bad at all. "What's that short for?" I asked. "Beauregard?"

His cheeks reddened. "That's one of my middle names. I don't use my first name."

One of his middle names? That deserved further attention. With my mission technically accomplished, I spared him any further embarrassment. If I wanted to know his whole name, I had ways to find it. I stuck out my hand. "Pleased to meet you, Officer Bo Holt."

This time, he shook it.

❋ ❋ ❋

"Sorry we were late," Scotty said as he pulled away from the library. "We forgot to allow for the daily Oak Grove traffic jam."

In the back seat, Lando chortled. "We had to stop for two red lights! The horror!"

"You should be grateful you're not dealing with a traffic jam in I-4." Scotty grinned and glanced my way. "Don't listen to him. He hates Orlando traffic. Why do you think he makes me drive all the time?"

Lando smirked. "Because you're my friend and I know you like to drive so I let you."

A fire truck lumbered down the street going the opposite direction and I craned my neck to watch it.

"You want me to follow it?" Scotty asked, tracking it in the rearview mirror.

"No." I turned back around. "No lights, no sirens. So, it's not an emergency." I pulled my phone from my purse and opened the police scanner app, anyway. After listening to three minutes' worth of chatter about Mrs. Barston's dog getting loose again, I closed it.

"Have you guys located the server where the zombies are winning yet?" I asked, breaking the silence.

"We're getting close," Lando told me.

"Today they took over the colony that maps to the area by the library if that helps."

In unison, Scotty and Lando shouted, "What?"

So, I repeated the whole story again. When we reached the house, Lando slid the door open and jumped out before Scotty even parked the van. "Send us that picture," Scotty said, once the engine was off. Then he dashed for the front door, abandoning me.

Not only did they leave me behind, they left their shopping bags in the van. But I didn't know what was new and what stuff they carried around with them. When I dug through the ones from the local grocery store, it felt as if I was sneaking where I didn't belong, but discovering a stack of frozen meals relieved me of my guilt.

They were glued to their computers when I pushed through the front door, carrying as many bags as I could. Each displayed a different map on their screen.

"We narrowed the hunt down to half a dozen servers," Lando said, not looking up. "Your information will give us everything we need to locate the right one."

I took my haul into the kitchen and set it on the counter. "I hope so," I said loudly. "This situation is getting on my nerves."

"You need help in there?" Scotty asked.

I did, but what they were doing was important. Besides, it gave me a chance to reorganize the kitchen. "I got it."

With all the frozen and cold food put away, I tackled the mishmash of other items. Snacks, mostly, but also items like soup and canned meats. If a zombie hoard attacked, they'd survive a few days before needing to forage for additional supplies.

"Harmony," Lando called. "Can you come in here?"

"Did you find them?" I put the last can of soup on the shelf and closed the cupboard door.

"No, but there's something else you should see."

I didn't remember a car crash scene in the game. But there it was, on the big screen, with graphics so well done it looked like a scene from a movie. Cars on fire, five or six police vehicles, lights splitting the darkness, ambulances, and fire trucks streaming water in an effort to control the rising flames. And yet, the setting seemed familiar.

"What is this, a prequel scene from the game? I don't see any zombies."

Scotty grimaced. "It's not the game, this is a live stream. From the interstate southeast of here. We've had a crawler running for several days now and it caught this almost right away. Whoever is streaming has the sound off."

"Holy shit." I leaned in closer to try to identify any of the people, but with the flashing lights creating a strobe-like environment all I could see were shadow-like figures. The stationary vehicles were a different story. The law-enforcement cars belonged to the sheriff's department or state police, but at least two of the fire trucks carried Oak Grove emblems. It took forever to hammer out a mutual assistance agreement between all the area agencies five years ago, and this was the first instance I'd seen it put into action.

Then I realized we hadn't heard from Eli yet. "Holy shit," I said again. "Eli's not involved in the wreck, is he?"

"God damn it." Lando pushed away from his computer to come stand by me and stare at the screen. "I can't tell if this is northbound or southbound traffic."

"On it," Scotty said.

I traced my finger over each vehicle on the screen. Pickups, sedans, semis, and minivans. Not a sports car in the mix, but one could be hidden behind a fire truck.

"Got it," Scotty said. "The feed from the state police. Give me a minute."

I forced myself to breathe. In. Out. In. Out.

An ambulance, emergency lights off, pulled away from the scene, driving down the shoulder. That was bad. Very bad. I offered up a quick prayer for whoever had died. And another that it was only one person.

I sniffed, fighting back the tears that hovered at the corners of my eyes. Eli had to be safe. He had to be.

Lando awkwardly laid his arm across my shoulders. "It'll be okay. Eli's a good driver. He'd react fast enough to avoid this mess."

If he had the chance.

"Northbound!" Scotty yelled. "The accident is in the northbound lanes!"

Fuck. My knees gave out, but Lando wrapped his arms around me and held me upright.

"Don't borrow trouble," he said. "That's what my mom would tell you. For all we know, Eli is still in Pittsburgh."

Logically, I knew he was right. Emotionally was a different story. I had to pull myself together.

"Didn't Eli say he expected a late night?"

Yes, and that's why Lando and Scotty picked me up, not him.

Scotty turned off the display. "You need a distraction. Let's play a game. How about going retro?"

Aliens. I could wipe out alien starships with the best of them. It took me a few minutes to get the feel of the old-fashioned controllers, but Lando and Scotty had the same issue, so we started out even. And stayed even. I wasn't sure if they were humoring me or if adjusting their play to the big screen threw them off as badly as it affected me. In any case, the aliens were winning.

Or perhaps it was because I only gave half of my attention to the game. The other half monitored the police scanner running on Scotty's system. A helicopter landed on the southbound lanes to transport a patient to Pittsburgh. Additional law enforcement set up detours around the blockage. Tow trucks lined up on the nearest on-ramp, waiting for the word to come in and clean up the scene.

When an alien starship landed a direct hit on my laser cannon for the third time, I dropped my controller on the floor. "I'm done. You two can keep playing, but I'm going to go read a book." Or something. Anything but wonder where Eli was.

Lando's gun got blasted and he dropped his controller to the floor. "I'm hungry and it's making me screw up. Anyone want to eat?"

I cataloged the contents of the cupboards and refrigerator, trying to decide what they'd bought that was fit for a meal and coming up empty.

"Chinese?" Scotty asked.

"One vote yes," Lando said. "How about you, Harmony?"

It had been ages since I ate takeout Chinese. "Chinese is good," I said. "My treat. Get whatever you want. Oh, and pick out something for Eli. That way you can take the blame if it's something he doesn't like."

Scotty grinned. "No problemo. He gets the same thing every time. Cashew chicken. We keep telling him he needs to try something new, but he doesn't listen."

While we waited for the food, Lando and Scotty went back to chasing down the zombies and I settled in a chair with the library book. Action adventure wasn't my usual genre, but as long as it was well-written, I'd read the whole story.

As I turned the page to start the fourth chapter, a tickle started at the back of my neck. I chalked it up to not knowing where the plot was going, a good thing in a suspense thriller. But a small part of my brain didn't believe it.

Chapter 30

The doorbell rang and Lando jumped to answer it. "It's about time," he said, grabbing my credit card from the cardboard box he was using as a table. "If I don't eat soon, I'll faint!"

I barely glanced up, more interested in the dogfight happening in the book than filling my stomach.

Until I heard the voice on the other side of the door when Lando answered it. "You don't look like the delivery guy," Lando joked.

"Is Harmony here?" Freddie asked.

Shit. My heart splintered. I could think of only one reason for Freddie to show up in person without trying to call me first. And it was bad. Definitely bad.

"I'm here," I said as Lando stepped aside to let him in.

"Good. I need to talk to all of you. Eli's not back yet? I didn't see your car outside."

I picked up the pieces of my heart and put them back where they belonged. "No, and I'm worried. I hope he didn't get caught up in the accident on the freeway."

"You know about that?"

"We caught the live stream."

"Yeah, we watched it at the station. I don't have a complete list of names, but your car wasn't part of the wreck. So Eli's safe."

That was the best news I'd heard in days. "So, what brings you here?"

He didn't answer, instead he turned to Lando and Scotty. "Have you two figured out who the local players are?"

Scotty shook his head. "Close. We're down to the final two servers. After that, it's a matter of finding which chat room they use."

"How long will it take?"

The doorbell rang again. Lando answered and this time it was the food. I smelled the spices from the opposite side of the room as he took the boxes and handed the driver my credit card. Even the alluring scent didn't revive my appetite.

"I'm sorry to interrupt your supper," Freddie said once the delivery man left. "But I need the information as soon as possible."

"What's going on, Freddie?" I asked.

"Did you see our fire department got called out to help at the accident?"

"Yes. What does that have to do with the zombies?"

"We're grasping at straws. We need to locate whoever was streaming and question them."

"Question them about what? Was there another fire?" Why was he avoiding answering me?

"Anything they can tell us about what they witnessed."

I closed my eyes, drew in a deep breath and counted to ten. "Freddie, what's going on?"

His shoulders drooped. "We lost another fireman."

Lost? Like in died? No firefighter from Oak Grove had been killed on duty as far back as I could remember. "What happened? Did one get injured out on the interstate?"

Freddie shook his head. "No. I mean lost as in disappeared. Vanished. One moment he was helping put away equipment at the firehouse, and the next he was nowhere to be found. Like he took a walk and didn't tell anyone. But no one believes that's what happened."

"What's Fiesker say?"

"Why would I bring him into this?"

"Because if anyone would understand the psychological aftereffects of working a scene like tonight's, he'd be the one. Maybe it's a form of PTSD or some other kind of mental breakdown."

It had been my suggestion, so I couldn't complain, but I hated the idea of Fiesker coming back to Eli's house. It was a combination of being ashamed the house was still unfurnished and my personal dislike of the man. But I couldn't let either of those reasons interfere with locating the missing man.

While Freddie waited for him outside, I hung over Lando and Scotty's shoulders as they worked. Each had the same map up with a different configuration of dots representing the colonies overrun by zombies.

"Which one is ours?" I asked.

Lando tapped his screen. "We're assuming this one based on the time frame the last colony got overrun. It's close to where the library sits in the real world. I'm working on accessing the logs of the chat rooms and forums."

"Have you got a list of the team members yet? With pictures? Now I've seen the culprits it'll be easier to identify them." It was frustrating being that close to success and having time run out.

"I wouldn't get your hopes up the kids can help find the missing guy," Scotty said. "My guess is that the two events aren't related. Same goes for the emails and texts."

"You think it's two different teams?"

"I don't think anything but the fires tie to the game. Come on, you know dedicated gamers. They won't get involved in anything that takes time away from the game."

I thought about my friends in the gaming club. He was right. "So we should stop looking for them and concentrate on identifying the people sending the emails?"

Lando's fingers moved across his keyboard faster

than I could follow. "We've hit nothing but dead ends in tracing those user names."

The aching in my neck heralded a major headache. Or a brainstorm. "Do you have a list of those names? I haven't been paying attention to that part of the project."

Scotty nodded. "We have the info saved to a document. I'll bring it up. Or do you want an old-fashioned print-out?"

A piece of paper to hold in my hand would be good, but I didn't want to appear to be computer-phobic. "Send it to my email, will you?"

He grinned. "Consider it done."

I didn't know what I'd do with the list, but having it would allow me to feel as if I was contributing to the effort. "Thanks."

Lando tapped me on the arm. "Harmony, do any of these guys look familiar?"

"What guys?" Freddie asked, coming in the door with Fiesker.

"Possibly the team responsible for setting the fires. The ID's are game names, but some of the pictures aren't 'shopped' enough to hide the features. Detective, why don't you help? You may have run into these kids in town."

I got to ignore Fiesker while Freddie and I squeezed together to stare at the screen and attempt to identify the faces behind the effects used to make them zombie-like. Not an easy task to ignore the fake blood and rotting flesh. But, as Lando said, some were less disguised as others, and I concentrated on those.

"This one," I said, pointing to the screen. "Can you make this one bigger? I need a better view."

Lando tapped a few keys and the picture doubled in size. "That's him," I said. "The boy who didn't want to set the fire."

"We get one, we can get all of them," Freddie said. "But we need a name."

"High school yearbook," I said. "But the library and schools are closed."

"It'll be online," Scotty said. "Give me a minute."

"Is that why you brought me here?" Fiesker snarled. "To show off in front of me and make me feel useless?"

"No," Freddie snapped, "Harmony suggested you might be the one with the knowledge to save a man's life. Is that enough to satisfy your ego?"

"Aren't you jumping the gun? How long has this guy been gone? An hour? Maybe he went out to get coffee or something."

"In the middle of a shift. Without asking anyone to go with him or telling anyone. That's not normal under the worst of conditions."

Fiesker sneered. "Unless he's running away from his mommy."

Expert or not, he'd gone too far. I executed a military-precise swivel, intending to march over to him and throw him out. Freddie must have read my intentions and stepped between us.

"I'm sure Chief Hinds and Chief Sorenson will be interested in your level of cooperation," Freddie said, deepening his voice. "I wonder if our DA will be comfortable filing obstruction of an investigation charge."

"Are you threatening me, Detective?"

I'd been on the receiving end of Freddie's 'bad cop' face one too many times, and it wasn't pretty. It made me glad I wasn't in Fiesker's shoes.

"No, pondering the situation. Something you seem unable to do. And I'm sure this conversation isn't being recorded."

Lando jumped in. "Oh, my bad. Did I forget to turn off the audio monitor I started earlier? Not that it matters because it's legal to record a law enforcement officer in the performance of his duties. You are on duty now, aren't you, Detective?"

I was pretty sure it was a bluff, but kept my expression flat. Did Fiesker resent me so much he'd refuse to help locate a missing person?

Freddie nodded. "Yes, this is official business."

Lando's broad smile seemed fake. "Good, that means we're legitimate."

Fiesker's eyes narrowed. "I don't consent to being recorded. Turn it off."

Lando punched a few keys and wiggled his mouse. He didn't really change anything, but it was a good show. "Okay, it's disabled."

"So, what do you want from me?"

Freddie took the lead. I gave the conversation half my attention and followed Scotty's progress with the other half. "Information. What do you know about the psychological factors that could play into a firefighter walking off the job?"

"I'm no psychologist, so don't quote me," Fiesker said.

"Agreed."

"Big one that comes to mind is workplace bullying. It's often tied to racism and sexism. I've seen no evidence of either here."

I was happy to hear that.

"Personal issues can come into play. Marital problems, finances, breaking up with a girlfriend." Fiesker shrugged. "Same as everyone else."

"What about PTSD?" Freddie asked. "Cops get it, and we have a psychologist on contract with the department we can refer our employees to if needed."

"It happens. One study claims up to a third of firefighters suffer from it. I think it's exaggerated. How many of those guys are saying shit just to claim disability? Supposedly, being young and single is a factor in who develops symptoms. I don't believe it."

Now I really didn't like him.

With one hand, Freddie rubbed the back of his neck. "Any ideas about where a firefighter might go to escape that's any different from a civilian?"

"Besides the bars?" Fiesker hesitated. "The guys I used to hang out with spent lots of time in the gym lifting weights to work off their aggression. Although I met one who was into meditation. He'd go sit in the park and watch the squirrels."

The squirrels were hibernating, but I had a contact to check the bars, once Freddie told us the missing man's name.

"I'll call Jake," I said. "He can get the word out to most of the other bars in town." If I could reach him. "I need a name and a picture to send him."

"Another expert?" Fiesker scoffed.

Freddie ignored him. "I'll get you a picture. Guy's name isPete Zamora."

Oh, crap. This had just gotten personal.

"I know him," I said softly.

"Of course you do," Fiesker said.

"How, Harmony?" Freddie asked.

Four sets of eyes fastened on me. "He volunteered at the library when he was in high school. He found the first brooch, and he's also the guy who came to me with the information concerning the emails and texts."

Lando whistled softly. "How familiar are you with him?"

"Not enough to help. We're only acquaintances who say 'hi' if we bump into each other in the grocery store. His parents still live in town. I suspect he's got a girlfriend, but I won't swear to it." I closed my eyes and examined my memory. "He seemed really proud to be a firefighter," I said as I popped them open. "I can't imagine he'd walk off the job. He wasn't that kind of kid."

"We've been in touch with his parents," Freddie said. "He talked to them yesterday. They didn't pick up any indication he was worried. His supervisor said he's never pulled anything like this before. He shows up for his shifts on time and hangs around the firehouse even on some of his days off."

That sounded like Pete. "Let me call Jake. He can at least spread the name around until you get me a picture."

Chapter 31

What I wanted to do was climb into Dolores and drive all over town looking for Pete. But Eli still wasn't back. And the police were already on it, with help from every free man from the fire department. So, I occupied myself with flipping through the yearbook online while waiting for Jake to return my call.

Once I identified the first boy, it didn't take long to find the others. The fact they all belonged to the gaming club at the high school made it too easy. I picked out the three I'd seen in the alley, and the rest was up to Freddie and Fiesker. Freddie decided it could wait until morning. Scotty and Lando were making sure the boys wouldn't gain any additional territory in the game and have any reason to set a new celebration fire.

I felt deflated. All that time and effort for nothing more than a bunch of stupid kids playing a stupid game. And we still had a missing man.

While Freddie and Fiesker debated the finer points of tactics to use to get the kids to confess, I wandered off to the kitchen. The Chinese food sat there, getting colder by the second. Thank heavens we'd designed the kitchen with a built-in microwave and the food would be almost as good warmed up.

But Jake beat me to it. "The sesame beef smells really good. You want some?" He handed me a plate.

"How did you get in here?" I hissed.

He jerked his head. "Back door. It was unlocked. Probably the resident ghost in action, which is fine with me. Your company makes me nervous."

I didn't believe him but couldn't prove him wrong either. I took the plate and surveyed my choices. Looked like Lando had ordered one of everything. I settled for an old favorite, sweet and sour pork.

Jake put both of our plates in the microwave and punched the buttons to start it. He leaned against the counter as we waited. "Your message said the missing guy's name is Pete?"

"Pete Zamora."

He shook his head. "I don't recognize the name. He must not hang out in the bars. Did you get a picture?"

I showed him the photo Freddie had forwarded. He shook his head. "Nope, he doesn't look familiar. Send that to me and I'll pass it around to my contacts."

The microwave beeped, and he handed me my plate. "Your help would be appreciated," I said. "There's only so much the police can do."

"And if this guy really wanted to disappear, there are ways to hide that make a person almost untraceable. At least for a few months. It gets harder the longer you are gone."

"Are you speaking from personal experience?"

He grinned. "Who, me?"

I knew better than to expect a straight answer from him.

"Did I tell you I heard about the job in Cleveland?" he asked before stuffing a forkful of rice into his mouth.

"Did you get it?"

I had to wait while he swallowed.

"No." He didn't appear too upset about it. "The guy's sister pressured him into giving it to his nephew. He doesn't expect it to go well and says once the kid has screwed up enough he'll give me a call. I won't hold my breath waiting."

Lando popped his head in the door. He eyed Jake up and down. "I thought I heard Eli in here."

Now that Lando mentioned it, I realized Eli and Jake had similar voices. "Have you two met?" I asked. Assuming they hadn't, I didn't wait for an answer. "Lando, this is Jake, Eli's cousin. Jake, Lando works for Eli."

Jake immediately switched into what I called his salesman mode, holding out his hand and plastering a not quite real smile on his face. "Eli has mentioned you. I'm glad to meet you."

I watched with amusement as Jake's charm worked its magic. Lando returned the smile and pumped Jake's hand. "Cousin, eh? Yeah, I can see the resemblance." He turned to me. "Do you have a minute?"

My mouth was full of food, but I nodded.

"I ran a search on the names used to send those emails and noticed something weird. I hoped you, as a librarian, could help."

That sounded interesting. I put down my plate and winked at Jake. "You want to join us?" I asked with my best hostess voice.

He grinned, knowing my game. "Nope. I'll hit the bars and spread this picture around, see what I can dig up. If I hit pay dirt, I'll give you a call."

"Be careful out there."

Jake gently touched my cheek. "I'm always careful, Angel." He nodded at Lando. "Nice to meet you. Tell Eli I said hi."

He left the way he came, reminding me to lock the door behind him.

Lando stared at me, his eyebrow arched so high it almost reached his hairline. "Angel?"

I blushed. "Long story. You should ask Eli to tell you it sometime."

The short list of email addresses stared at me from the big screen, and my neck itched as I stared back. What was I missing?

"Here's the thing," Scotty said. "Our search keeps getting hits from fan fiction sites with these names. Or names close to them. We've been ignoring them because they seemed bogus. But we don't have anything else to go on."

The itch turned into the beginnings of a headache. "What's the author's name?"

"We didn't look. Give me a second."

While he pecked away at his keyboard, I studied the list, hoping for a brainstorm.

"Caboodle," he said. "James Caboodle. Looks like he writes action novels."

"I know who he is. He's Pete's favorite author."

The conversation between Freddie and Fiesker stopped. "What did you say?" Freddie asked.

I didn't answer right away. I was too busy looking for where I'd put the book I was reading. It was right where I left it, on the side table of one of the lawn chairs. I flipped through the pages, looking for names. And there they were, on different pages and in different chapters, but laughing at me in black and white.

"This is Caboodle's newest book," I said handing it to Freddie. "Pete got hooked on his stories when he worked at the library. We talked about this one the day of the fire here."

"Did the people who sent the emails know that?"

"It's a hell of a coincidence."

"What if Zamora has been the target the whole time?" Fiesker asked. "And the emails to the other guys was a cover to make it seem less suspicious?"

I couldn't wrap my brain around the idea. "Why?" I asked. "What's so different about Pete?"

"If the emails came from one person, I'd suspect a case of unrequited love." Fiesker rubbed his chin. "From a group? I don't know."

Freddie scrunched his lips. "Guys, can you bring

up one email from each name and show them all on the screen at the same time?

What was he up to?

"Sure," Lando said. "Hold on."

It was only a minute before the list of names disappeared and six emails took its place.

"Now, forget the names. Read just the emails. Notice anything?"

"They all sound the same," I said. "Like the people who wrote them got together and wrote them at the same time."

"Or one person wrote all of them," Fiesker suggested.

Freddie nodded. "That's what struck me. So your theory of someone having a major crush on Pete is a possibility."

Overwhelmed, I sat in the nearest chair. "You think someone walked into the fire station and abducted Pete without another firefighter seeing them? That doesn't sound possible."

"They've already reviewed the security tapes. The cameras don't cover every portion of the truck bay and there's no record of him leaving."

"What are the chances he left with someone he knows?" Fiesker asked.

Freddie tilted his head. "At this point, pretty high."

"But not willingly," I said, memories I wished I could forget flooding back.

"You think he was drugged?"

"It would explain a lot. Like why he didn't put up a fight or contact anyone and tell them he's okay."

"Now you're an expert on using drugs to control people?" Fiesker sneered.

I should have expected his cooperation would be short-lived. What I didn't expect was how the three other men in the room reacted. They formed a wall between me and Fiesker, protected me, Freddie in the middle, Scotty and Lando on either side. Lando's fist clenched and unclenched in time to the rapid beating of my heart.

"You just found the limits of my patience." Freddie's strangled voice was so deep it was a growl. "You need to think before you speak."

"All I said…"

"Shut up!" Freddie roared.

I was glad all I could see was his back. I'd never seen him that angry. He took two stiff steps forward. Lando and Scotty moved with him. Fiesker took a step back.

"It's none of your business," Freddie said, "but Harmony is the survivor of a drugging and abduction. If she's willing to share her experiences to give us insight into this case, I'll take them. They are more valuable than anything book training can give."

Freddie pushed his shoulders back and rotated his neck, cracking it. "I'll ask Chief Sorenson to assign one of the other detectives to work with you for the rest of the arson case. We're almost done and I have more important things to do. Now, I suggest you leave. This is private property and you aren't welcome anymore."

Fiesker grabbed his coat from the back of the chair. "I'll be filing a complaint."

If Fiesker meant that as a threat, it didn't work. Freddie answered calmly. "That's within your rights. I imagine Chief Sorenson will request the state police to investigate, so expect to hear from them."

Without even a 'good night,' Fiesker stomped out the door, slamming it behind him. No one talked while we listened to him start his car and pull out of the driveway.

"Well, wasn't that fun?" I asked, wondering if Fiesker would follow up on his threat.

"Sorry about that, Harmony," Freddie said, "bringing up your personal business, but I've had it with him. For a minute, I thought he might actually be useful and then he had to go and blow it."

"He came up with some good ideas." I don't know why I felt compelled to defend Fiesker.

"And we need to move on them. So, let's look at the particulars. Whoever grabbed Pete knows his favorite author, his email address, and phone number. That adds up to a friend or relative."

"And if it was a friend, Pete wouldn't worry about going to talk to them outside the firehouse."

"I need to get back to the station and check his phone records again. Find out who he calls most often and who calls him. Question the guys at the fire station about who he hangs out with. Too bad he doesn't have Eli's tracker on his phone." Freddie pulled on his coat and zipped it halfway. "I'll talk to you tomorrow."

When he'd left, it hit me like a brick, just how drained I was. It was late, Eli still wasn't back, and I had to make it through one more day at the library. I couldn't think straight, and couldn't even go home and sleep in my own bed. Not that I'd be able to sleep, because I was worried about Eli. Why hadn't he called?

"Security system set?" Lando asked Scotty.

"Give me two secs."

Security system? I hadn't put a security system in the house and I hadn't noticed an alarm box by the front door.

"I'll text Eli the code." Lando turned to me. "You'll need it too. Hopefully, the app will work on your phone."

"What security system?" I asked. "What app?"

"Something new we installed today. Remote monitoring of the house, inside and out. Only on the first floor, of course. Eventually, we'll expand to cover the yard too. Your keys will still work but the system will send an alert to everyone's phones when you use them. With all the equipment we've installed, we need to cut the risks of someone breaking in."

I'd have to warn Jake. I doubted he'd be able to beat the system and didn't want him taking any unnecessary risks.

"Done," Scotty said. "Give me your phone, Harmony, and I'll set it up for you."

I handed it over. "Which one of you wrote the program?"

"Eli wrote the basic shell. The two of us collaborated on fine-tuning the code. If he decides to market it, it'll make him rich."

Lando chuckled. "Richer. I doubt he'll sell it because the set-up is complicated. He's considering a stripped-down version for the average user."

"Damn," Scotty swore softly. "That's it. You need a new phone. We'll get you one tomorrow."

"I work tomorrow."

"Saturday then. Before we leave."

Chapter 32

A lump formed in my throat. I knew they'd leave eventually, but I enjoyed having them around. More importantly, would Eli go with them?

Scotty handed my phone back. "We've been keeping an eye on the weather. If we don't get out of here in the next few days, we'll be stuck when the next system moves in. And our job here is done."

"Besides," Lando said. "I'm tired of the cold and snow. I'm ready to get back to sunshine and sandy beaches."

"And tourists and mosquitos," I joked, hiding my dismay.

"You can come play tourist any time. If Eli is gone, I'll kick out my roommate and you can stay with me. I'll take you to all the fun places he won't. Like coleslaw wrestling."

"Are you kidding me? Coleslaw wrestling?"

"Yeah. Women in skimpy bikinis fighting in a kid's swimming pool filled with coleslaw. I bet you could beat any of 'em."

He was right. Eli would never take me there. "If I put that on my bucket list, I know who to call."

All three of our cell phones buzzed in succession. I got to the text first, a group message from Eli.

Big Steelers game tonight. The roads are a disaster. I'll find a hotel to hole up in. See you tomorrow.

My phone buzzed again with a second text.

I'll call you when I get settled. Love you. I hoped that hadn't gone to the guys, too. But they were putting their phones away, so it came to only me.

Be safe. I texted back. *Love you too.*

"You guys want to help me put the food away?" I asked, pushing myself out of the chair. I needed to stay awake until Eli's call.

Lando stuffed his phone into his pocket. "Sure, if you help us kill off some zombies afterward."

It sounded like a fair deal. I wouldn't mind harassing a bunch of egotistical high school boys for an hour or so.

I got a rundown on how the security system worked before going to bed. If I got up in the morning before the guys, I'd be able to disarm it when I left without waking them. Which was a given—the getting up before them part. But one of them would have to get up to take me to work. They were still wiping out the zombie horde when Eli called, and I went upstairs to talk in private.

"You sound stressed," I said as I crawled under the covers.

"Things didn't go so well today," Eli said. "I

don't know what happened, it was like we started from scratch. I can't figure out if politics was involved or what, but I finally got a signature on the dotted line. Then I didn't have the patience to deal with drunk drivers."

I made the swift decision not to tell him about the evening's events and stress him more. "We need to celebrate when you get back. Where can I take you for dinner?"

"As good as that sounds, I have to take the guys out. They pulled some last-minute miracles this afternoon and I want to treat them to a fancy meal. I was thinking about taking them—and you—to The Grove."

The Grove is the fanciest restaurant in town. The kind of place people take their dates to impress them. The place I'd planned to take Eli to for a romantic dinner. "That sounds like a great idea," I lied. "Did they bring the right clothes?" You didn't go to The Grove in jeans and a t-shirt.

Eli chuckled. "You'd be surprised at how well those two clean up. I'll call and make reservations tomorrow."

I mentally inventoried my closet, deciding what to wear. Eli had already seen me in every nice dress I owned, and there was no time to go shopping. He'd have to deal with a repeat. Thinking about it made me tired and I yawned.

"Don't start, Buttercup." He yawned, too. "Look what you made me do."

Even though he couldn't see me, I grinned. "It's not the company. It's been a long day."

"Yeah, but if I was there, I'd find the energy to stay awake a little longer."

"Just a little?" I teased. And then ruined everything by yawning again.

"Go to bed. And fall asleep thinking about me."

Which I did.

It was cold. Too cold. I tried to pull the covers up, but my hands wouldn't move. My feet felt like rocks. I pried my eyes open. The nightlight was out. No moonlight crept through the crack of the curtains. I attempted to turn over to wake Eli, but nothing budged.

Sweat poured down my forehead. It dripped into my eyes. I yelled, hoping Lando or Scotty would hear me. No sound came from my mouth. The darkness grew blacker.

I tugged at my hands again, but my wrists were tied to the chair. I pulled, but they wouldn't come loose. The ropes dug into my skin. Blood seeped from the wounds. On the far side of the room, a shadow in the shape of a man muttered to itself. My brain urged me to run but there was nowhere to go. The shadow morphed into a familiar face. Fiesker.

With a start, I bolted upright and opened my eyes. The nightlight spread its comforting little blaze of brightness. It had been months since my last nightmare. I focused on the memory of a mountain lake my parents had taken me to when I was ten and tried to match my breathing to the lapping of the small ripples against the shoreline. The one counseling session I'd gone to after my abduction had been a waste of time because the psychologist had never treated someone in my situation. Meditation was more useful, and I didn't need to pay anyone.

The nightmare robbed me of any chance of crawling under the covers and going back to sleep anytime soon. I pulled on my robe and padded my way down the stairs to the kitchen, remembering seeing a box of mint tea in the cupboard. Not my first choice, but it would do.

While waiting for the water to heat, I fired up my laptop. It had been a long time since I'd casually surfed the internet. Watching videos of babies and puppies on the big screen should help me relax. First, I wanted to check if the video of Jake had been reposted. If so, I'd get Lando and Scotty to do their thing and get it removed before they left.

I got distracted by new videos of the crash but could only stand to watch a few seconds of each. The knowledge that someone died at the scene intruded into my study of the event. It was safer to scan old videos of fires. No one had gotten hurt.

After a few minutes of flames crawling through dead grass, I was bored. But the people at the locations—I could spend hours cataloging their expressions and body language. I searched for the faces of the three boys I'd seen in the alley but didn't spot them. All the faces I didn't recognize were a sad reminder of how library usage kept shrinking no matter how many events we sponsored or how many outreach programs we tried.

But it wasn't 'we' anymore. As of quitting time later, it was all Janine, the other staff, and volunteers.

Speaking of the volunteers, the camera zoomed past a face that looked familiar. It was hard to tell because of the heavy coat and the hood pulled over their head. I backed up the video a few seconds to replay it. The second look confirmed it. Rena Oleksandra.

Well, that was a weird coincidence, but she might have wandered down the street and stopped to check out the action. Or took a break from work to gawk at the firemen. I wasn't sure where that particular fire was. Once upon a time, someone had mentioned where her 'real' job was, but I couldn't think of it at the moment.

The next video was of the Axcel fire. I'd avoided watching any of them as they struck too close to home. As long as I was exorcizing old demons, I might as well face down a new one at the same time. I rubbed the back of my neck, trying to ease the dull pain that had started.

It took a moment to orientate myself to the spot the cameraman shot the scene from. They were at the opposite end of the block from where Eli and I observed the disaster. There'd been a larger crowd at that end, and the backs of heads frequently blocked the view of the action. The person doing the filming moved through the gathering, trying to get better shots. There were some good ones of the firefighters and one nice one of the water brigade in their purple vests. With Rena among them.

The ache at the back of my skull turned into a roaring headache.

She appeared in about half of the videos, proof of absolutely nothing. After all, that's what the water brigade did, show up to fires.

My headache got worse as I tried to recall if she volunteered at the library at the same time as Pete. Then I remembered the rumors of how she'd asked to change her shifts to be the same as his, even though she was a few years older, and how the volunteer manager squashed the idea. But those were only rumors.

And it didn't explain how she got his phone number and work email. Volunteers didn't have access to the personal information used when patrons signed up for cards. And Pete's card had been active since his high school days.

But once a year, the fire department sent a couple of firefighters over for children's story hour, the last time being just before I took over for Janine. *If* they had passed out business cards, and *if* Rena had been there that day, and *if* Pete had been part of the group, then *maybe* there was a way she'd gotten their emails.

It was too many *ifs* to prove anything. And it still didn't account for the text messages. I was tired, on edge, and jumping to conclusions. But I imagined Pete in a dark room, gagged and tied to a chair, praying for rescue.

The correct thing to do would be to go back to bed and call Freddie in the morning to tell him about my suspicions. What I wanted was to take Dolores and cruise past Rena's home, looking for signs of anything out of the ordinary. That was impossible because Dolores was in Pittsburgh with Eli. And I didn't have access to the keys to the van or know where Rena lived.

At least that was easy to fix. I didn't even need to log into a police database to get the information. All I needed was to enter her name into any one of the many sites on the internet that provided 'true and accurate' background information. The address came free. Beyond that, they charged for publicly available data. With Rena's name being fairly unique, it took less than a minute to find her listing. What would I do with it?

Only one person I could think of would be up and fully functional this time of the night. In fact, he was probably at a bar, helping the bartender close while enjoying one last free drink. And he had a car.

Jake.

I sent him a text first. *Are you up?*

He answered. *Yes?*

I didn't want to take anything for granted, in case he'd found a 'friend' to spend the night with. *Are you available to come here?*

Your place or Eli's?

Eli's

5 minutes

That gave me enough time-barely-to get dressed and outside to meet him. I didn't want him to try to get in and have the new security system wake up Lando and Scotty.

It took him seven minutes. I was outside putting up my bun when he pulled into the driveway. I hopped into the car and fastened my seat belt. "Head for Poole Street. We can talk on the way."

"Where's Dolores?" he asked, looking both ways before pulling into the street.

"Pittsburgh. With Eli. He got stuck down there after the game."

"The Steelers won." He made the needed right turn.

"Good."

"What's up?"

"Remember Rena Oleksandra? The library volunteer involved in the accident the night you played traffic cop?"

"Yeah. What about her?"

"I think she's involved in Pete's disappearance."

The brakes of the Charger squealed as he pulled to the side of the street. "What?"

"I don't have proof. That's why I want to go scout out her house. Just peek in a few windows and see if anything looks weird."

He grinned. "Even for you, that's quite a stretch. How did you come up with this crazy idea?"

"I watched the videos again. She kept popping up in them. What if she showed up at the firehouse after the accident last night with bottles of water to give to the firefighters? And what if she spiked one and gave it to Pete? He wouldn't see anything out of the ordinary about a friendly face offering him water."

"That almost makes sense."

"The only thing I can't figure out is how she got the firefighters' personal phone numbers."

He looked over his left shoulder and pulled back onto the street. "That's easy. She works at the cell phone store in the mall."

Chapter 33

"I topped off the minutes for my phone last week and Rena was the one who cashed me out." Jake slowed at a stop sign and waited for the one other driver up that time of the night to go by. "Is Freddie going to meet us at her place?"

"I didn't call him."

Jake slammed on the brakes again. "Why not?"

"We can't sit in the middle of the street and argue." The lack of other cars didn't mean anything. We were still obstructing traffic.

He rolled to the side of the street and put the Charger in park. "Is that better? Now talk."

I stared out the windshield. "I don't have any evidence. That's why I want to go look around. If I find something worthwhile, I'll call him. I don't want to wake him up if it turns out to be nothing."

"I'll do almost anything for you, Angel, but I can't do this." He reached out and tucked a stray lock of hair behind my ear. "I'm a convicted felon. How would it look to one of Oak Grove's boys in blue if I was caught prowling around someone's back yard in the middle of the night?"

I hadn't considered that. "Freddie won't be able to get a warrant based on my guess."

"He might not need one. If he sees something suspicious and believes a life is in danger, he doesn't need to wait for a warrant."

"I don't want to wake Freddie up without a good reason."

With a gentle hand, Jake turned my head, so I had to face him. "Do you trust your gut, Angel?"

Was I overreacting based on my experience? We didn't even know for sure that Pete had been abducted. He might have gone for a walk. A very long walk, at this point.

I pulled my phone from my purse. "Let's do this," I said. "I'll call Freddie."

He turned on his blinker, looked over his shoulder, and pulled back onto the street. Doing it by the book. "Have I told you how proud I am of you?"

What? I didn't have time to ask because Freddie's phone rang. I held up a finger to acknowledge his statement.

It took three rings before Freddie answered. He fumbled with his phone and I thought, for a second, that he'd hung up.

"Harmony? This better be good." He yawned noisily. "I only got to sleep a few minutes ago."

If I was right, he'd thank me. If I was wrong, he'd never trust me again.

"I think I know what happened to Pete and where he is."

There was dead silence at the other end.

"Freddie? Did you hear me?"

"I heard you. I wasn't sure if I was awake enough to respond politely. What kind of trouble are you in?"

"None, yet. Jake convinced me to call you before we showed up at Rena's house."

"Jake? Where's Eli? And who's Rena?"

"Eli's in Pittsburgh. And Rena is the library volunteer I think abducted Pete."

"Jake is with you? Put me on speaker."

I punched the button. "You're on speaker, Freddie."

"Jake? Has Harmony been drinking?"

Jake laughed. "No, she's sober. At least I can't smell anything on her breath. And yes, she's serious about this. She's analyzed it and I can't find any flaws in her logic. Except for motive. I haven't got a clue why she suspects Rena would do this."

That had been bothering me, too. Then I remembered what Fiesker had said. "Unrequited love. I bet if she uses social media she'll have lots of pictures of Pete on it."

"Can you get Lando or Scotty to check?"

"We're not at Eli's," Jake said. "We're sitting at the corner of Pine and Herald. I refused to go any further until Harmony called you."

Freddie muttered something about 'opposite day' and 'prank TV.' From the sound of it, he'd moved to the small office in his house, because the click of the old mechanical keyboard he favored came through clearly.

"How do you spell her name?"

"R-E-N-A. O-L-E-K-S-A-N-D-R-A," I said.

He muttered again, something about a waste of time. "Got her. And Pete isn't the only one she's posted pictures of, but he wins the award for the most."

I pantomimed to Jake to turn shift gears and drive. He nodded.

"Go home, Harmony. We'll handle it from here."

He knew me better than that. I hung up on him.

"Where to, Angel? All you told me was the street name."

"453 Poole Street. And step on it." I figured we'd get close before Freddie finished the calls he'd need to make and called me back. We had a head start, after all.

I doubted Rena would recognize Jake's car but wasn't going to take the chance and made him park a block away. With my phone on silent, ignoring Freddie's calls would be easy. I left my purse stuffed under the front seat but tucked Betsy into my waistband. Jake rolled his eyes at me but said nothing. Smart man.

There were no signs of the police when we stood on the sidewalk in front of her neighbor's house. Rena's house was totally dark. Not even the porch light was on. All the other houses had lights so, the electricity wasn't out.

"Does she own a dog?" Jake whispered.

She was one of the few volunteers I never made friends with. "I don't know."

"Easy way to find out." He knelt and felt around, finally coming up with a stick. "I need a rock, but this will have to do."

"Wait." I remembered seeing a soda can in the gutter and retraced my steps a short distance until spotting it in the pool of light cast by the street light. I wished for a tissue to use to pick it up but didn't find one in any of my pockets. At least the cold air should have killed off some of the germs. Still, I wrinkled my nose as I pinched the edge between my thumb and forefinger to pick it up and carry it back to Jake.

"Use this."

He didn't have any qualms about potential germs and snatched it from me, then throwing it in one smooth motion. It pinged as it struck glass and then fell to the ground. I wasn't sure what he expected.

He waited a few seconds. "No barking," he explained. "So, either no dog or it's deaf."

If he said so.

"If she's even home," I said.

"That's her car in the driveway. She hasn't got it repaired yet."

He made a good companion for a nighttime stealth mission. I didn't find that comforting.

Down the street, headlights glared. "Play along," Jake hissed, before wrapping his arm around my waist and pulling me close. As the car flew by, going too fast for the neighborhood, he bent his head towards mine. Instinctively, I raised my face towards his. I should have expected it, the moment his lips touched mine, but hoped it was part of the charade and it would only last a fraction of a second. Instead, he crushed our mouths together. For a moment, I gave in, remembering how good of a lover he had been. But my heart belonged to Eli and I pulled away.

"No fair," I said.

He chuckled. "It worked, didn't it? All the driver saw was two people. He couldn't see our faces and identify us later."

I wasn't sure why that mattered. We weren't doing anything illegal.

Another car turned the corner. I identified it right away as Freddie's Mustang and when Jake tried to repeat his maneuver I resisted. "Not this time, Jake. You had your one shot."

"Can't blame a man for trying."

I could, but it wasn't worth the argument. Besides, I needed Jake for the moment.

Freddie pulled up alongside us and parked. "What are you two doing here?"

"Watching the house and waiting for you," Jake said. "What took you so long? And where's everyone else?"

Freddie ignored the questions. "What have you seen?"

"Nothing," I told him. "The place is darker than black. You'd think there'd be a light on in the house somewhere."

He nodded. "You stay here. I'm going to check around back. If you see anything, yell."

I tracked him as he scooted along the side of the house. He stopped, and the rusty gate groaned as he opened it. I reached behind me to check if Betsy was still in place. If anything was going to go wrong, it would be then. No dog barked, no light flared from inside the house, no curtain moved. It worried me, and I didn't understand why.

I lost track of him when he slipped around the corner of the house. How long should it take for him to come around the other side? I listened for any sign of a problem—screaming, cursing, a gunshot—but the night remained still.

Until the gate creaked again and Freddie came back the same way he'd left. I waited not-so-patiently for him to rejoin us. "Find anything?" I asked.

He shook his head. "Nothing. That house is closed up as tight as the old five-and-dime. Either she's got blackout curtains, or she's covered every window with black garbage bags."

It sounded suspicious. "So, now what?"

"I'll try the direct approach. Knock on the door and say there's been a request for a wellness check, that a friend was concerned about her mental well-being." He raised an eyebrow. "You are worried about her, correct?"

"Oh, absolutely."

"Good."

"I'll cover the back door," Jake volunteered.

Freddie eyed him.

Jake raised his hands to shoulder level, open palm out. "I'm not carrying. I figure if Rena sees someone skulking around her back door, she'll be less inclined to leave that way. She'll think it's another cop."

Jake's understanding of how the criminal mind works scared me.

With a jerk of his head, Freddie indicated the back yard. "Two minutes," he said.

Jake took off at a slow run, and I waited for the creak of the gate. Instead, he leaped and sailed over the fence.

"Showoff," Freddie muttered. He waited a few more seconds before heading towards Rena's front door, leaving me behind. Once again, I was the third wheel.

I considered sitting in the Charger where I could mope in peace. It didn't seem fair. After all my hard work, I wouldn't be part of the rescue. I comforted myself with the thought that at least I'd be close by and moved to stand by the edge of her yard.

Freddie pounded on the door. "Police! Open up!"

Nothing happened. No one came to the door and Jake didn't yell from the back yard. Freddie knocked again. "Police! Open the door!"

Was that someone peeking out from the window near the back of the house? Or a figment of my imagination? Because they were there and gone.

"Freddie," I said in a stage whisper and pointed at the window. He nodded and pounded on the door. "Police! We're coming in!"

He took a few steps back and rushed the house. His foot hit squarely next to the lock. The door vibrated but didn't fly open. He shook his head and stepped back again.

I don't know if the second attempt had more force behind it or what, but he was successful. He stopped for a moment, pulled his revolver, and disappeared inside.

Then the screaming started.

Chapter 34

Three voices shredded the stillness of the night, one female and two males, competing for attention. Down the street, a dog barked, and a chorus of howls rose to join him. In the distance, sirens wailed. I prayed help was on its way. But why was Rena the one screaming for help like her life depended on it?

I knew better. I did it anyway.

With Betsy in hand, I shouldered my way through the partially closed front door. And stopped in shock. I expected to see Pete tied to a chair, half out of it. Instead, on the floor next to the worn-out sofa, he and Freddie wrestled, striving for control of Freddie's gun. And no sign of Rena.

Jake burst through the back door and ran down the hallway. He stopped short and we exchanged a look of helplessness. If I shot at Pete, I might hit Freddie. Besides, I couldn't force myself to shoot Pete.

But if Pete got a hold of Freddie's gun, someone might end up dead. And I wouldn't let that happen.

Pete yelled something about 'fire' and 'everyone out.' I didn't understand. The house wasn't on fire and I didn't smell smoke.

He let go of Freddie's gun hand long enough to punch Freddie's shoulder. Then he rammed his head into Freddie's chest. With his free hand, Freddie shoved back. Not nearly as hard as he could have. It dawned on me he didn't want to hurt Pete either.

Rena's screaming turned into loud wails. Jake disappeared into a room off the hall and her sobs stopped. That helped. A little.

Most of Pete's blows missed Freddie. It seemed as if he moved in slow motion, giving Freddie time to avoid them. But Freddie wasn't able to get the upper hand in the fight. Pete was too strong.

I decided to try something foolish. Very foolish. I dropped my hand, so Betsy hung at my side, half-hidden. "Pete, can you help me? I need some books moved." I prayed my voice would break through his drug-fogged brain.

He paused for a second before throwing a punch at Freddie's face. Freddie moved fast enough that Pete hit the floor instead. "Get out," Freddie panted. "Call 911."

I wouldn't leave him. I tried again, using the calm voice I use when talking to our teenage volunteers, despite my heart racing. "Pete, have you straightened the shelves in the children's section yet?" Would he remember my voice and trust me?

He turned his head to stare at me. "Miss Duprie?" He shook his head vigorously as if trying to make sense of my presence.

I was smart enough to know that if he went after Betsy, I wasn't strong enough to stop him. I kept my distance and sat in a nearby chair, so I didn't loom over him.

"Hey, Pete, what are you doing? Do you have time to help me?"

"Miss Duprie?" He rolled off Freddie. It was progress.

"I can help you, Pete." A promise I hoped to keep.

"What are you doing here?" He sat up and stared at me.

"Looking for you."

"Am I lost?"

From the corner of my eye, I watched Freddie inch away, crawling backward. "You were, but I found you."

Pete blinked and shook his head again. "Where are we?"

I didn't know how to answer the question. "It doesn't matter. What matters is we want to get you somewhere safe. Will you let us help you?" A spasm ran through his entire body. I wanted to hold him, but instinct told me it was risky.

"An ambulance is on its way," Freddie whispered. "Keep talking to him."

I worried two ambulances were needed, one for Pete and one for Freddie, but didn't say that out loud. Instead, I rambled on about the library.

"Have you tried out the new kiosks yet? They're real easy to use. I had one of the older patrons tell me they're better than the card catalogs." I didn't wait for an answer but kept talking. "The kids still play with the old helmet the department left at their last visit. I bet we have some potential new firefighters in the making."

Pete swayed. "Lots of fun." His words slurred.

So, he had been part of the group. That answered one of my questions. It didn't tell me what was taking the ambulance so long.

"Miss Janson will be back starting Monday. She'd like it if you dropped in to say hi."

"Yeah." He closed his eyes and slumped forward, then collapsed on the floor.

Freddie reached Pete before I could. "He's still breathing. The ambulance should be here any second. I requested a silent run. I didn't want the sirens to upset him."

Three ambulances showed up. Turned out that Jake had been communicating with 911 much of the time. At least, once he'd worked Rena out of the duct tape securing her to a kitchen chair. She didn't appear to be hurt other than some minor scratches and bruises, but the EMTs insisted she go to the hospital for a thorough checkup before being transferred to a holding cell at the police department for questioning. Freddie read Rena her rights before the paramedics loaded her into the ambulance, because she was already spouting off about what she'd done, moaning how it had all gone wrong. Several police cars arrived with the ambulances, and an officer accompanied her to the hospital.

"Did Rena really think her plan would work?" I asked Freddie as my best EMT buddy Lee looked him over for a second time.

"You mean drug him into submission, and when the fog cleared he'd pay attention to her and fall in love?" Freddie moved the ice pack from one side of his face to the other. "Sounds flawless."

Lee chuckled. "Except for the bit about her either buying the wrong drug or him having an adverse reaction to it. I've heard about it in training, but have never seen it in person."

That was the EMTs' theory, anyway. Until the hospital ran blood work, there'd be no way to prove it.

"You'll have to ask her what book she got the idea from," I told Freddie. "So, I can remove it from the shelves." I yawned loudly. "Speaking of, is it okay if Jake and I take off? There's enough time for me to get an hour's worth of sleep before heading into work. Don't want to ruin my reputation on the last day."

"Where is Hennessey?"

"He's waiting for me at his car. There are far too many police types hanging around for him to be comfortable. No offense," I added, winking at Officer Holt as he walked through the room. I'd done my research on his whole name. Alfonso Aloysius Beauregard Holt. No wonder he didn't use his first name.

Freddie chuckled. "Go home, Harmony. I'll contact you and Hennessey later for your official statements."

"I'm ready," I said, sliding into the front seat of the Charger. The engine was running, and the car was toasty warm.

"Ready for what?" Jake asked, stretching. He must have been taking a catnap.

"Bed. Then a shower and clean clothes. And a ride to the library. In that order."

"I can help with all of that," he grinned.

I yawned. "Just take me home."

He shifted into gear and pulled onto the still busy street. "Which one, Angel?"

There'd be no Eli to cuddle with. "My place."

"Mind if I crash there? In the front room, not with you, unless you want me to. That way you don't have to worry about me falling asleep and not waking up to give you your ride." He graced me with one of his trademark smiles.

The way he phrased it, I couldn't take offense. "The easy chair is all yours."

❋ ❋ ❋

With the help of several cups of coffee, I made it through the morning. The Oak Grove rumor mill apparently hadn't picked up on the night's shenanigans yet, because no one cast sideways glances my direction. No more than usual, anyway.

I was on edge, hoping for Eli to show up and half-expecting Freddie. Or someone from the police department. At some point, I'd have to give an official statement as to my part in the rescue. At least I'd finally got an email from the steampunk company. They'd been unable to find anyone beyond vendors that had bought a large number of the brooches. Rena must have gotten her supply from one of them.

I also hoped for word on how Pete was doing. The hospital wouldn't release his private medical information, but at least I wanted to know if he was okay.

I spent most of the morning wandering the stacks to get one last look, one last touch, of what had been my kingdom for far too short of a time. It felt like saying goodbye to a lover. Until the mail came, nothing else needed to be done. Everything was ready for Janine's grand return.

And I was stuck. At least until Eli showed up and returned Dolores.

It was almost lunchtime when Jake strolled in the door, looking his normal cocky self. After dropping me off, he must have gone home and slept more. He waved my direction, but Mabel grabbed his arm and said something to him. He nodded and followed her. That was weird. Unless she had something heavy she wanted moved. It wouldn't be the first time he'd put his muscles to good use and helped us out.

Then Danielle wandered down from the third floor. She helped on the main floor when no patrons needed assistance in the children's area. She stopped in front of me, put her hands on her hips, and eyed me.

"You look like heck," she said. "Didn't you get any sleep last night? Whatever, you're going to take a break now. Why don't we go hide out in the conference room for a few?"

It sounded like a marvelous idea and I followed her to the basement. Converted into a bomb shelter in the fifties and back to useful space in the seventies, it was the quietest spot in the library. A great place to relax.

I thought I heard voices as we walked down the stairs, but it must have been a figment of my imagination. There weren't any meetings scheduled.

Danielle opened the door and held it for me. That was nice of her. Until I realized I was walking into a room full of people. The large banner hanging from the back wall that read 'Thank You' was the giveaway that this wasn't a meeting.

I held it together long enough to scan the room to see who was there. Several members of the board, most of the staff, and a bunch of volunteers. Janine, of course. And Jake hovered in one corner, beaming from ear to ear.

When Janine threw her arms around me, I lost it. I blamed it on the lack of sleep, but I hadn't expected any recognition.

"I've been delegated the task of making an official speech," Janine said, pulling out of the hug. "But the normal platitudes can't express how much

I appreciate everything you've done for both me and the library. So, no speech, just a bunch of us that want to say thank you."

And it was enough. The hugs, the handshakes, the glimmer of tears in other people's eyes. It would get me through the rest of the day. Maybe even a week or two.

It was enough to distract me from remembering that I still needed to deal with official police reports. At least until Chief Sorenson showed up at the library.

When he jerked his head my direction then headed toward Janine's office, I had to rush to stop him. Janine had stuck around and was in there with several members of the board of directors. The Chief and I needed to find another place to talk.

So, the conference room would have its second unscheduled meeting of the day. All signs of my farewell party had been moved to the break room and the room was clean and soulless. Much like I feared my conversation with the chief would be.

I let him choose his chair first, then sat across the table from him. I took the bull by the horns and started the interrogation.

"Since when does the responsibility for taking my official statement fall to you?" I set my glasses on the table and rubbed my eyes.

"I'm not here to take your statement. In fact, I haven't determined who will be. Your answer to my question will decide."

Puzzled, I said, "You haven't asked me anything yet."

From the coat pocket, he drew out small stack of papers, unfolded them and laid them in front of me. "I understand today is your last day of work here at the library. This is an official job offer. It's only part-time, and we can discuss how your hours will be configured later. I want you to report directly to me as a data analyst. You won't need to go through the academy because you won't have police powers. Oak Grove is a small city, Miss Duprie, but crime is a growing concern. I believe you are well-equipped to help me tackle the problem."

I knew my answer before I even read through the paperwork. The salary offered was good and the idea of making my own hours even better. The best part being that I wouldn't need to leave town. "What does this have to do with determining who I give my statement to? Can't Freddie do it? Is he all right?" I was worried he got hurt even though he denied it.

Chief Sorenson raised a hand to stop me. "Detective Thomason is fine-mostly. Nothing more than bruises. However, since Mr. Fiesker raised the possibility of filing a complaint, I'm playing this one by the book. Detective Thomason will be interviewed by an assigned officer from the State Police, and so will you if you agree to work for me. Otherwise, I'll have another detective take your report."

"I don't know how much Fiesker got paid," I grumbled, "but he wasn't worth it."

"That's not our call to make."

"Do you ever get tired of being a politician, Chief?"

His standard stoic expression vanished, replaced by one of weariness. But only for a second. "Between you and me? All the time, Miss Duprie."

I slid the papers back to him. "There's your answer. I can't play that game anymore. Even doing it for a couple of months here at the library was enough to make me crazy. I'll be glad to continue helping with your monthly reports and one-off data analysis projects, but I won't put myself at the mercy of the city council any longer."

One side of his mouth rose, and he took the papers and stuffed them back into his pocket. "I can't say I blame you. Expect a call from Detective Ortiz in the next few days. It'll be routine and nothing to worry about."

The chief didn't seem upset. Or he was hiding it.

He stood. "One other thing, Miss Duprie," he said. "They found a few more of those pins and a steampunk outfit at Oleksandra's house. Not like we needed more evidence, but it's good to close all the threads of an investigation. She hasn't revealed her motivation for leaving them behind like a trail of breadcrumbs for the birds, but she'll tell us sooner or later."

Chapter 35

With my shiny new cell phone clutched in my hand, I watched the black van ease out of the driveway and onto the street. "I worry about them making it back to Florida without breaking down," I said, leaning against Eli. He'd be taking an early flight back on Monday, but at least we'd get a day and a half alone. Well, not all of it alone. We were making a trip to the local furniture store to shop for real chairs and a sofa. And a washer and dryer, and a kitchen table, and a desk or two.

He chuckled. "It may look like a piece of crap, but Lando sank a lot of money into the mechanics. He said keeping the rough exterior was part of his cover. Besides, they promised to take the interstate all the way back." He slipped his arm around my waist. "I feel like a bad boss because I'm not going with them. I'm always preaching teamwork and here I go making excuses for myself again."

"They're probably tickled to death you're paying for the trip back and aren't monitoring their spending. Wait and see where they eat and stay the night before you feel guilty."

"Am I going to need to monitor your expense reports?" he teased.

This wasn't a conversation I wanted to have standing outside in the cold and there was no putting it off. I took him by the hand and led him up the three stairs to the front door. "We need coffee. And to talk." In that order.

Smart man that he is, Eli didn't pester me until we both had filled cups in our hands. The warm coffee gave me an extra bit of courage. "So, what's going on?" he asked.

I blew across the top of my cup and leaned against the kitchen counter, trying to look casual despite the butterflies in my chest. "What you said outside, about me working for you. For the record, you haven't officially asked me, unlike Chief Sorenson, who presented me with a very attractive offer yesterday."

Eli winced. "You accepted?"

It gave me a bit of joy to see him squirm. "That's police business I'm not at liberty to discuss. However, I'm willing to hear your counter-offer."

"You're serious," he said, his eyes wide.

"You spent how many hours negotiating the business deal in Pittsburgh? Am I not worth at least the same level of consideration?"

He set his coffee on the counter and took my cup from my hands and put it on the counter too. "A day isn't enough time for me to show you how much consideration you are worth." He leaned in to kiss me but I turned my head and he ended up with his lips on my cheek.

"That's number one in the negotiations. We need to figure out how to separate business and personal matters. When I'm on the clock and when I'm not. Who I answer to when I'm working. Since I don't even know what my duties will be, I don't have a clue where to draw the boundaries. But I won't do sales. That's non-negotiable."

"You want to be treated as a valued employee who earns her money and isn't just the boss's girlfriend."

That summed it up pretty well. "I've always worked for what I have and don't intend to change, not even for you."

His eyes twinkled although he didn't smile. "Well then, Miss Duprie, I expect you to report to my office in Florida a week from Monday for training. I'll arrange your flight and accommodations. That will give me time to pull together an official job description and salary offer and start your background screening, a requirement for my employees. Agreed?"

"Can't we do it through the video conference system?" I didn't want to bring up my reluctance to fly. "I'll need the hands-on experience before I use it for client meetings. If I am to be included in meetings."

"There'll be paperwork to sign."

"Mail still exists."

He crossed his arms, puffed out his chest and stared at me. "Are you challenging me, Miss Duprie?"

I couldn't match his size, but my stare wasn't to be trifled with. "Every step of the way, Mr. Hennessey. But only in private. In public, I'll support you unless I think you're about to make a huge mistake. And then we can work out a signal, so I don't need to say anything. Which I doubt I'll ever use because you're a smart man."

His mouth quivered. Was he trying not to laugh? I needed him to take me seriously or the arrangement would never work.

"Do you know why I want you to come to Florida?"

"You mean besides to get me in your bed? No."

He uncrossed his arms and leaned in until our foreheads touched. "I want to introduce you to the rest of the team. Watch how they work so you're familiar with our operations. You met almost everyone when you visited last summer, but I want you to sit in the open area and get a sense of the business. I don't want you shut off in an office, I want you in the middle of everything. And, of course, in my house and in my bed after hours. We'll deal with my dream of having sex in my office another time."

"Boundaries," I whispered, restraining myself from finding a way to make his fantasy come true.

"I know," he groaned. "But I've never seen this tough negotiator side of you before. It's hard to resist."

"We still need to discuss how things will work here. I refuse to be banished to an upstairs room or use the back door when you hold business meetings.

I won't play the sweet little woman you send to get more drinks from the refrigerator or make coffee. Don't expect me to be your secretary or your mother.

"And I won't be moving in. I'll come over for meetings and stay when you're in town, but otherwise, I'll keep my place. That way I don't become part of the furniture or spend my nights listening to the ghost in the walls." Or end up homeless if we broke up.

"We have ghosts?"

Out of all the things I'd mentioned, he wanted to talk about the ghost?

"I've never seen it, but I hear it. I figured it was mice in the walls at first, but after we had the exterminator go through the entire house, the noises still happened. It quiets down when the house has people in it. It likes company."

"You're not the type to believe in ghosts."

I wasn't. "Spend a few nights here by yourself, then tell me what you think."

"I'll take you up on that. But not tonight. Tonight I want to spend with you." Eli untied the ribbon around my bun. "But I'm honored. The amount of thought you put into this shows how much you care about us. I'm not happy with the not moving in part but it makes sense. Just like you coming to Florida make sense."

I tilted my head. "Are you really negotiating the terms of my employment at the same time you're trying to seduce me?"

He stuck his hands behind his back. "I assumed

we were done bargaining. I accept your terms as long as you accept mine."

"All right, if the weather holds I'll drive down."

"Fly and I'll rent you a car to use. That way I won't worry about you getting stuck in a snowstorm somewhere."

"You're one to talk." Twice he'd caused me days of worry because he'd gotten stuck making the drive from Florida.

"Guilty as charged. I'll send the corporate jet for you. I'll even come along."

With him along to hold my hand, I might be able to handle a short flight. "Agreed. We still need to negotiate salary, working hours and benefits, but we can do that once you get a handle on my job description." If he thought I'd been tough on him so far, he wasn't ready for what was coming.

A smile lit up his face and he held out his right hand. "It's been a pleasure doing business with you. Shake on it?"

I should have expected what came next. With our hands clasped, all it took was a tug and I tumbled into his arms.

"I've been waiting for this since I got here," Eli said, his voice deeper than normal. "The whole house to ourselves and no interruptions. All we need to do is set the security system and turn off our phones."

"What happened to buying furniture?" Not that I had any desire to wander through the most boring store in the city, but Eli wasn't interested in used desks and chairs.

313

"I didn't know you were that kind of woman, Buttercup," he said, stroking my cheek. "One who would give up this rare opportunity in favor of shopping."

I sighed. "You're too easy, Sweetie. You've got to keep up. I was teasing."

"Were you kidding about the ghost, too?"

A gust of winter wind howled as it brushed by the house. Perfect timing. Without saying a word, I clung to him, pretending to be scared. He wrapped his arms around me and held me tight. I couldn't help myself and giggled. He squeezed tighter.

"You're crazy." His breath rustled the hair on the top of my head. "That's one reason I love you."

"What are the others?" I asked, running my hand down his thigh.

"You want a list? You'll have to wait. This is all about showing you." His lips descended on mine with a ferocity I strove to match.

"You don't think the ghost will mind if we ignore it?" he asked with a grin when we stopped to catch our breaths. "I'm about to break some boundaries."

He didn't give me enough time to answer before our mouths crashed together again.

Epilogue

"What will happen to them?" I asked Freddie, staring through the one-way window of the interrogation room at one of the boys who set the fires. The little room was crowded because his parents and a public defender shared the space with him and Detective Ortiz.

"Unless one of them cracks and admits guilt, nothing." Freddie rubbed a hand across the top of his head. "We have no physical evidence to link them to the scenes. Even Fiesker wasn't able to find anything."

After dropping Eli off at the airport, I'd come to the station to give my official statement to Ortiz about Pete's rescue, but had picked a bad time. He'd be tied up for several hours interviewing the suspects. "Is Fiesker still hanging around? I thought he'd worn out his welcome."

Freddie coughed. "He's been assigned an empty office at the fire station to use until he finishes his report for Chief Hinds, and then he'll head out for his next assignment. Rumor has it that his brother, who he's been staying with, is tired of him, too."

So, it was his brother's cat he'd been buying food for that day in the grocery store. "I wonder how much of the glory he'll lay claim to?"

"If we end up not being able to prosecute the kids, there won't be any glory to claim."

"It doesn't seem right they'll get away without some punishment."

"Look at the expressions on the parents' faces." Freddie nodded toward the window. "They aren't buying his story. He'll be in the doghouse for a long time."

I supposed it would have to do. That and Lando had pulled his magic and gotten the kids' accounts banned. They couldn't play the game anymore without a new user name and starting from scratch.

"Let Detective Ortiz know I was here, would you?" I asked Freddie. "I don't want him to think I'm avoiding him. But I've got errands to run." And cleaning to do. And just sitting back and relaxing and reading a book. I was a free woman for a week and planned to enjoy every moment.

"I'll pass the word along."

"Thanks." I turned to leave, but he caught me by the sleeve of my coat.

"Oh, and Harmony?"

"What?"

He smiled. "Stay out of trouble, okay? At least for a little while?"

"Me?" I winked. "I'm just a small town ex-librarian, how could I possibly get into trouble?"

The End (for now)

Other Books in the
Harmony Duprie Mysteries Series

THE MARQUESA'S NECKLACE

Harmony Duprie enjoyed her life in the quiet little town of Oak Grove—until her arrest for drug trafficking. Now she has to figure out who is behind the sinister incidents plaguing her, and why.

HER LADYSHIP'S RING

Harmony Duprie is back, and so is trouble in Oak Grove.

Her ex-boyfriend Jake is out of prison and a suspect in a murder. Can Harmony clear Jake's name and solve the mystery of her own heart?

THE BARON'S CUFFLINKS

What starts as Girl's Night Out ends in murder, and Harmony Duprie is a suspect.

She's innocent, of course, but with no alibi, the sheriff's department won't remove her from the list of suspects. But caution isn't Harmony's middle name and she plunges head first into danger to defend her honor.

Books in
The Free Wolves Series
by P.J. MacLayne

WOLVES' PAWN
Book 1

Dot McKenzie is a lone wolf-shifter on the run. Can she survive when she becomes a pawn in a pack leader's deadly game?

WOLVES' KNIGHT
Book 2

Tasha Roeper knows what it means to protect your own. Torn between tradition and a changing world, will Tasha risk everything to save a friend—including her own life—when old enemies arise?

WOLVES' GAMBIT
Book 3

Free Wolf Lori Grenville has made it her life's mission to help unhappy shifters escape from overbearing alphas and dangerous situations. She hasn't failed in a mission yet. This one may be the exception.

P.J. MacLayne
can be reached at

WEBSITE
PJMacLayne.com

FACEBOOK
facebook.com/pjmaclayne

TWITTER
twitter.com/pjmaclayne